VENOM RISING

BOOK 4 THE SOVEREIGN CODE

TAMAR SLOAN

HEIDI CATHERINE

SEQUEL HOUSE

CHAPTER
ONE

ECHO

E cho rubs her eyes, too weak to ask River if he can see what she's just noticed. He inches his way forward, his feet dragging rather than stepping. She follows, each movement sending aches reverberating through her depleted body.

It's only been a handful of hours since the Worker released them into the Extinction Zone. This falls well short of the lifetime Echo hoped to spend by River's side when they ran into the nothingness filled with blind confidence. But it's more than she feared they were going to get when Oren first captured them, so for that she's grateful.

She parts her cracked lips, trying to form some words in her parched mouth.

River hears her struggle and turns to her. If it weren't for the fact she hasn't let go of his hand this whole time, she'd wonder if the person beside her had switched places with the guy she loves. His face is coated with orange dust. His hair is standing on end in stiff tendrils. His green eyes are bloodshot.

"Look," she croaks, tilting her chin to point to the horizon. "There."

River squints as he tries to focus. Then he sees it. His eyes widen and he draws in a breath.

Since they set off, they've seen a few shimmering stretches of land in the distance that turned out to be nothing more than a trick of the eye. The first had them running at twice the pace. The second, cautiously marching forward. The third, walking at a slow but steady rate. They don't have the energy left for another disappointment.

"It's different," she says, forcing her voice to cooperate.

River nods. This apparition is rising from the earth, transforming the horizon into a jagged line with a point in the middle. Could there possibly be something out here in this land of nothingness?

They stumble as they walk, dizziness gripping Echo's senses as the unforgiving sun beats down. They both know if this turns out to be nothing more than another mirage, it will also be the end for them. It's going to take everything they have left to find out.

River's hand is bone dry, and Echo squeezes it weakly. Their bodies gave up the idea of producing sweat to keep them cool long ago. Their cells need to hold onto the little moisture they have left. They need to find some water and they need it very soon.

Echo's legs buckle and her grasp on River breaks. She tumbles to the hard ground, wincing as the gravel scratches her knees. Her head spins as she tries to get up. The temptation to give into the fatigue burns like fire in her belly. If she could just lie down on the earth and let it swallow what's left of her, this nightmare would end.

They shouldn't have walked this far. They should have found their way back to the Green Zone and taken their chances there. Or the Dead Zone. Out here is certain death. It's called the Extinction Zone for a reason. But it's too late to turn back now. She's not even sure they could find their way. Everything looks the same. For all she knows, they're walking in one giant circle.

River's face looms before her. He hauls her to her feet, and she knows she can't give up. Especially not now that hope is hovering in the distance. They might be in the Extinction Zone, but they're most certainly not extinct.

"It's a building," says River, pointing at the horizon. "Tall, like the Sting."

Echo rubs at her eyes. She can see what River's talking about but surely it's not a building. Maybe it's a rock formation or a dead tree. It's just that...it does look an awful lot like a building. Like a squarer version of the Sting.

Unlocking some energy from deep within her depleted reserves, Echo takes River's hand and they shuffle forward. Each step is bringing them closer. And each step confirms what River just said.

Over the crest of a gentle hill, the spire of a building is visible. Echo doubts it's inhabited. Nobody could possibly survive in this vast nothingness, but maybe the building has water stored somewhere. Just a mouthful of liquid would make the difference between death and survival.

River pulls Echo along in his desperation to get there. She wishes she could keep up. But his legs are longer and he has more stamina thanks to years of good nutrition in the Green Zone. It's impossible to match his pace.

"Go," she tells him, not wanting to slow him down. Maybe if he finds water, he can bring some back to her. "Go on."

"No." He tugs on her hand. "I'm not leaving you."

If she could spare any energy for talking, she'd call him stubborn. But she can't, so she drags herself up the hill, which doesn't seem so gentle anymore. It's a brutal challenge, which she's not at all sure she'll pass.

River reaches the top a few heartbeats before Echo. The gasping noise he makes has her pushing forward to stand directly beside him. It takes several long moments before she's prepared to believe what she's seeing.

There's a vast garden, stretching across the earth like an old woman's shawl. It's different from the neatly curated crops in the Green Zone with its precise rows and symmetrical patterns. This garden is filled with plants, but some are scraggly and fighting for life, and others are growing wild, in need of a decent prune. The haphazard plantings give it a neglected feel, and Echo's certain this garden was once so much more than it is now. Yet, still, it's bearing fruit and Echo can see orange and avocado trees dotted around tomato plants with heads of lettuce sprouting from the soil beneath. Trails of bean sprouts and passionfruit are winding around the branches of a peach tree and Echo's reminded of her promise to never eat a peach again after watching Clover kiss River. That promise will be broken the moment she can get close enough to sink her teeth into the fruit's juicy flesh.

Right in the center of the garden is a square concrete building that's around a dozen stories high. Its windows have been boarded up and it's either swaying slightly in the faint breeze or Echo is. Neither Echo nor the building are in great shape.

She pinches herself, deciding it's very possible she's imagining this whole thing. Although, why then is River standing with his mouth open and eyes wide as he scans the terrain?

This has to be real. There's an abandoned oasis in the middle of the Extinction Zone. In all the times she looked through the net and imagined what was out here, never—not ever—did she imagine anything like this.

"Where are all the people?" River narrows his eyes as if he expects someone to jump out at them.

"There are no people," says Echo, certain nobody has set foot in this garden for a very long time.

A smile spreads across River's face. "You hungry?"

"I could eat." Echo returns his smile, feeling a renewed sense of hope as they charge down the hill with energy they didn't possess moments ago.

Echo lets go of River's hand to run to the peach tree, the shade embracing her as it welcomes her beneath its canopy. She plucks a piece of fruit and closes her eyes as she takes a bite. The juices run down the back of her throat and she moans with the sheer pleasure of her thirst being quenched.

"Eat this," says River, holding a tomato out. "Tomatoes have more water than a peach."

Echo finishes the peach and takes a bite of the tomato, wincing when the juice squirts her in the eye.

"Do you think there's water in that?" River points to two wooden buckets underneath the tree beside them. One is turned over, but the other stands upright.

"I hope so." A drink of water would be bliss. Echo's muscles are aching. It's going to take a lot more than a belly full of sustenance to recover. Or a drink of water. Sleeping for a month may help.

"It's empty," says River, going to the bucket and picking it up. "Oh, hold on. There's some at the bottom."

He sniffs at the water. Seeming to decide it's safe, he takes a cautious sip. Echo knows if it weren't for his fear that there may be something wrong with it, he'd have given it to her first. The thirst she thought she'd quenched takes over like a beast inside her and she finds herself putting out her hands and pleading for her turn.

"It's good." River nods as he hands her the bucket. "I had plenty. You finish it off."

She knows for a fact that he only took a small sip, so she resists the urge to drain all the liquid from the bucket, stopping herself at one gulp.

"Seems I've had plenty, too." She hands the bucket back to him.

He rolls his eyes, not believing her for a moment, then takes another sip.

"River!" Echo shouts, her heart rate picking up when she sees something moving on the side of the bucket. "Stay still. There's a bee."

River freezes and after two terrifying seconds, the bee loses interest and flies away. He lets out a long sigh.

"It's attracted to the water." Echo takes the empty bucket and sets it down away from River. They'd been so focused on getting food and water, they forgot to watch for bees. Echo might be Immune, but River isn't. If they're going to survive out here, they really need to do better than that.

"Do you think that's what happened to all the people?" River asks. "Did the bees win?"

Echo shudders as the abandoned garden suddenly feels eerie. Is this what the Green Zone would look like if the bees outlived the humans? "I think so."

"We should check out the building," River says, clearly not wanting to give this terrifying thought too much airtime.

Echo nods. They need to rest and it will be safer indoors where there are fewer bees. Not to mention the pollen they're surrounded by. She highly doubts there's any serpentwood growing here. And if River's breathing becomes labored, there's no Clover to jump out and save him. Which is both a blessing and a curse...

They pick their way down the overgrown path, picking more fruit as they go, and Echo tries to imagine what this garden would have been like when it was cared for. Clearly, someone had put effort into establishing a sustainable food source.

"Who do you think lived here?" she asks, struggling to make sense of any of this.

"I've never heard of anyone surviving out here," says River. "As far as I've been told, all of Earth's last survivors live in either the Green or Dead Zones."

"As far as you've been told," she quotes back to him.

"Yeah." He shrugs sadly. "Exactly. Which could mean anything."

"Maybe there are still some survivors?" She peers ahead toward the building. "We should be careful."

River nods. "If there's anyone here, I'm sure they won't turn us away. We can help tidy up their garden to earn our keep. Maybe teach them a few techniques to get more out of their harvest."

Echo stops on the path, wincing as her exhausted body aches in protest at the change in movement. "We can't stay here, River. Too many people are counting on us."

"I know that." He puts an arm around her, encouraging her to step over a prickly vine and continue down the path. "But we will need to stay for at least a little while. Just until we regain our strength. Then we can figure out how to get back."

She nods, knowing he's right. It's unsettling to think that while they're here in this strangest of places, life is going on back home. Chase and Flora will be figuring out how to test Daphne to see if she's the Sovereign. Makk will be running around delivering messages. Oren will be figuring out his next evil move. And all this time, poor Nola and Vern are still stuck in the Hive. That's if they've managed to survive for this long, of course.

But while Echo and River are here in this overgrown garden, it almost feels as if none of that exists.

Almost.

"Do you think Oren's fed the Vulnerables?" River asks.

"I hope so," she says. "I'm sure Chase has figured something out. Or maybe Flora's had Nectar break a hole in the net to bring food back for everyone. They might be having a feast right now."

River smiles. He's still coated in dust, except now he has a trail of clean skin at each corner of his mouth where the juice from the tomato dribbled down. Echo brings her fingertips to her own face to realize she must look the same.

"You look beautiful," he says.

She laughs, knowing that can't possibly be true.

They step onto the cracked concrete slab that rings the building. Tall weeds have sprouted in the crevices and the main entrance door has fallen off its hinges and is lying broken and pushed to one side. The building looks even taller now that they're standing at its base. Echo's pretty sure it was her that was wobbling earlier, not this monolithic structure. It's survived for hundreds of years out here. It's not going to topple now. At least, she hopes not.

"Hello?" calls River as they pull aside a large piece of heavy cloth hanging in the doorway and step inside the building. "Is anybody here?"

Echo blinks as her eyes adjust to the darkness. The air is stale but it's much cooler inside, which is a relief.

"Hello?" River calls again, his voice bouncing off the concrete walls.

They're standing in a vast open space that was likely once an opulent foyer like in the Sting. This one has been stripped bare by the passage of time. There are no floor coverings, nothing attached to the roof or walls, and not a single piece of furniture. A wide staircase sits in the middle of the space, winding its way to the above floors.

"Look." River points down. "Footprints."

"They could be old," says Echo, studying the muddy outlines. "All they really tell us is that people were here once, which we already knew. Someone had to plant that garden out there."

"Hello?" River calls out louder this time. "Is anybody here?"

They go up the stairs, calling out every now and then, not wanting to take anyone by surprise. The first floor is just as empty as the ground one. Although, with the windows boarded up, it's a little hard to see all the details. They continue up the stairs again and Echo begins to struggle, barely making it to the landing on the second floor. Her legs are aching, and her feet are covered in blisters from walking so far.

"I can't go on," she says, gripping the railing. She wants to tell River to go ahead but knows he'll never leave her.

"Let's find somewhere to rest." He takes her hand and leads her into the darkness. They reach the far corner of the open space and River sits down and leans against the wall. Echo collapses onto his lap and he wraps his arms around her.

"River," she says, feeling the grip of sleep begin to claim her the moment she rests her head on his chest.

"Shh," he hushes.

For a moment, she thinks he's warning her that someone is approaching. But the building remains silent. River wants her to sleep. He's looking out for her just like he always does.

"I'll keep watch," he tells her. "You sleep."

Echo's eyelids close like they weigh as much as one of Makk's lellephants. An hour ago, she thought she was about to die. And now she has food. Water. And finally, the chance to rest. Which is more than anyone in the Dead Zone has.

And that's why they can't possibly stay here.

They have to regain their strength.

They have to go back.

And then, they have to fight.

CHAPTER

TWO

RIVER

R iver rests his head back against the hard wall, wishing it was cool rather than the gentle warmth it emanates. His bones ache. His body feels like the desperate wish for water will always whisper through his marrow. His skin threatens to crack like parched soil at any second.

But he's holding Echo. They're alive.

And for now, that's a gift he's not going to underestimate.

Each step through the Extinction Zone had felt like a step closer to their end. The sheer size of the bleak nothingness they were trekking across had reminded him exactly how insubstantial their lives are. It had dwarfed his dreams of something so lofty as Immunity for all. Continuing to walk was all they could do, no matter how fruitless it felt.

Watching Echo wilt as each hour passed had been the hardest part. Her shoulders had been the first to droop, then her chin. As the sun and thirst had taken their toll, her feet had dragged through the dirt, leaving scuff marks. He knew within a matter of hours he'd be holding her dead body in his arms.

River draws her closer, simply focusing on the sound of her

11

even breaths. Her hand is curled around his arm, holding him even in sleep. They've been through so much together. Their love was truly forged in a crucible of adversity, danger, and division.

Which only makes it all the more precious.

His eyelids sink shut as the effort to hold them open becomes too much. Everything suggests this oasis they've found is abandoned. A relic of the days when humanity lived wherever they wanted. Now, the buildings they built are gone, save this crumbling monolith. The gardens they tended are wild and overgrown. The bees have claimed it back.

Which means for now, they're safe.

Echo can eat and drink and sleep. She'll survive.

A slow, relieved breath leaves River's lungs. Despite it all, he almost smiles. They'll rest tonight, and tomorrow they can discuss their plan. They need to heal and regain their strength.

And then they need to go back.

He has no idea where they'll hide or how they'll continue to be part of the fight for Immunity, but all he knows is they have to be there. He doubts Oren has reinstated the rations to the Dead Zone. River can't sit here in a pocket of plenty while others starve, and Echo would feel the same. She fought the injustice the moment she saw the glaring divide between Dead Born and Green Born.

Sleep invades River's mind like a slow-moving mist, and he allows it to envelop him. Tomorrow will come. Now is for rest.

An image rises, defined by the sort of detail only a memory can give it. The familiar warmth and security he'd always associated with their family room in the Sting washes through him. The soothing white walls. The comfortable gray furniture with the flashes of green his mother insisted on decorating with. The window that gazed over the Green Zone.

Yet River's sad, curled up in his mother's lap as he watches his father pick up a sick Flora. Her skin is red and puffy, covered in a sheen of sweat.

Their father presses a kiss to his young daughter's head. "My little Immune will be fine," he promises lovingly. "Daddy will make sure of it."

Flora smiles up at him despite her flushed face and raspy breathing, probably not hearing their mother correcting their father in a quiet voice as she says, "Green Born, not Immune."

A pang of jealousy tugs at River before he can stop it. Their father's affectionate moments are few and far between, which means they cherish each and every one of them. It's clear that's exactly what Flora's doing.

His father looks to his mother. "The infirmary has everything she needs."

He exits and River curls tighter into his mother's lap. He and Flora don't spend much time apart. The room feels bigger and whiter without her.

His mother holds him, brushing his hair back from his tear-filled eyes. "Flora will be fine. Daddy will look after her."

"The medicine was supposed to help her, Mommy!"

They were playing two days ago when Flora knocked one of the water bottles onto the tiled floor, smashing it. He'd managed to catch her before she fell, but in trying to regain her balance, Flora stepped on one of the pieces of glass, cutting her foot.

Their mother was there to wipe away her tears, bandage it up, then give her the medicine that stops an infection.

"She must be allergic," his mother soothes. "Nothing Daddy can't fix. Flora will be back with us before you know it, I promise."

River sighs, trusting his mother with every cell of his being. Her warmth wraps around him protectively and he burrows into it. Their father's affection may be sporadic, but their mother's love is as constant and enduring as she is. He'll always cherish that.

Pain slices through River's consciousness. The moment is... tainted somehow. But before he can figure it out, he discovers he's alone in the living quarters.

He's still dreaming, but this time he's all grown up.

The older version of himself walks to the large window that looks over the Green Zone, his mind divided between the calm serenity this dream evokes and the uneasiness his consciousness can't quite shake. Even in his dream, a part of him knows the Sting isn't safe.

But the sight that greets him washes everything else away.

The same gardens and crops and fields surround the Sting, yet on a grander scale. The lush vegetation extends as far as he can see. There's no Dead Zone. No Extinction Zone.

Just one, beautiful expanse reaching to the horizon.

People move about below, but they're not dressed in the white suits he expects. They're wearing colors, vibrant cobalt, stunning crimsons, sunny yellows and lavish emerald. They've chosen to wrap themselves in the colors of life and celebration.

"Beautiful," River murmurs, his hand brushing the glass.

But a beauty he never could have imagined. It's brighter, bigger, deeper.

The door opens behind him and he spins around, the part of him caught up in this dream future pulling up a welcoming smile.

The part of him that knows this is nothing but a wish is ready to fight.

Echo stands in the doorway, a dazzling smile gracing her face. Her hair is a little longer, her body filled out in a way that makes his eyes roam over her curves. She opens her mouth to speak but he doesn't hear it.

His entire focus is now on the child by her side.

A dark-haired child with green eyes. A child smiling just as broadly and blissfully as their mother.

"Wake up!"

River jolts at the rough male voice, then stops when something sharp presses into the side of his neck. His eyes go from shut to wide open as his disorientated mind catches up with what's going on.

They're not alone.

And the new additions aren't happy.

Echo tenses in River's lap and he knows she's awake. He'd look down to confirm but the man standing over them has a long-handled scythe pressed against his neck. The look in his eyes says he's ready to swipe.

"We come in peace," River says, his voice raspy.

Echo turns slowly so she's facing their newfound foes. "We mean no harm."

The man presses the scythe a little harder against River's throat. Luckily, the blade is dull and dirt-stained, leaving his skin unbroken.

Although the abandoned building is dark, River can make out the face of the man standing over him, and the shapes of the several others behind him. Their skin is so pale they almost glow. If the pinch of pain at his neck wasn't so real, he'd think he was still dreaming.

"Are you here to be Remembered?" the man demands.

At first, River has no idea what the man's talking about. But then he realizes.

Remembered is the opposite of Forgotten.

"Yes," he says quickly. "We want to be Remembered."

The man steps back suddenly, thudding the base of his long-handled scythe on the cracked cement floor. "Then you shall be."

River feels Echo tense, probably thinking this is too easy.

15

Still, they cautiously scramble to their feet, keeping their backs to the wall.

"Who are you?" Echo asks.

A woman pushes past the man, tsking. "I told you they were just more of them, Manu. Look at them, they barely made it."

The woman smiles, revealing a mouth full of teeth that are actually darker than her skin. Wild, matted hair covers most of her face like a mane and she's also carrying a long-handled tool, but this one has a flat piece of iron on the top. "My name is Lyra. Welcome." She waves her arm to the others behind her. "We are the Moon Workers."

"The Moon Workers?" River repeats, his mind working in overdrive. Yet no matter how hard he tries to think, he's sure he's never heard of them.

Lyra nods, her mass of hair rustling. "Night is clear. Night is true."

Two other voices join her in the final line. "Night is safe."

River wishes his brain could keep up with what's going on. Who are these people and what are they talking about?

Echo gasps softly. "Safe from bees."

Manu hisses and leaps back, waving his scythe. "We do not speak of them!" he shouts in panic.

"You will wish them on us!" someone else screeches.

River clamps his mouth shut even though he wasn't the one who spoke. These people are clearly terrified of bees, acting as if they'll attack any second, yet don't have the sense to keep their voices down.

A few tense seconds pass but then Manu relaxes, even smiles. "Welcome to the Moon Zone."

Clearly named after these pale people.

"The zone of peace and unity," Lyra adds. "No division, no war. Just food and shelter for all."

River and Echo glance at each other. They've stumbled upon the very thing they've been fighting for?

Or is he still dreaming...

"Come," Lyra says, her face soft with compassion. "You must be hungry and thirsty."

River realizes she's right. He's not sure how long they slept, but his stomach is already clamping around the familiar feeling of emptiness and his mouth is coated in sandpaper. "Thank you," he says, meaning it.

Echo nods. "Yes, thank you."

Lyra beams. "We'll get you tools so you can work the gardens. They're so beautiful at night."

Manu is also grinning in his moon-colored face. "Night is clear. Night is true."

Everyone speaks at once again. "Night is safe."

He turns and heads for the stairs and practically bounces down them. The man seems to jump from emotion to emotion in the space of a blink.

Lyra follows him, indicating they do the same. River and Echo hold each other's hand as they have little choice but to do that. Although only minutes ago, these people were ready to kill them with dirty tools, and they're now acting as if they've just accepted them into the fold.

They've only just moved away from the wall when River sees one of the Moon Workers slip in front of a woman who's more swaying than walking. There's something familiar about the slope of the man's shoulders...

"Ruff!" River gasps.

Thinner, paler, his hair longer and unkept, but definitely Ruff.

That's how these Moon Workers know of being Forgotten. Others have escaped before River and Echo and managed to make it here. Including Ruff.

Except he hunches down, not answering.

"Don't try to hide," Echo says. "We know it's you, Ruff."

The Moon Workers still as if she just threw an insult at them. They slowly turn, pale lips curling in their pasty faces.

Ruff quickly separates, glaring at them. "My name is Samir," he says, practically hissing the words. "I've never met you before."

River shakes his head, confusion once more making it spin. "You're most definitely Ruff."

A jolt shoots through the Moon Workers. Manu growls, another thuds his tool on the floor.

Ruff's eyes widen with panic as he scans them. "My name's Samir! Nothing else!" He turns to River and Echo. "That is all I will be remembered as."

A small seed of understanding takes root. Ruff has been Forgotten. That man is essentially dead. He's now Samir.

Although that doesn't explain why these people are so angered at hearing Ruff's original name. But now's not the time to be finding out...

River smiles as he consciously unwinds his body. "Sorry, Samir. I must've been confused."

"We're pleased to meet you, Samir," Echo adds, her face softening. "We're looking forward to working in the garden with you all."

The Moon Workers also relax, seemingly mollified. They continue to make their way down the stairs, now breaking into song.

"Night is clear. Night is true."

Ruff—Samir—joins in, hoisting his pointy-ended tool with others as they exuberantly shout the final line. "Night is safe."

Uneasiness once more slides down River's spine as the same words filter through his mind. He's been with these people for less than twenty minutes and he already knows their chant.

He glances down at Echo as they go to follow and he sees the same turbulence in her dark eyes.

They've found a zone that claims to be everything they ever wanted. Peaceful. United. Accepting of all. Yet it's nothing like the dream of the future River just had. Nothing like *any* dream he's ever had.

Because it certainly doesn't feel united.

Or safe.

E cho steps into the darkness and breathes in the fresh air of the Moon Zone. Lyra was right. The garden is beautiful at night. Without the beating sun and threat of bees, peace blankets the earth. Beads of dew hang from leaves, sparkling like crystals in the light of the stars, and crickets chirp in a rhythmic hum.

"Come," says Lyra. "You need water and food before you start work."

Work is the last thing Echo feels like doing, but she nods agreeably. They need to prove their worth to these Moon Workers. And repay their debt. Not that she thinks the debt of saving their lives can ever be properly repaid. Had they not stumbled across the Moon Workers with their overgrown garden and falling-down tower, she and River would surely both have collapsed and perished on the scorching dirt.

They follow Lyra a few steps, only to be stopped by Manu shouting.

"Stop!" He puffs as he catches up to them. "Our new arrivals need names."

"Sorry." River holds up a hand. "This is Echo. My name's River."

"No!" Manu's face pinks up in the moonlight and he shakes his head firmly. "Those are not your names. Do you understand?"

Echo looks over at River, seeing he's as confused as she is.

"If we ever hear those names again, you can go back to where you belong," says Manu. "Samir is lucky we didn't send him away earlier when you spoke of his former self."

"I made a mistake," River says quickly. "Please, don't blame Samir for that."

Manu nods. "The place you came from, forgot you. Here, we're prepared to remember you. Always. But it's the new you that we'll embrace."

Echo nods, even though this concept doesn't sit comfortably with her at all. The person she is today is made up of all the parts of her that have come before. To shed those memories like an unwanted skin would make her a completely different person. Although, perhaps that's exactly Manu's point.

Manu points at Echo. "You are Luna."

"Luna," she repeats, liking the name, even though it doesn't at all feel like it belongs to her.

Manu moves his extended index finger to River who gulps with expectation. "And you are Celeste."

River's eyebrows shoot up. "Celeste? Are you s—"

"You heard me." Manu smiles, his anger of only moments ago appearing to have evaporated into the night air. "Welcome to the Moon Zone, Luna and Celeste. Now, it's time to turn you into Workers."

Echo gasps, thinking of the giant mechanical bees Oren uses as his slaves, then reminds herself these people call themselves Moon Workers. And no matter how many reservations

21

she has about them, she'd rather face a group of pasty humans than a beast that's been programmed to kill.

"Before I get their tools, they need to eat," says Lyra. "They're still recovering from their journey. We must go easy on Luna and Celeste for now."

"Of course." Manu turns and walks away.

"Thank you," Echo says to Lyra. "We promise to work hard and do our part as soon as we've recovered some of our strength."

"Of course." Lyra flashes her stained teeth through the matted hair covering her face and motions for them to follow her through the garden.

"How many people live here?" River asks, looking around at the people harvesting their crops. It's becoming clear why the garden seemed abandoned. The people are showing little respect for the plants they're working with, which in fairness is partly due to the fact it's difficult for them to see what they're doing in the dark. If only they could see what a mess it looked like in the day, they might take more care.

"We had thirty-six Moon Workers at the last census," says Lyra. "Thirty-eight now that you're here."

Echo nods, not sure why a census would be needed for such a small number. "Are there any children?"

"We call them Moon Borns." Lyra glances up at the tall building. "We have five of them at the moment. When they turn twelve, they'll become Workers."

"And you all live up there?" River points at the building.

"We live on the top floor," Lyra explains. "It's safer up there."

A dozen questions flood Echo's mind as she tries to decide which one to ask first. "And you only come out at night?"

"The night is safe." Lyra trips on an overgrown plant, and Echo stifles a smile at the irony. "Oh, look. Carrots!"

Lyra pulls on some stalks and four carrots slide from the soil. She hands one each to Echo and River and puts the other two in her pocket.

Echo cleans the carrot with her already dirty shirt then takes a large bite, enjoying the crunch.

"Aren't you going to eat one?" she asks Lyra.

"Not with these teeth." Lyra chuckles. "I'll give these to the Moon Borns."

"I don't see anyone planting," says River cautiously as he looks around. "I'd be happy to teach—"

"We're fine, Celeste." Lyra's tone is firm. "Mother Nature cares for us. The birds spread the seeds, just like they have for thousands of years."

"Which means they're also eating the fruit," Echo points out.

"Listen." Lyra drops her voice to a whisper. "You'd be wise to keep your suggestions to yourself. Especially around Manu. I know how you do things in your world. And I think we can agree it hasn't turned out so well."

"Can't argue with that," says Echo. "Can we, Celeste?"

River smirks. "No, Luna. We sure can't."

"The water's just around here." Lyra points to the rear of the building. "We collect it from the gutters when it rains. It's been a dry spell lately, so we need to be conservative."

Echo's about to suggest that leaving buckets tipped over in the garden isn't exactly conservative but decides to remain quiet. It seems the less they say right now, the better.

They turn the corner of the building to see half a dozen large water tanks have been set up with pipes connected to them. Echo looks up, noticing the pipes run all the way to the top of the building in jagged lines, the original guttering having rusted away.

"Clever," says River. "We have a similar system in..." He

clears his throat, wisely deciding this isn't a story worth telling right now.

Echo quickly finishes her carrot, keen for some water to wash it down. Lyra heads for the closest tank and plucks a bucket from a pile stashed to the side. She puts it underneath a tap and twists it. Except, nothing comes out.

"This one's empty," says Lyra without looking up at them. "I told you we need to be careful with our supplies."

"The ground's damp." River squats down and touches the soil. "Could the tank have leaked?"

"Our tanks don't leak." Lyra goes to the next tank. "This one will have something in it."

Echo crouches beside River and feels the soil for herself. He's right. It's most definitely damp, which is strange given the dry spell Lyra just spoke about.

Lyra quickly discovers the next tank is also empty. And the next one. And the one after that.

River stands. "The ground—"

"Shh." Echo pulls on his shirt. "No suggestions."

He nods. They need to let Lyra come to her own conclusions about what's happened here.

"Manu!" Lyra's voice rattles through the night air, her panic clear in the high pitch of her tone. "Manu! Manu!"

Several people come running, including the man who appears to be their leader, despite their insistence that everyone is accepted as equal.

"What is it?" Manu asks, waving his scythe. "Is it the new arrivals?"

"No," says Lyra, pointing at the tanks. "They're empty. And the ground is damp."

Several Moon Workers rush forward, checking the taps and cursing when nothing comes out.

"Who did this?" Manu booms. "We have a saboteur!"

"It was Nikini!" a woman shouts.

"How dare you?" another woman replies, launching herself at her accuser and knocking her to the ground.

Echo expects someone to dive in and break them apart, but everyone is too busy looking around at each other with their own suspicions.

"I saw Amaris here earlier," a man growls. "He was with Titus."

This starts an all out brawl as the Moon Workers throw punches and swing their tools, accusing each other of bringing their colony to ruin. It's hard to make sense in the darkness of everything that's taking place, but it fills Echo's gut with fear and dread.

She presses herself to River's side as they step backward. It's no wonder the population of this place is so small if this is the way they handle disputes.

"Should we try to stop it?" Echo asks, dragging her hand through her filthy hair only for her fingers to get tangled. It's no wonder Lyra barely bothers to push hers back from her face.

"How?" River asks, his eyes darting around in desperation. "They don't want our suggestions, remember? We'll just be attacked, too."

Lyra weaves through the melee, ducking to avoid a pickax that's flying through the air.

"I have to get you out of here!" she gasps. "Hurry. They'll turn on you next."

"Where can we go?" River asks, taking Echo's hand as they prepare to run.

"It was the new people!" a man shouts. "I knew we couldn't trust them!"

The brawl pauses and for three beats of Echo's heart, silence envelops them as two dozen sets of eyes focus on them.

"Get them!" a woman screeches.

To Echo's horror, the Moon Workers charge forward, emerging from the shadows with an almighty roar.

Turning around, Echo and River find more of the angry mob behind them. They're completely surrounded. Echo's breath comes in gasps as her brain races to come up with a plan to get out of this impossible situation.

"No!" Ruff hollers, racing over to stand in front of River and Echo, using himself as a human shield. It's the exact opposite of when Oren had been threatening their lives and Ruff had ratted them out.

Lyra stands at their backs, protecting them from behind.

"It wasn't them," says Ruff. "They only just arrived. These tanks would take hours to empty."

"They've been here for hours," a man grumbles. "And the tanks were already half empty. They had plenty of opportunity."

"Why would we empty them?" Echo asks. "We were thirsty. We're *still* thirsty."

"You're wasting your time interrogating these two," says Ruff. "You should be looking for the real culprit."

"Samir," sneers Manu. "You seem quite sure about Luna and Celeste's innocence. It's almost like you know them."

Ruff shakes his head. "I don't know them. The day I was welcomed by the moon was the day I was born."

Ruff's voice has changed since Echo last saw him in the Dead Zone. He'd always been so sure of himself, to the point of arrogance. Is it possible since arriving here that he's learned to be humble? Or is he simply afraid?

"Who did it then?" Manu asks, directing his question at Ruff. "Was it you, Samir?"

Ruff raises a hand and points it at a woman at the back of the mob. "It was Chandra. Look at her knees. They're covered in mud. And her hands are washed clean."

The crowd turns to inspect the woman Ruff has identified. She holds up her palms, which are indeed clean, and she begins to shake. "I didn't do it."

There's a dark flash and Echo yelps as she sees the pickax that Lyra had ducked to avoid earlier sailing through the air.

"Watch out!" she shouts.

But her warning is too late and the ax lands in the center of Chandra's chest. She drops to the ground as a moan rattles from her throat. The moan quickly becomes garbled as blood fills her lungs. Then she falls silent.

The Moon Workers set down their tools and bow their heads, forming a circle around her blood-soaked body.

"Come on," whispers Lyra. "We must join them."

Echo shakes her head, not wanting any part of this strange ritual.

"We must," hisses Ruff. "Trust me."

Echo never thought in her life she would trust Ruff after what he did to them, but she finds herself following Lyra, pulling a shocked River along with her.

They join the circle and the Moon Workers link hands around Chandra.

"Night is clear. Night is true. Night is safe," they chant.

Echo clears her throat and joins in, relieved to hear River do the same. "Night is clear. Night is true. Night is safe."

It wasn't too safe for Chandra, Echo thinks as she repeats the words over and over.

Without warning, the Moon Workers stop their chant and release their hands. Two of them go to Chandra and pick up her body, carrying it off into the darkness, while everyone else heads into the garden and gets back to work.

Ruff walks away without a word, like he hadn't just saved their life.

"It's like it never happened." River shakes his head. "They just killed that woman."

"She tried to kill us," says Lyra. "And if it doesn't rain soon, she'll have succeeded."

"But why?" asks Echo. "Why would she empty the tanks?"

"She was crazy." Lyra shrugs as if what she just said is of no concern. "Crazy people do crazy things all the time."

"Lyra," says River, lowering his voice. "Are we safe here?"

"Come on," Lyra says brightly as she ignores River's question. "Let's pick some cucumbers. They're great for thirst when there's no water. When we're finished working, it's time to remember. Remembering might help you understand a few things around here."

Echo and River follow Lyra down the path with no idea what she's talking about. But they have to trust her. Understanding what's going on around here has got to be a good thing.

Because the dozen questions Echo had earlier have now expanded to at least a hundred.

Is this Moon Zone really the place that saved them? Or is it the place that's going to bring them down?

FOUR

RIVER

River and Echo spend hours working in the haphazard
gardens alongside Lyra and the others. Harvesting is
slow going in the dark, and River almost trips over a root or a
fallen branch more than once. At the same time, it doesn't take
long for his stomach to be full and content in ways it hasn't
been since he left the Green Zone. In fact, as he bends over to
rustle through what smells like a tomato bush, his belly almost
complains. His body's no longer used to the amount of food it's
currently digesting.

His thumb impales the soft, squishy flesh of a rotten
tomato and he grimaces, quickly drawing his hand back. It's
not the first time it's happened, but it's still an unwanted
surprise. "So much waste," he mutters under his breath.

"Shh." Echo sighs. "Even if it's true."

So many bushes and plants they've come across have had
soft fruit tucked amongst their leaves in various stages of
decomposition. River's stepped on at least three rotten cucumbers. Echo stumbled and fell, hands first, into a pumpkin that
was more mold than fruit. The moment River shucked a corn

29

cob, a giant caterpillar landed in his palm, making him jump. The corn itself was little more than a dried-out cob.

"They can't see everything they're missing," River says, deeply uncomfortable with the food that's being left behind.

He straightens, narrowing his eyes as he can barely make out Lyra not far away. Actually, he can hear her more than see her as she's humming their chant.

"Night is clear. Night is true. Night is safe."

River wipes his hand on a nearby leaf, having no idea what sort of plant it belongs to. His stomach might be full and content, but his mind is a whirlwind of uneasiness. There's something wrong with the Moon Zone.

Very wrong.

Echo also stands. She goes to move closer, trips on something, and crashes into him. River catches her, close to smiling, until he almost slips over as his foot lands on something slimy. They quickly right themselves, holding each other to make sure there are no more surprises.

"We'll get you some tools for tomorrow night," Lyra says, now sounding closer. "The long handles are good for keeping steady." There's the sound of a stick whacking leaves. "And you can use them to sweep for anything that could trip you up."

Like the blind woman in the Green Zone who River's mother delivered food to.

"So, Lyra," River starts, knowing they need some answers. "What do the Moon Workers do during the day?"

"Sleep," Lyra responds quickly. "Night is safe."

If River could see more than a few inches in front of him, he'd glance at Echo to get a gauge of that answer.

"Do you ever miss the sun?" Echo asks, suggesting she's conscious that Lyra's answer isn't what she expected either.

"Night is safe," Lyra says, her voice dropping.

River shakes his head. "But does anyone ever go—"

"Night. Is. Safe." Lyra bites each word off, clearly communicating the topic of conversation is over.

River clamps his mouth closed, even more uneasy with this new colony they've found. If they don't go out during the day to stay safe from bees, then that explains their pale complexion. But surely that's going to have an impact on them beyond that. Humans aren't designed to be nocturnal.

The sound of the chant wafts over and Lyra joins in. River grits his teeth. It's fast becoming stuck on a loop in his head. Somewhere to his left, he's pretty sure he can hear Ruff singing along with it.

Echo shakes her head. "I just don't understand."

River doesn't either. These people are happy, yet paranoid. Safe, yet prisoners of the night. Accepting, yet regimented.

And they killed one of their own without conscience.

"Danger!" Manu screams. "The sun is coming!"

River glances to the east, narrowing his gaze again as he tries to see if there's even a sliver of dawn on the horizon. But it's as black as the rest of their surroundings.

"Quick!" Lyra gasps, herding River and Echo toward the building. "The sun is coming!"

Around them, the Moon Workers rush past, the sound of dropped fruit and vegetables peppering the ground. One or two cry out in panic. Someone shoves Echo in their haste, and River helps to steady her. The people have gone from happy, singing gatherers to a panicked, rushing mass in the space of a handful of words. Now they know how that bucket of water they'd found when they arrived got kicked over.

"Hurry!" Lyra hisses. "It's too dangerous out here!"

River and Echo allow themselves to be hustled toward the door, quickly being swallowed by the crowd that bottle-necks trying to get through. He holds tight onto her, everything feeling out of control once again.

Except the moment they're inside, everyone calms. The tension in the air dissipates as if it never existed. Someone even giggles.

"Come, Luna, Celeste," Lyra says beside them.

River grits his teeth. The more that name is said, the more he hates it.

Knowing that's the least of their issues, he waits to see what these strange people are going to do next. The thought of unwinding enough to sleep feels impossible right now, yet the moment he thinks that, a wave of exhaustion washes over him, as if it was waiting for permission. Echo sags against him and he pulls her in close. They're still recovering from nearly dying in the barren plains of the Extinction Zone.

Footsteps clatter up the stairs, indicating that's where the Moon Workers are going. A soft song accompanies them as they ascend, creating a rhythm as their feet take each step.

Night is clear.

Night is true.

Night is safe.

Without realizing it, River finds himself muttering it along with them. He stops the moment he's aware of what's happening.

Echo squeezes his hand. "It's practically a form of indoctrination," she whispers.

She's right. Those three lines are worming their way into his mind, feeling more and more true with each repetition.

River thinks they're at about the tenth floor, so not too far from the roof, when the Moon Workers take a sharp right rather than continuing up. Holding tight onto Echo, he senses more than sees that they step into a large space. The people around them spread out, several yawning loudly. A group of children enter the room and run to their parents.

Suddenly, a strident voice rings out. "Hey, that's my mat!"

"What?" a female snaps back. "It's always been my mat. You sleep over there!"

"No, I definitely sleep here."

River's instantly tense, wondering if someone's about to be mobbed and killed again. Being around the Moon Workers is like being in a powder keg and you never know when someone's going to strike a match.

Light flares to life behind them and River spins around, stepping in front of Echo. Manu is standing on the other side of a large, open room, holding a flaming torch beside him. "It's time to remember," he announces.

It's like the fight never happened as everyone quickly sits on one of the many mats lined up along the walls.

Lyra claps her hands in excitement along with several others. She looks to River and Echo. "It's time to remember!"

Yet River and Echo don't answer. They barely glance at her. They're too busy trying to understand their surroundings.

Every inch of the walls and ceiling are painted with the same line, over and over.

Night is safe.

Some in yellow, some in black, they're all different sizes and different handwriting. It creates a glaring, bee-colored cacophony of the same three words, making them inescapable. It almost hurts to look at, but no matter where River glances, it's slamming into his senses.

Night is safe.

The only wall not covered in the propaganda or graffiti—River's not sure which is a more appropriate term—is the one Manu is standing beside. The stretch of concrete has been painted with a mural, divided into four sections.

"Come, Celeste," Lyra says, touching his elbow. "You and Luna can sleep beside me."

Still reeling from the garish décor, River and Echo sit on a mat woven from dried reeds near the opposite wall. "Thank you," River murmurs, not entirely sure how much he means it.

The Moon Workers have been generous in sharing what they have.

Yet they seem completely unaware of how strange their existence is.

Manu waves his torch as he stands beside the first scene. Clearly created by someone with talent, it's a stark contrast to the crudely painted words it's surrounded by.

"In the beginning, there was food for all," Manu announces, dancing in a strange pirouette as he illuminates the first panel of the mural.

The same building they're in is the backdrop, the gardens they just harvested at its base. But this time, they're ordered and well kept. People walk through them in white suits, smiling and peaceful. River blinks as he realizes it reminds him of the Sting and the Green Zone.

"Food for all!" the people repeat, throwing their hands up in the air.

Manu moves onto the second scene with a leap and a flourish. "But the superbees came. Not everyone survived. Many were Vulnerable."

This painting looks similar at first, but as River focuses more closely, he notices the differences. There are fewer people, and...round stones are dotted through the gardens. Lines have been scratched onto them, like the people of the Dead Zone do to remember their ancestors. His stomach tightens as he wonders if those were any of the protrusions he tripped on while they were out there tonight.

The Moon Workers throw their arms out wide and River has to lean out of the way as Lyra's hand flashes past. "The Vulnerables needed to be protected. One Zone for all!"

"River," Echo whispers. "This is..."

He squeezes her hand in answer. They're watching the origins of their society unfold. And it was a time where the Immune cared for the Vulnerable, rather than cast them aside. It's the goal they're working toward.

One Zone for all.

Echo draws in a sharp breath, and River finds he does the same as his gaze falls on the next panel of the mural.

The image has morphed again. This time, it's less green, more bare. The building is boarded up. The crops are sparse and dying. The rounded stones are becoming more numerous.

River or Echo would definitely have tripped over one of them.

The Moon Workers slap their hands on the floor. "Not enough workers!" they cry, slapping again. "Not enough food!"

River's still and silent as he processes that. With only the Immune to care for the Vulnerables, the society struggled to survive. He draws Echo closer to him, even as he knows this is one thing he can't shield her from.

The knowledge that their dream was brought to fruition generations ago.

And failed.

Manu stomps his feet in time to the slapping as he moves to the final scene. The vegetation around the building has now shrunk. It's browner. Patches of round stones are scattered around. Scoring grounds are cropping up.

And a group of people are in the Extinction Zone, walking away.

"The Immune left," Manu cries, waving his torch manically. "We were Forgotten!"

"Forgotten!" the people wail. "Forgotten!"

River's chest aches. His eyes burn as he stares, unblinking, at the final scene.

The Immune left to create another Green Zone. They built the Sting.

And a Dead Zone for those who failed the Confirmation.

"But we found a way!" Manu dances around the room, the light of his flame flickering over the three-word sentence that ensured these people could survive, irrespective of whether they're Immune or Vulnerable.

Night is safe.

The Moon Workers lift and drop their arms as if they're worshiping the words they're surrounded by. The same words they're now singing out loud.

Manu reaches the mural again and smothers the flames of the torch with a length of material. "Now rest, Moon Workers. Tomorrow night we will rise again as one."

Lyra sighs, the sound full of happiness and contentment, then curls up on her mat. The others do the same around the expansive room. River finds he can barely move, let alone lie down. Beside him, Echo's just as frozen.

Soft snoring quickly fills the air. Someone groans as they roll over. Lyra's still in the way only someone in a deep sleep is.

Echo's the first to break the shocked stupor they're in. She tugs on River's hand. "Come," she whispers.

River follows, even though he has no idea where she's thinking of going. Anywhere away from the black and yellow words waiting in the dark, away from the mural of shattered dreams, is preferable right now.

Moving carefully and silently, they slip out of the room, Echo leading River to the stairs. But rather than going down, she goes up.

A single flight of stairs and another thick piece of material hanging over the doorway, and they're on the rooftop. They don't go far, considering it's dark and they have no idea what they're surrounded by. To River's surprise, Echo's the first to sink to the warm cement floor. He joins her, even more surprised when she curls up with her head in his lap.

Echo's exhausted. This is all taking far more of a toll on her than he realized.

"Oren was right," she chokes out.

River strokes her hair back from her face, hating that what she says is true. Their ancestors tried to save everyone, and it was a disaster. They almost killed them all.

Yet surely the answer can't be living in the dark, slowly going crazy without even realizing it.

"Echo," River says, realizing something.

"Immunity is the key," she breathes.

"Yes. Everyone can be outside. Everyone can work."

"Everyone can survive," she finishes.

No more segregation. No needing to live nocturnally.

"We have to leave, River," she says. "We have to tell the others."

They have to find the Sovereign and the Code, now more than ever.

He chews his lip, knowing Echo's right, but also conscious that right now, she probably doesn't have the strength to trek back to the Green Zone. Or Dead Zone. Or wherever they're going to hide as they figure this out.

"We'd have to go during the day, when they're asleep, in case they try to stop us," he says, his mind working. He registers the faint hint of dawn on the horizon, which gives him an idea. "But the bees will also be out, which leaves me at risk of being stung."

Echo tenses, clearly not liking the sound of that.

He presses his lips to her forehead. "Unless we leave on a day where it's raining. This dry spell has to break, eventually. Bees don't fly when there's no sun, it messes with their navigation systems."

Echo relaxes as she pats his chest. "You're very clever, you know that?"

"I don't know about that," he says, chuckling. "In fact, there's only one thing I'm sure of."

She angles her head up. "Oh?"

"How I feel about you." He brushes a kiss over her nose. "I love you, Echo."

Her teeth flash in the dark. "I love you, too," she says, her voice thick.

Both with emotion and exhaustion.

River settles down next to her, resting her head on his shoulder and making sure she's comfortable. "Get some sleep. We'll have to return below before the sun gets too high."

Echo doesn't object. In fact, she's asleep almost as quickly as Lyra was. River holds her as he watches the sun slowly rise, casting its light over the Moon Zone. Below them, the bees would be waking, flying out to complete the work ecosystems can't survive without. The same bees the Moon Workers will do anything to avoid, including living in perpetual night as their minds and bodies slowly waste away.

A few days will give Echo time to recover. To become strong again.

Because they have to go back.

Somehow, they have to stop history from repeating itself.

CHAPTER

FIVE

ECHO

E cho wakes with the afternoon sun on her face and River at her side. She snuggles in closer, feeling more alive than she has in a long time. Her body has been fed and rested. And her mind has had a chance to sort out the jumbled events of the last couple of days.

She puts her hand to the locket her father gave her, remembering her promise to plant the seeds back in the Dead Zone. It's a promise she intends to keep. She's clearer on that than ever now.

The Moon Zone isn't a haven. It's a chaotic assembly of lost souls. She needs to go home. Because she's not Luna. She's Echo. And River is most definitely not Celeste.

"Hey." River presses his lips to her forehead. His voice is gravelly, and it tugs at Echo's insides as her heart expands with the depth of her feelings.

"Hey, yourself," she replies, tilting her face to kiss his lips.

Just as she's losing herself in the moment, a dark cloud crosses the sky, extinguishing the bright rays of the sun.

They pull apart and look up. There's a single gray cloud that's covering the sun like a blanket.

"Surely that's not rain already?" River's eyes are wide. "Did Mother Nature hear you?"

"One cloud doesn't mean rain," says Echo, not wanting to get her hopes up. She'd thought they might have to wait days or even weeks before they could make a run for it but if the rain comes today, they could escape this place far sooner than either of them expected.

She sits up and glances around, seeing that the rooftop is nothing more than a vast concrete space.

"It's not quite Eden, is it?" River's brows raise as he takes in their surroundings. "Such a waste. They could grow all kinds of crops up here."

"That would attract the bees," Echo points out.

"Then they should sleep up here." River gets to his feet and stretches. "A bit of sun would be good for them."

"Night is safe, Celeste." Echo grins as she waits for River's reaction to the name he hates so much.

He pokes out his tongue and shakes his head. "Do you think that's why they behave so strangely? Is it the lack of sun?"

"Maybe." Echo shrugs as she stands, joining River at the edge of the rooftop. Having grown up in a zone drenched by sun, she's never really considered the impact of living without the benefits it brings.

"When we were growing up in the Sting, our diets were carefully managed to make sure we got enough vitamin D, given we weren't allowed outside" says River.

"What does vitamin D do?" Echo asks, far from an expert on various vitamins. "Is that what causes the scurge? If you don't get enough, I mean."

River shakes his head. "That's lack of vitamin C."

"I didn't know I was getting a spelling lesson." Echo smirks. "C. D. Are there vitamins A or B?"

"There are actually." He smiles. "But lack of vitamin D can make you tired and weak. And depressed."

"Oh." Echo grimaces. "That actually makes sense. No wonder they're all snapping at each other."

"Night is safe, Luna." River lifts a brow.

"Until everyone loses their minds and starts killing each other," she adds.

River sighs. "Unfortunately, I can't see them chanting that."

"Nor can I." Echo looks down at the unkempt garden that rings the building, then the never-ending nothingness that lies beyond. The Moon Workers were left behind by the rest of the world. Forgotten. And now they're determined to be remembered, if not by everyone else, then themselves.

And once Echo is far away from here, she'll most certainly remember them. Just perhaps not for the reasons they would like. The strange ceremony they held last night in front of the murals had been enlightening. It showed what can happen when Vulnerables and Immunes live under the one roof. And if this is the result, then it's far from a good solution. They need another way. One where everyone is Immune. One where everyone can safely live beneath the sun's light.

"We should go down and get some more food," Echo suggests. "I'm starving. If you wait on the ground floor where it's safe from the bees, I'll bring you back something."

River pats his stomach. "I'm still full from last night, but I'm sure I can fit something in."

"We should eat as much as we can." Echo looks to the sky again, studying the solitary gray cloud. "We need to be ready to run."

"Maybe we should hide a bag of food somewhere." River

41

heads to the stairwell and holds back the thick piece of material that acts as a door.

Echo follows and stands on the top landing, blinking as her eyes adjust to the dim light. River slips his hand into hers and it's almost as if this helps her see better. It certainly helps steady her and gives her strength.

"Where are you going?" a voice hisses.

They spin around to see Lyra on the stairs.

"We thought we'd head down to the garden," says Echo, bracing herself for Lyra's reaction. "We'll be careful."

"No." Lyra turns on a torch and shines it in their eyes. "You must wait. Night is safe. Day is for sleep."

"Then why aren't you sleeping?" River asks, shielding his face.

"I can't sleep." Lyra lets the torch light fall and crosses her arms. "Sleep is hard sometimes."

River reaches out to touch Lyra's arm. "Maybe if you got a little sun, then—"

"Night is safe," she snaps. "Let me show you what I mean, if you don't believe me."

Echo shoots River a look and the torchlight is quickly shifted to the stairwell as Lyra takes a few steps down.

"Come on," she says, sounding almost excited. "Don't you want to see?"

Echo isn't at all sure she wants to see anything else this zone has to show her but finds herself gripping the handrail and taking the stairs. Lyra leads them past the floor where the Moon Workers are sleeping and continues down another floor where they emerge into a large open space.

Echo squints, wishing Lyra would hold her torch still so they could get a better look at where they are.

"What is this place?" River asks.

"It's the census room." Lyra gives a little laugh like this

should have been obvious. "Manu added your names last night."

"Can you shine the light around?" Echo asks.

"I can do better than that." Lyra walks across the room and presses a switch. Light pours into the cavernous space.

"You have electricity?" River asks, his jaw dropping open.

"It's solar power," Lyra explains. "We only have it on this floor. The census is important. The Moon Zone remembers everyone."

Echo looks around and draws in a sharp breath. Just like the floor above, the concrete walls have been covered in text. Except the writing is smaller and the words are arranged in long columns. She steps closer to get a better look, wishing her literacy skills were stronger. Perhaps a spelling lesson on the roof might not have been such a silly idea.

"Apollo," she sounds out, looking at the top of one of the lines of text. "Callisto. Mona. Aruna... Are these names?"

"That's right," says Lyra, proudly. "This is a list of those who were Forgotten. And all who came after them. Now they're Remembered."

"There are so many people," says River, standing a little further down the wall.

Echo notices small symbols have been drawn beside each name. "What do these drawings mean?"

Lyra points to one of a sun. "Jericho died in the day. So did Hala." She moves her finger down to a symbol of an insect. "Crescent was stung by a bee." Then she points at a knife. "Perdita was stabbed."

River gives Echo a look of alarm.

"But look here," says Lyra, claiming back their attention. "Here's another sun, which means Vikesh died in the day as well. And Sasi, and Hang, and Kuu. Just look at all the suns."

Echo looks down the list, seeing that Lyra is right. More than half the names have symbols of the sun beside them.

"So many suns," Lyra muses. "And not a single moon. Night is safe."

"Where are our names?" River asks.

"At the end of the list, silly." Lyra flashes her brown teeth and moves down the room. "You only just arrived."

They follow Lyra. The final column only has symbols next to about half the names. The other half have blank spaces, ready to record their deaths, however they may happen. At the end of the column, neatly scrawled, are *Luna* and *Celeste*.

Echo scans the list, looking for Chandra, the woman who'd allegedly drained the water tanks. Finding her name, she sees she has an ax drawn beside her name. Which is accurate. But also completely deceptive. She points at it and River nods, not needing to say out loud what she knows he's thinking.

Chandra had most definitely died at night. Yet, conveniently, she has an ax as her symbol instead of a moon. It seems those who die in the day get a sun and those who die in the night get another inventive symbol. Are the Moon Workers really so brainwashed that they can't see this census is simply another part of the propaganda being leveled at them?

"Look! Here's me." Lyra points at her own name with pride. "I'll always be Remembered. I'm so happy you found us, so that now you can be Remembered, too."

"Lyra," says River, gently. "We can't stay here. You do realize that, don't you?"

Lyra's eyes fly wide open. "Nobody leaves here. You can't leave here! We need more Workers. We must all be Remembered!"

"There are people who need us back home," says Echo. "Their lives depend on us. They remember us, too."

"But you're my friends," says Lyra, panic rising in her voice. "You're mine!"

River glances at Echo, then at the stairs. She gives him a subtle nod to show she understands. They knew they might have to run at short notice, but it seems the time has come a lot sooner than they expected.

"I can see what you're planning," Lyra growls, switching from happy tour guide to menacing prison guard in a blink. "You're going to leave me! But if you try to escape, I'll tell Manu. Then you'll have a knife drawn beside your names. He doesn't like people to leave. Is that what you want?"

"They're not our names." River pulls back his shoulders and narrows his eyes. "This is Echo, not Luna. And my name is River. You can't erase who we are. If you want to remember us, then remember us for who we really are."

Lyra gasps, stumbling backward as if River's words physically repel her.

Echo takes her chance and runs to the stairwell, relieved when River follows. They race to the landing and are about to head down when Ruff jumps out at them.

"Go up!" he whispers as he holds them back. "They're waiting for you at the bottom of the stairs. Manu is going to kill you! He heard you talking."

"Is there another way out?" River rakes his hands through his hair.

"Traitor!" Lyra bursts out the door and sees Ruff talking to them. "You have betrayed us, Samir!"

Ruff groans, knowing he's just as dead as they are now. He steps forward, gripping Lyra by her filthy shirt collar. "My friends and I are going up the stairs," he growls. "And you're not going to stop us, or you'll end up with my fist drawn beside your name. Do you understand?"

Lyra yelps, trying to wriggle away. "I understand."

Ruff lets go of her and grabs River and Echo by the arms, hauling them back up the stairs with surprising strength. They emerge onto the rooftop to find the gray cloud has been chased away, leaving nothing but blue sky.

"Great," Echo groans. "Even if we can get down, we can't go far in this heat."

"No choice." Ruff races to the edge of the roof. "Manu will kill us if we stay here. We'll have to climb down one of the water pipes."

"Stop!" River holds up a hand. "That won't work. It's not strong enough."

"No choice," Ruff repeats, throwing a leg over the edge of the roof. Echo's not sure what's taken place since Ruff arrived here, but it can't have been good. He's clearly terrified of Manu. So much that he'd rather fall off the roof than face him.

Ruff grips onto the water pipe, testing it to see if it will hold his weight and it pulls away from the building, taking Ruff with it. Echo screams and River grabs Ruff by his belt just before he's flung to his death and hauls him back to safety. The pipe hangs loose in the air a few feet away from the concrete and wobbles.

"What are we going to do?" Echo's heart pounds as she looks around. Surely, there has to be a fire escape or ladder somewhere. Anything!

The curtain at the stairwell is pulled back and Manu and the other Moon Workers burst onto the roof, guarding the only exit as they advance forward, waving their gardening tools. Echo's seen firsthand what damage those tools can do. And she doesn't plan on being the next victim.

"There's no way out," Manu shouts. "We fed you. We remembered you. We asked for very little in return. And this is the thanks we get. You've forced us out into the day. We could die out here!"

"Night is safe!" the Moon Workers chant, glancing up at the sun in terror. "Night is safe."

"Kill them and we can return inside," Manu commands.

Two men march forward, waving axes.

Echo links hands with River, hating that their legacy will be two names on a wall to be remembered by. And it won't even be their own names.

Just as the men are about to close the gap, a loud thrumming overhead has everyone stilling. Echo pivots and lets out a moan to see a familiar shadow growing in the sky.

"It's a Worker!" River gasps.

An enormous set of wings is powering one of Oren's mechanical beasts through the air at impossible speed. The machine lands on the concrete roof and turns to Manu with her antennae twitching.

Manu screams, running for the stairwell, his people tripping over themselves to follow. They disappear behind the curtain and the Worker spins around to face River, Echo and Ruff. She scans them with all five of her evil eyes. Then she tilts her head. And the glowing disc on her back lights up.

Echo draws in a gulp. Oren has found them.

And this time, there really is no escape.

CHAPTER

SIX

RIVER

E cho steps around River as his arm shoots out, already predicting his innate need to protect her. She stands beside him, defiant and strong as always, even in the face of a giant mechanical bee that's been sent to finish them off.

Oren must've figured out they survived, which doesn't bode well for Reed. River should've guessed that at the slightest suspicion he and Echo were alive his father would do anything he could to finish what he started. If the Workers can be programmed to target a person's unique combination of DNA, of course a Worker could be sent to track them down.

And dispatch them.

Somewhere behind them, Ruff is whimpering even as his teeth chatter, giving the petrified sound a strange, almost rhythmic beat.

Except the Worker doesn't move.

She stands on the roof, still and glittering in the afternoon sun. River's never seen one in the daylight, and he has to admit it's an impressive sight.

And a terrifying one.

The black is darker somehow, but also shinier. Her size seems to have multiplied. Every angle and joint and masterfully designed moving part is on display.

Including the disc glowing a brilliant silver on her back. Silver!

"Nectar?" River asks in shock.

The Worker bee whirs in response, her jaws twitching as if she just spoke.

Echo takes a step forward. "Nectar!" she gasps in surprise.

"Stay back!" Ruff screams. "That thing will kill you!"

"No she won't," Echo says without glancing over her shoulder. She takes a few more steps toward the robotic bee. "She's a friend."

River leaps to her side, not entirely sure he agrees, even if this Worker has been reprogrammed by his sister.

Echo stops in front of Nectar, angling her head up to look in her metallic face. "Flora sent you, didn't she?"

Nectar whirrs again, and River has no idea what that means. In the past, it's always been to communicate, "I can't wait to end you."

Behind them, Ruff moans brokenly. River's sure that if Manu and the other Moon Workers weren't somewhere below waiting to kill them, Ruff would've disappeared the moment Nectar turned up.

Echo angles her head, studying Nectar. "But why are you here, huh?"

Nectar simply stares back, the lights in her large eyes flickering in the same repetitive pattern.

Echo takes another step forward and extends her hand.

"Echo," River says in a low voice. "We don't—"

Her palm brushes over Nectar's nose and the effect is instantaneous. The robotic bee lowers her massive head, the loudest whirring so far rumbling from within her metal chest. River reaches out to grab Echo's hand back, ready to face the Moon Workers rather than this deadly machine, when a small piece of metal slips back from the center of Nectar's forehead.

A small, black circle is visible.

"Run!" Ruff screams, mirroring the same word that just ricocheted through River's mind.

A beam of light spears from the black hole, fracturing out. Several of its rays land on Echo before River can yank her out of the way. His heart screams a denial. There's no way Oren would be taking any more chances. He'll end them quickly this time. With finality.

An image of Flora appears, partially overlapping Echo. "River! Echo! If you're watching this, that means Nectar found you!"

Echo leaps to the side, her eyes just as wide as River's. Simultaneously, they step around to stand beside Nectar, gazing at the holographic image of his twin. Flora smiles at them, the image clear and detailed enough that the relief on her face is evident.

The smile grows across her face. "It was Echo who touched her, wasn't it?" she says knowingly. "She's more of a risk taker."

River almost rolls his eyes at the teasing note in his twin's voice. It's mostly annoying because she's right. Beside him, Echo nudges him with her elbow. "It's a freaking robotic bee, okay?" he grumbles under his breath.

Echo giggles and River can't help but smile. The sound will always fill him with joy, no matter what. He's here, fighting this fight, in part so he can hear that sweet sound more often.

Flora clasps her hands, looking serious again. "Once Reed got a message to us that you were in the Extinction Zone, I worked as quickly as possible. Nectar's been programmed to track your DNA. Even the smallest trace is all she needs." Her face twists. "I just had to hope I wasn't too late."

River's stomach tightens. She would've been if it weren't for the Moon Zone.

"Nectar is programmed to return you at dusk, so we can hide your arrival. I can't wait to see you, River." Flora blinks. "Oh, and you too, Echo."

The recording shuts off and the image of Flora disappears. Beside him, River hears the faint buzz as the cover slides back over the small projector in Nectar's forehead. He and Echo turn to each other.

"We're being rescued," she says, blinking as she tries to process it.

"By a Worker," Rivers adds, just as astounded at that unexpected twist.

Echo wrinkles her nose at him. "By Nectar," she corrects.

"Don't you start," he huffs, his lips twitching with a smile. "She's not some...pet."

Echo pats the side of Nectar's neck. "Don't you listen to him," she coos. "He's like his sister. Doesn't trust easily."

Nectar whirrs in response, then shuts down.

No doubt waiting for dusk when she'll take them back to the Dead Zone.

Ruff takes a cautious step forward. "You can't seriously be thinking that thing is going to save you."

River arches a brow at him. "You could go back downstairs if you like?"

Ruff tucks his arm in as if wanting an inch more distance between him and the Moon Workers. Yet he glances at Nectar, just as anxious. "What is it?" he whispers.

"A deadly, killing machine," Echo says, patting Nectar again. "That's been reprogrammed to be an ally."

"She's practically a friend," River says dryly.

Echo grins up at him. "Exactly."

"You can't be serious," Ruff rasps.

"You heard Flora," Echo says. "Nectar will be taking us back at dusk."

Ruff reels back. "You can't be thinking of returning. They'll kill you!"

River snorts. "They've been trying to do that from the beginning." It didn't stop him and Echo then, and it won't now.

Ruff looks back at the material covering the door, no doubt thinking of the murderous Manu somewhere on the other side. Surely he realizes he can't stay, even if returning to the Dead Zone is dangerous.

He looks back to Nectar doubtfully. "We're going to ride it?"

River blinks, realizing that's logical. Being carried by those metal legs like they did in the Sovereign graveyard would get uncomfortable over time. Then he wonders if Nectar even has the ability to carry three of them... Flora planned for only River and Echo to return. She has no idea they have Ruff with them.

"Yes, we are," he says firmly. They'll make it work. They have to. Leaving Ruff behind to be butchered by Manu isn't an option.

Echo glances up at the sun, squinting. "At dusk," she says. A small frown pulls down her brow. "Looks like that rain is coming after all."

River follows her line of sight and registers the dark clouds accumulating on the horizon. Seems they would've left today, with or without Nectar.

"Dusk is exactly when the Moon Workers will return," Ruff mutters.

Echo rolls her eyes. "Less doom and gloom, Ruff. Let's focus on the fact we're going home in a few hours."

"She's right," River agrees. "We'll use this opportunity to rest, then get out of here."

And go home.

He realizes both the Green Zone and the Dead Zone flash through his mind at the word *home*. Somehow, he's now a product of both.

And when they become one, when everyone is Immune, then it won't matter, he tells himself. There will be no more choosing. No more who is right and who is wrong. Just equality.

And peace.

Echo slips an arm around his waist. "We're going back," she whispers, her eyes shining.

"To fix this," River says, tugging her in closer.

Discovering the Moon Zone has shown them where they came from. How the Green Zone and Dead Zone were founded.

Now, they forge where this is going.

Ruff snorts quietly as he makes his way to the edge of the building. He settles himself down against the low wall that circles the top, away from the door and Nectar. "The foolishness of youth," he mutters under his breath. "Dreamers, the lot of them."

"Let's stay with Nectar," Echo says to River, ignoring Ruff.

He glances at the giant metal body that's as unmoving as a mountain. "Great idea," he says dryly.

Echo grins, tugging him toward Nectar. Ducking, they slip underneath her head and make themselves comfortable under the black thorax, leaning against one of her legs. River can't help but think of the other times they've been this close to a Worker.

It usually involved fighting for their life.

Yet he implicitly trusts his twin. Flora would do anything

for those she loves, and that includes him. Which means trusting this metal beast...

River settles his arm around Echo. "Rest," he suggests. "We have a few hours before dusk."

"Are you sure?" she asks as she sinks further against him.

River nods, smiling. "We're about to ride a giant metal bee. You'll want your strength for that."

Echo tucks her head into his shoulder. "I love you, River," she murmurs, her voice already thickening.

He presses a kiss to the crown of her head. "And I love you. Now, sleep."

To his surprise, that's exactly what Echo does. As River listens to her steady breathing, he can't help but worry. Although he's glad Echo's resting, he didn't actually expect her to take him up on the offer. The Echo he knows is always ready for the next attack. Probably because there's always been one coming.

The Extinction Zone took more of a toll than he realized. Or maybe it's also the cumulative toll of all three zones. They've certainly been through a lot. Or she's unwell... Pushing away the worrying thought, River keeps scanning between the also-dozing Ruff, the covered door to the stairs, and the horizon. The first two don't change. The last is what ends up keeping River's focus.

As the time passes, the clouds come close, dropping lower as they grow darker. The sight makes him nervous. Not because he's worried about rain. But because it's harder and harder to tell when the cusp of dusk will be here. There's no way of knowing when Nectar is going to come back to life.

And when the Moon Workers are going to return.

Ruff snorts and jolts awake as if River's thoughts just disturbed him. His gaze snaps to the door as he vaults to his feet.

Or he heard something.

River's pulse goes from slumbering to screeching through his veins. "Echo—"

He's just grabbed her shoulders when two things happen.

A torrent falls from the skies, instantly drenching them.

And Manu leaps past the material acting as a door, the Moon Workers spilling out after him.

River jolts to his feet, bringing Echo with him. She stumbles, then quickly rights herself. She's beside River as they move in front of Nectar.

The Moon Workers spread out, their tattered clothes sticking to their bodies as the rain falls in a steady thrum, and River realizes one thing hasn't happened.

Nectar is still powered down.

"They must die!" Manu screams, waving his scythe. "They do not respect the night!"

The Moon Workers shout their agreement even as a few glance around nervously. River realizes it must not be quite dusk. They're out here earlier because of the rain.

He steps forward, holding his hands out placatingly. "There's no need for anyone to die. We're about to leave."

"Never!" Manu screeches. "No one leaves the Moon Zone! This is where you're Remembered!"

River doesn't even bother trying to reason with that. Dead isn't better than Forgotten. "Echo, climb on Nectar." They need to be ready to leave the moment they can.

"I will," she says, her voice low. "Once she's awake."

River tenses. "I really think you should—"

"Silence!" Manu shrieks. "You have brought the giant bee of death upon us! Attack!"

Except the Moon Workers don't move. Most of them are staring at Nectar, waiting for the beast to charge.

"Attack! They cannot get away!"

No one moves. River holds his breath, hoping just the presence of Nectar will stop blood from being shed. The moment she powers up, they can get out of here.

Except Manu lifts his scythe into the pounding rain. "I will not be a coward!" He launches forward, rivulets running down his pale face and into his matted beard. "I will protect the night!"

Adrenaline flashes through River's veins as he also breaks into a run. He can't fight. He has no skills in combat. But he's not going to sit by and let Manu attack Echo. He's taken two steps when a new sound joins Manu's screaming and the rain pounding on the cement roof.

A gentle, unmistakable whirring.

Nectar's eyes flash with light, making the Moon Workers shy away, most of them covering their faces as if they're about to be burned.

River instantly changes trajectory, discovering Echo was already beside him and is doing the same. Nectar hunkers down as they draw close, lowering herself so they can climb on.

"Ruff!" Echo shouts. "Hurry!"

Her words are almost unnecessary. Ruffs shoves past River in his haste to get to Nectar, leaping on a split-second before Echo.

"No! I won't let you leave!" Manu shouts.

River turns around, his blood icing at how close the man is. A blurred movement has him flinching back as the scythe slices through the rain. River doesn't think. The moment the dirty blade is past him, he leaps forward, shoving Manu.

The man stumbles, then slips, landing on his backside. River turns back to Nectar, blinking through the water pouring down his face, and finds Echo has her hand outstretched.

"Get on!"

As if Nectar knows the danger, or more likely because Flora programmed her to get going quickly, her wings snap out. Raindrops splash and fracture on their midnight surface. Ruff leans forward, wrapping his arms around her neck, looking almost as pale as the Moon Workers.

River grabs Echo's hand, noting how slick it is. Nectar's wings become a blur, sending a spray of water over him, but he doesn't let go. In fact, Echo tightens her grip. She leans back, hauling him up.

River leaps, knowing there's only one chance at this. Nectar's slowly inching into the air.

The moment his feet leave the roof, Nectar lurches down, her legs clattering on the cement and making River stumble backward, releasing Echo's hand.

Nectar surges up again as he regains his balance, his heart plunging as undeniably as the robotic bee did. The three of them are too heavy. Nectar won't be able to lift off.

River already knows what that means. He's going to be left—

"River!" Echo screams.

A lancing pain explodes across his shoulder and he staggers to his knees. Through the agony, he hears Manu cackle maniacally. "You will be remembered, Celeste!"

River groans. He hates that name. Yet it's now going to be his legacy. That thought is enough for him to lurch to the side in case another blow is coming before spinning around, preparing to defend himself. He may not be able to get away on Nectar, but at least he can fight for his name.

"My name is River!" he shouts, wishing there weren't two Manus swimming before him.

Manu slashes the scythe again and River goes to duck, except he has no idea which way. There are now three Manus.

He blinks rapidly, bringing them back into focus and one person, only to discover it's too late.

The scythe is arcing down toward his head.

"No!" Echo screams. "River!"

River braces himself for the pain. At least his true name was the last one to pierce the air.

With a shout, Ruff shoots past River, bowling straight into Manu and knocking him over. One of the Moon Workers cries out, but no one moves.

"Get on that thing," Ruff screams. "Hurry!"

River doesn't question the reprieve he was just granted. Spinning around, he finds Nectar's now a few feet off the ground. He runs and vaults, focusing with everything he has as he catches Echo's hand. With one mighty yank, she helps him settle behind her.

River grasps her waist as a mighty roar sounds below them. Ruff lifts Manu and carries him to the edge of the building, then throws him over. He turns around, not bothering to watch the man's demise. There's a faint thud, then just the steady roll of rain.

Ruff turns to the Moon Workers. "I am Samir. I refuse to be Forgotten." He thumps his chest. "But I also refuse to hide any longer!"

The Moon Workers stare at him, several with their mouths open. Lyra is the first to move. She steps forward. "What else can we do?" she asks, her hair plastered to her face.

Ruff hesitates, a flash of uncertainty crossing his features.

"You can harvest in the rain," River shouts. "There are no bees, just like the night."

The Moon Workers glance at each other, faces wet and mouths slightly open.

A slow smile spreads over Lyra's face. "We could see where we're going."

"I could pick the ripest peaches!" says a man next to her.

"I'm scared..."

River doesn't hear the rest of what the woman says as Nectar spins around. Her body angles forward, making him and Echo clutch even tighter. A heartbeat later, she shoots forward, slicing through the sheets of water falling from above.

Leaving behind the Moon Zone and whatever was just unfolding.

And taking them to the Dead Zone.

Where they have even less idea what they're about to face.

CHAPTER
SEVEN
ECHO

At first, riding on the back of Nectar is terrifying. Thankfully, Flora attached a strap around the mechanical beast's neck and Echo grips it with white knuckles, her stomach dropping with each dip and churning as they soar higher. She holds her breath, unsure if she wants to scream or throw up.

River has his arms around her waist. It's comforting, as well as providing constant reassurance he hasn't fallen off. Which is a very real risk given the speed they're moving. They'll be back in the Dead Zone in no time at this rate.

Nectar flaps her wings, their constant beating sending droplets of rain bouncing as the wind rushes at Echo's face. She squeezes her eyes closed, wanting to shield them but not daring to let go of her tight hold. Especially given River is depending on her to stay steady.

Just as she wonders how long her heart can continue to pound at this rapid rate, something miraculous happens.

The rain stops.

The setting sun chases away the clouds on the horizon.

And Echo opens her eyes wide.

Spectacular streaks of orange fan out and Echo gazes in awe as the sun disappears. The moon, which is already high in the sky, takes its turn at ruling the sky.

Nectar flies on, navigating the fading light with expert precision and a large white bird soars past. They swerve to avoid it and River lets out a whoop of joy as their altitude drops, filling Echo with a new sense of exhilaration. This must be exactly what it feels like to be an eagle, or to sit in one of those flying machines people used generations ago.

"Look!" River shouts directly into her ear. "We're nearly there already!"

Echo turns and sees the Green Zone lit up by the shimmering glow of the Sting that rises proudly from the center of a world made from deep shades of green. Directly beside the Green Zone is a sea of darkness, the net encasing the Dead Zone barely visible in the limited light. The inequality between the zones is even more stark when viewed from this perspective and Echo shakes her head at the injustice of it all.

How might this look when they've managed to make everyone Immune? There would be no net for a start. And the green fields would spread beyond their current boundaries as they discover ways to regenerate the earth. The Betadome would become just another orchard. And maybe a new Sting could be built to replace all those falling down buildings of the Dead Zone. Nobody would ever lose their family again in the same way as Chase.

Now *that* would be paradise.

"River, look," Echo gasps. The wind takes her voice, carrying her words far away from the ears they were intended for.

A moonbow has burst from the sky and colored light is stretching across the expanse ahead in a wide arc. There's crimson morphing into oranges and gold. Then sparkling emerald merging with blues and purples, finishing in a ribbon of deep violet. The phenomenon crosses both zones with the far end meeting the rolling nothingness of the Extinction Zone.

River grips Echo tighter and leans forward to press his cheek to hers.

"It's welcoming us home," he says directly into her ear.

She smiles, knowing the exact opposite is the truth. Why else would there be a need to arrive at night if they were truly welcome?

"It's beautiful!" she shouts, unsure now if it's raindrops or tears that are wetting her face as they're swept from her eyes by the constant movement of air.

"You're beautiful!" River calls back.

Nectar flies closer to the moonbow. Except the nearer they get, the further it seems to move away. It's like a dance of seduction where the partners can admire each other, but never touch.

Then Nectar changes direction and the moonbow slowly fades, leaving the night sky as a backdrop to a spectacular display of twinkling stars. Echo relaxes into the experience of flying, taking in the magnificence of the world, and just how insignificant she is as part of it. Then she reminds herself that even the tiniest of things can have a major impact. She only needs to look at the size of a bee sting to be sure of that.

A particularly bright star catches Echo's attention and she wonders if it's still alive or she's seeing the light it emitted many years ago. If she and River can bring Immunity to the world, they could be like that star—the impact they make on the world being felt long after their deaths.

Nectar approaches the Dead Zone from the opposite side to the Green Zone, heading for the scoring grounds. The night wraps them in a cloak and they land outside the net. The

Worker lowers herself to the ground and Echo and River climb off with wobbly legs.

"That was..." Echo can't find the word to describe what they just lived through.

"Yeah." River slips a steadying arm around her. "It really was."

Nectar goes to the net and uses her front legs to work on the threads, seeming to unravel it somehow.

"How is she doing that?" River asks, peering into the darkness.

They go closer to get a better look and see that Nectar is indeed cutting through the net. Her claws work quickly and with amazing dexterity, and a large hole is quickly formed. She goes through to the Dead Zone, turning to Echo and River as she waits for them to follow.

They scurry through and Nectar gets to work repairing the damage, stitching the net together until it looks like nothing ever happened.

"That's incredible," Echo breathes.

Flora and Chase appear out of the shadows. River embraces his twin enthusiastically while Echo gives Chase a quick and awkward hug.

"It worked!" Flora squeals. "I knew Nectar could do it. She's amazing!"

"We can't thank you enough," says Echo. "Your timing was perfect."

Flora claps her hands. "Excellent. It's such a relief to have you both home."

Home. That's exactly what the Dead Zone has always been to Echo and Chase. It seems the same word now applies to River and Flora. It's a thought that warms Echo's heart. Her home is River's home. And their future is together.

"I hope you've thought of somewhere good to hide us," says River.

"Don't worry," says Chase, returning to Flora's side. "Nectar's taken care of that."

"Is there anything Nectar can't do?" Echo asks, laughing.

"Not much." Flora's teeth flash in the moonlight. "Come on. I'll show you."

They pick their way around the scoring grounds, trying to avoid stepping on any of the marked stones, which would feel disrespectful to the person it had been laid for. It's an eerie place at night, but Echo can see why Flora and Chase chose it. Nobody comes here apart from on the Night of Keeping Score. It's kind of amazing that Chase is here at all. It seems he's had to come to peace with this place. Maybe some healing has happened amongst all this heartache and pain.

There's a large pile of rocks over the other side of the grounds that have been stacked up near the net. This is where people can look for a stone to use as their marker, although many already have other stones in mind to use. It's where Echo found the stone she gave to Reed to keep score for his cousin. The same stone he used to hit River over the head...

"You want us to hide behind a pile of rocks?" she asks Flora, not feeling at all confident in this plan.

Flora's laugh tinkles through the night air. "Just wait."

Nectar comes over and shifts a few stones out of the way, revealing a large metal plate. The Worker lifts it and heads down into a tunnel, the glow of the silver disc on her back lighting the way.

"It's a bunker," Flora announces proudly. "Nectar made it."

"Good thinking," says River, his voice filled with awe. "The Alphadome is far too risky."

"Exactly." Flora heads into the tunnel behind her Worker. "We need somewhere Oren has no idea exists."

Echo and River follow Flora, with Chase taking up the rear. As they descend into the earth, an uneasy feeling wraps around Echo's spine. Are they going to be nocturnal like the Moon Workers, hiding in the bunker during the day and only daring to come out at night? They already know what that would do to the state of their minds.

"It's only for a little while," River whispers in her ear, sensing her discomfort. "Just until we work something else out."

They emerge into a space that looks very much like the Alphadome minus the large glass enclosure in the center. It even has a tunnel to what should be the crypt and an opening to what Echo assumes is a LaB. If it had white walls, Echo would wonder if somehow she's been transported to the actual Alphadome.

"I had Nectar copy the floorplan," says Flora proudly, seeing her confusion. "She used the Alphadome as a blueprint."

"But how could she have done this in such a short space of time?" River asks. "It hasn't been more than a couple of days."

"She started work before you left," says Flora. "And she works quickly."

There's a humming noise coming from the LaB. "And she hasn't finished yet," says Chase. "She still has to dig out Flora's LaB."

Echo leans forward and sees the LaB is little more than an alcove. Nectar is in there digging, soil flying behind her as she works.

"She should be finished by morning," says Flora. "Chase and I will go to the Alphadome to get the rest of my equipment. There'll be no need to go back there at all after that."

"We've set the crypt up for you," says Chase, motioning for

them to follow him down the corridor. He waves a torch, lighting their way.

Echo shoots River a concerned look as they follow.

"Don't worry," Chase laughs. "We're not using it for dead bodies."

They emerge into a replica of the crypt, although without all the shelving, the space looks larger. There's a large sleeping mat and some essentials, including a water jug, a bucket and some clothes. The chain of plastic flowers that Jupiter had hung in Nola's hut has been strung across the roof, and Nola's chair sits off to the side.

Echo's jaw drops. "How did you—"

"Nectar," says Flora, following them in. "We thought it wise to rescue whatever we could from Nola's hut before anyone else moved in. Even though I still don't understand why you're so attached to that filthy chair."

Echo realizes they haven't had a chance to tell Flora who exactly Nola is. That the filthy chair she just wrinkled her nose at belongs to her own mother. The very person Flora came here to look for. But this feels like something River needs to talk to her about, so Echo lets it go for now.

"See," says Chase. "I told you it's different from the crypt. Unless Oren comes down here. I wouldn't mind putting his body on a shelf. Or Daphne's."

Echo's ears prick up at the potential Sovereign's name. "Have you thought any further about how we might go about testing Daphne?"

Flora nods. "Once I have my LaB set up, we can talk about that. Right now, you need to rest."

Exhaustion grips Echo at the idea of sleep. Chase leaves them with the torch and follows Flora back down the corridor. Echo and River collapse onto the sleeping mat and lie on their backs, their hands finding each other's and their fingers inter-twining.

"My sister is a genius," says River. "I mean, I always knew she was smarter than me, but this is next level."

"She's amazing," Echo agrees. "We're just lucky she's on our side. We'd still be running through the Extinction Zone in the rain if it weren't for her."

"What do you think the Moon Workers are doing?" River asks.

Echo thinks about this for a moment, knowing they'll need to tell Flora and Chase everything in the morning. "I think Ruff has quickly taken Manu's place as leader. Maybe he's teamed up with Lyra. Maybe they'll start to venture out a little more during the day. Things will get better."

"I hope so." River sighs. "They were good people, as odd as they were."

"They sure were," Echo snuggles into his side, enjoying the bliss of not having to move. "Odd, I mean. More so than good."

It doesn't take long for them to drift into a deep sleep. Echo dreams of running, and flying, and moonbows, and clouds.

She's not at all sure what tomorrow is going to bring. But one thing she's certain about is that she's not spending it underground.

EIGHT
RIVER

W hen River blinks his eyes open and finds himself in semi-darkness, a moment of panic grips his throat like a fist. Endless nights can't be what his life has become. It's only a matter of time before he loses his mind like the Moon Workers.

He sucks in a sharp breath and the scent of soil fills his lungs. A scent very different to the stale air of the building painted endlessly with the words *night is safe*. It reminds River he's in the bunker.

They escaped the Moon Zone. They flew on Nectar, searing into his memory one of the most magnificent sights he's ever seen. There's no one he would want to be part of that memory more than Echo.

She sighs beside him, her head resting alongside his, her soft breath creating a lulling rhythm. The gentle glow of the torch caresses her soft skin, the relaxed line of her lips.

A smile spreads across River's face, that same feeling he had on top of Nectar filling his chest once more.

Turns out you don't need to be flying on a mechanical bee, trying to touch a moonbow to get it.

All River needs is to be beside Echo.

Her eyes flutter open, and his smile grows to a grin. He'll never tire of waking up beside this girl.

"River," she whispers. "Why aren't you asleep?"

"I slept." He pulls her close and kisses her forehead.

"Is it morning?" she asks, pressing her own kiss on his chin.

"No idea." Kissing her one more time just for good measure, he stretches his back and sits up. "I haven't heard Flora and Chase leave yet."

"Should we go with them?" Echo asks, also sitting up and running her fingers through her hair. "You know, stay out of sight and see what we can do to help."

River understands her need to do that. They came back to fix this. To finally find the Sovereign, then the Code. But he shakes his head. "We have to stay down here during the day. Oren can't find out we're alive. And you remember how the people turned the last time they saw us."

Echo chews her lip, eyes scanning the room, then lighting up. She jumps to her feet and darts to the pile of clothes that Nectar brought over from Nola's hut and finds a cap and a scarf. "Then they won't see us," she says, taking her hair out of her braid and pulling it across her face, securing it with the cap so she can peek through at the front. Then she tosses the scarf to River.

"You look like Lyra," River laughs as he catches it.

Echo grins. "Just as long as I don't look like me."

"This isn't a good idea," River says, even as he's tucking the scarf around his face.

"Well, I'm not staying down here all day." Echo puts out her hand to help River up. "Not after what we saw in the Moon Zone."

"I know what you mean." He slips his hand into hers and hauls himself to a stand. "But you have to promise me that you'll be careful."

Echo wrinkles her nose at him. "I'll be as careful as you."

He shakes his head, acknowledging that's all he can really ask for. After a long drink of water from the jug Flora left out, they creep down the corridor and wait in the shadows. Several long minutes pass and Chase and Flora emerge from what seems to be a fully dug out LaB and head for the exit.

Echo and River wait a few minutes for them to leave, then follow, keeping hidden as best they can. They emerge from the bunker, the morning sun already a full orb in the sky.

Even as River feels open and exposed out in the scoring grounds, he can't help the rush of goosebumps over his skin as the warm sunlight flows over him.

Beside him, Echo tilts up her face. "We were part of the sky last night, River," she murmurs.

"And even that wasn't as magnificent as you," he says, his voice husky.

Echo lowers her gaze to his. She smiles. Sways toward him. And presses her hand to his heart. "It was magnificent because we were together."

Which is the truth.

Her gaze moves past him as her brow wrinkles. "Where are Flora and Chase?"

River glances over his shoulder, seeing that the distance between them and the village is empty. "They moved quickly," he muses. "Which means we'd better do the same."

Echo nods and they break into a jog, moving along the winding paths of the scoring grounds. A smell assaults River's nose as they get close and his stomach rebels. He looks to his left, seeing the door in the net where the Vulnerables leave their dead, unaware their remains are actually being taken to the Sovereign graveyard.

Echo slows. "There are normally one or two bodies waiting for collection," she says, her gaze also drawn to the gruesome sight.

Today there are dozens. A breeze whips up and the smell of decay hits them like a wall of nausea, making his stomach somersault.

"River," Echo whispers as her eyes fill with tears. "This is terrible. Oren is starving them."

"Which is why we came back," he reminds her.

She nods, her jaw tight with determination. "And why we're not staying hidden all day."

They turn away, moving toward the nearest hut, now somber. This is most definitely why they came back.

How they stop the starvation is something they've yet to figure out.

They've just reached the hut when there's a flurry of movement and River's scarf is yanked so hard, he stumbles and almost falls over. Echo's right beside him, then spins around, eyes wild and ready to fight.

"River!" Flora gasps as she plants her hands on her hips. "What are you doing here? It's not safe!"

River's heart drops back down from where it lodged in his throat. "That's never stopped us," he says, adjusting his scarf back over his face. "We're here to help."

"Plus, we're wearing disguises," says Echo, pulling down her cap.

"Then how did we know it was you?" Chase asks as he appears beside Flora, rolling his eyes.

"You knew we followed you and were waiting," Echo shoots back.

Chase huffs. "Get back behind the hut, will you?"

River rolls his own eyes. "Which is where we were a second ago."

They all press themselves against the rough wall, listening intently. There's no movement within, nor is there in the alleyways and streets beyond.

Flora lets out a breath. "The Dead Zone is even quieter than it was before."

Because people are dying faster than ever.

Which is probably what Oren always planned.

"Oren's going to pay for every Dead Born lost," Chase says with gritted teeth.

Flora rests a hand on his arm as he practically vibrates with anger. "We'll get what we need out of the Alphadome, then we'll find the Sovereign."

"We need to hurry," River adds. "Oren isn't going to just let the Alphadome fall into Dead Born hands."

In fact, starving the Dead Borns ensures there's no rebel army to stop him from seizing it back.

And they need the equipment in there. The queen bee venom. The adrenacure. The medical supplies.

With grim faces, they make their way through the village. Just as Flora noted, it's quieter than ever before. Like a graveyard. If they don't do something, the entirety of the Dead Zone will have a stone in the scoring grounds.

They've just reached the last of the huts before they need to make a run for the Alphadome when River pauses. His gaze is drawn to the Betadome looming in the distance where a large group of Vulnerables are gathered. Some are holding onto the net, staring at the food that's so close yet so far away. Others are lying in the dirt and River wonders if they'll ever be getting up again. More are pacing and raking at their hair.

The scene reeks of desperation as these poor people cling

72

onto whatever life they have left. Guilt tugs at River's insides. He's part of the reason this is happening.

"Look," Echo hisses.

River, Chase and Flora turn to see what she's pointing at.

The black door to the Betadome is swinging open, the blast of smoke filling the void. What steps through isn't Oren or Daphne or guards in white suits.

It's far more terrifying.

Four mechanical Workers emerge, legs rippling in chilling unison as they carry large, bulging sacks in their powerful jaws.

The Vulnerables back away, many running into the village screaming. This would be the first time they've seen these terrifying beasts. River can still remember the ice that flooded his veins the first instance he and Echo watched one emerge in the Hive. His understanding of the world changed drastically that day.

And it now has for the Dead Borns.

Many run into the village, screaming. A few of the braver souls approach with curiosity, while more people come out from their huts to see what the commotion is about and stand back at what they must feel is a safe distance.

"Should we warn them?" River asks, images of those four soulless beasts rampaging through the village, killing and destroying, filling his mind and making him feel ill.

"No." Flora holds up her hand. "They haven't attacked. Let's watch for a moment."

River and Echo glance at each other. Just because Nectar's been reprogrammed, doesn't mean these Workers aren't a threat.

The Workers spread out in a line and River prepares to run, already wondering what he can use to smash the glowing discs on their back. Beside him, Echo is thrumming with kinetic energy.

The Workers set down the sacks and food spills out onto the dirt. Apples roll down the incline, along with oranges, plums, peppers and carrots.

"Food!" a Vulnerable calls out to those standing back. "We're saved!"

"Oren's feeding them," Echo gasps.

River shakes his head, trying to understand what they're witnessing. "But why is he using the Workers?"

People run forward and soon there's a crowd as Vulnerables push and shove, each trying to get what they believe to be their fair share, or more. Some people stuff food into their pockets, others directly into their mouths. A few remove their shirts—both male and female—and quickly fashion them into bags.

River and the others stay perfectly still at the edge of the village, eyes glued on the scene of chaos before them. There's so much shouting, color and movement it's hard to know what to focus on first. People are getting crushed in the frenzy and he's certain more bodies will be piled up at the net before this day is over.

Maybe that's what his father's planning. Oren's killing just as many as he's saving with this unexpected offering of food.

The Workers retreat, heading for the black door, where they collect new sacks of food to bring to the people. These ones are filled with celery, beets, beans, and more. If the people could only establish some order, they'd see there's enough food for everyone, but instead they grab wildly at the offerings at the expense of each other and themselves.

"Why is he doing this?" Chase asks, voicing the suspicion they're all feeling.

"He wouldn't have poisoned it, would he?" Echo asks.

"I don't know why he'd do it this way," Flora says. "It's going to be something else."

"Is he teaching the people not to fear the Workers?" Echo asks.

River's brows shoot up. That is something his cold-hearted father would do. If the Vulnerables learn to associate good things with Oren's evil machines, he could use them to attack when they least expect it.

After several more trips back to the Betadome, the Workers retreat through the black door and don't return. All that's left behind is trampled dirt. Even the sacks the food was in are gone.

The people disperse, taking their hauls back to their huts, many of them squabbling on the way about who has more. A few fights break out as some make a dash for it, trying their best to hold on to what they have.

"Now's a good time," says Flora. "While everyone's distracted."

River looks at her, confused, then remembers what they're doing there.

They need the supplies so they can test the Sovereign.

Without waiting for agreement, Flora darts forward and sprints across the open area to the Alphadome. River and the others quickly catch up. They reach the hatch and Flora throws it open, ducking in. Chase is the next to enter, running down the stairs.

River and Echo follow and as they move through the hatch, he's aware this is likely the last time he'll ever go down here. He can't say he's unhappy about that. This place is filled with some of the worst memories of his life.

"Let's just get what we need and get—" Chase's words are cut off by a grunt.

Flora's reached the bottom of the stairs and stopped, frozen, causing a domino of crashes behind her.

"What is it?" Echo asks.

"I..." Flora lets out a moan, not moving forward any further.

"You what?" River tries to lean out to see what's happened. He freezes when he registers the digital counter attached to the wall on the other side.

Three minutes just reduced by a second. And then another.

"There was a wire," says Flora, her voice shaking. "It was across the landing. I felt it snap."

River's veins turn to ice. His heart is nothing but a cold, hard lump lodged behind his ribs.

It wasn't the people who'd been distracted by the delivery of food.

It was them.

While they'd been watching the Workers, Oren rigged this place with explosives.

"We need to get out of here," says Echo. "This place is about to blow."

"No!" Flora cries, darting into the Alphadome. "We need the supplies!"

NINE

ECHO

"Flora!" Chase's voice is filled with anguish as he reaches out. But he's too slow and Flora's already darted toward the LaB, determined to take whatever supplies she can before the Alphadome explodes.

Echo's not going to make the same mistake as Chase, and she grips tightly onto River. "Stay here. We don't have time."

"Maybe we can disarm it?" he suggests.

She cocks an eyebrow. "In less than three minutes?"

River looks at her in panic, and she realizes there's nothing she can do to stop him following Flora. He's never abandoned his twin before. He's not about to start now.

"Fine then!" She lets her hand drop. "But if you're going in, so am I."

A fresh wave of panic crosses River's face, but he nods his agreement. "We'll be fast."

But just as they're about to run forward, Makk appears at the top of the stairs.

"Get out of here, Makk!" Echo shouts, pointing at the timer

which is now at two minutes and forty-three seconds. "The place has been rigged with explosives."

"You're alive!" Makk's eyes are almost as wide as his grin.

"Not for long if we don't move!" says Echo, accepting their disguises really aren't very effective.

"Is Chase in there?" Makk asks, pointing to the LaB.

Echo nods as River marches away. "And Flora."

"I'll keep count," says Makk. "Get whatever you need. Hurry!"

Echo scurries after River and they run to the LaB. Flora is wildly throwing items out of cupboards while Chase stuffs them into empty drawers he's pulled out of the cabinets.

"Here!" Chase shoves a drawer at River, who sidesteps so that Echo is forced to take it. He wants her safely out of here as fast as possible.

She puts out her hands, but only because she plans to carry it to the stairs and come back for more.

"Two minutes, twenty!" Makk shouts from the stairs.

Echo runs out with the drawer and Makk steps aside so she can take it up the stairs. Dropping it on the top step, she barrels back down, having to press herself against the wall when River comes charging up with another drawer.

"Get outside!" River says as he passes. "You too, Makk."

Echo doesn't bother to answer, saving her energy to get back to the LaB as quickly as possible. Chase is waiting for her with another load and Echo grabs it, circling around the glass dome in the center of the room as she passes River and goes back up the stairs.

"Two minutes!" Makk calls.

"When it gets to one minute, you need to leave," she shouts over her shoulder. She'll drag him out of here if she has to. There's no way she's going to allow him to blow up with this place. His life has barely begun.

She dumps the drawer on the top step, only this time she doesn't see River on her way back down.

"What's happening?" she shouts as she runs back to the LaB.

River is carrying a tray loaded with glass jars filled with chemicals.

"I'll take that," she says, trying to relieve him of the tray. "I'm the only Immune."

"I won't drop it." He surges forward, refusing to let her take it.

"One minute, forty!" Makk shouts. "Stop talking!"

Chase and Flora emerge from the LaB. Flora has one drawer, while Chase has two stacked on top of each other.

"Go!" Flora yells. "Move!"

"One minute and thirty seconds!" Makk shouts, turning to run up the stairs now that he can see they're all coming out.

River goes first, balancing his tray with expertise. He takes to the stairs and Echo follows him up. She can hear Flora puffing behind her and assumes Chase is taking up the rear.

Makk flings open the hatch and River races out of it, while Echo and Makk quickly collect the drawers they left at the top of the stairs. Flora tumbles past and they follow, landing on the dirt with a thud.

Echo and Makk carry what they can while River manages his tray of jars.

"There's still a minute left!" Makk puffs. That should give them just enough time to clear the area.

"Chase!" Flora screams. "Chase!"

Echo turns to see Flora has gone back to the stairwell and is standing at the top, looking down. He still hasn't come out yet.

There's a loud rumble as the ground begins to vibrate underneath Echo's bare feet.

"Get down!" she shouts. "Now!"

River sets down his tray and Echo tosses the contents of her drawer onto the dirt and places it upside down over the jars to protect them. Then she throws herself on top of it as River gathers closer, pulling Makk to his side. Together they shelter from whatever it is that's coming at them.

"Flora," River whimpers, knowing there's nothing more he can do for her now. "Flora!"

A shimmering gush of energy bursts from the stairwell, and Flora is sent flying backward, her feet dragging across the ground with her toes pointed out while she clutches a drawer to her chest.

Chase shoots out of the entrance a moment later like he's riding a wave. His arms and legs beat at the air as he tries to stabilize himself. The items he was carrying are sent scattering as shockwaves reverberate and a jet of bright orange flame licks out at him.

Flora comes to an awkward stop, skidding across the ground as Chase's empty drawer crashes beside her and splits open. River jolts as if he's going to run to her, but he seems to change his mind as he wraps himself tighter around Echo and Makk.

Several yards away, Chase lands and tumbles as he tries to bring himself to a stop. Echo winces, certain he must have some broken bones. He rights himself and crawls weakly in Flora's direction as a surge of heat sweeps across the already scorched land. Echo turns away to shield her face.

There's more rumbling and dust rises from the earth like a reverse-gravity snowstorm. It swirls around them and soon Echo can't see anything as she coughs, trying to find some air amongst the dirt she's breathed into her lungs.

"Makk," she chokes out. "Are you okay?"

"It wasn't time," he says, seeming confused. "We still had another minute. I was counting. I always count right."

"You do," says River, also coughing. "It was another one of Oren's tricks. He was hoping we'd still be down there when it went off."

"But doesn't he think you're dead?" Makk asks. "He must've been trying to kill Flora and Chase."

Echo squints through the dust, hoping Oren hasn't succeeded with exactly that. It's impossible to tell what shape Chase and Flora are in after their dramatic exit from the Alphadome.

River disentangles himself from their huddle and gets to his feet.

"How are you alive, anyway?" Makk asks. "My dad told my mom that Oren got rid of you."

"He did." Echo helps Makk up and feels for River in the cloud of dust. "But it turns out we're not that easy to get rid of."

"You're just like a cockroach." Makk wraps his arms around Echo's waist and buries his face in her stomach. She splutters out a laugh at this unusual compliment and hugs him back, glad they'd been able to find their way home.

"Flora helped us," says River, putting one arm around Echo and the other around his young cousin. "She saved our lives and got us back home."

"She must've needed you for something," says Makk, making Echo wonder why he doesn't seem to like Flora. They need to make sure he spends some more time getting to know her so he can find out how great his other cousin really is.

A breeze picks up the dust, creating mini tornados, and the three of them walk cautiously forward, scanning ahead for either Flora or Chase.

"There," says Makk, pointing.

Echo is about to tell Makk he's mistaken and that's nothing more than a misshapen rock, when she realizes it is indeed them. Flora is sitting, bent over Chase, who has his head in her lap.

"Chase!" Echo rushes forward, not wanting anything to have happened to the first best friend she ever had. He's like a brother to her, and she's not prepared to lose him. River is right beside her, desperate to see his twin.

But Makk is faster than they are, and he reaches his hero first, squatting down as he glares at Flora.

"What did you do to him?" he asks her.

Flora doesn't answer. She's too busy slapping Chase gently on the face, trying to rouse him. He opens his eyes and looks at Echo and smiles. Then he turns to see Flora and his entire face lights up. She leans further forward and presses her lips briefly to his, then covers his face with more kisses.

"Thank goodness you're alive," she says, her voice breaking with emotion.

"Lucky for you," says Makk.

"Makk," River admonishes. "We're all on the same side here."

Echo nods, realizing River has noticed Makk's behavior toward Flora, too. But there's no time now to wonder what it means.

"Get...the stuff," says Chase, his breathing so labored his words are hard to catch. "I dropped...it."

"He's right," says Echo. "We can't let all this be for nothing."

"But it's gone everywhere!" Makk looks around. "We'll never find all of it with this dust everywhere."

Flora takes something from her shirt pocket. It reminds Echo of the small device Oren had used as a pager. She presses a button and it emits a quiet beep.

"What is that?" River narrows his eyes.

"I'm calling for Nectar." Flora tucks the device back in her pocket.

"Maybe we should have brought her with us in the first place," says Echo, looking in the direction of the scoring grounds.

Flora returns her attention back to Chase, lovingly caressing his cheek. "We were trying to be inconspicuous."

"But how about now?" Makk asks. "Won't it be spic... uous?"

Echo has to admire the way he doesn't shy away from new words.

"The dust will cover her," says Flora. "She can get in and out before it clears. Besides, it's not like anyone is going to be frightened of her anymore."

"Come on." Echo starts to gather canisters of venom and adrenacure scattered nearby while River heads over to where they left the tray of chemicals.

Nectar appears minutes later, seeming to have scurried around the village rather than flown. Flora leaves Chase momentarily to program something into a panel on her side and the giant bee gets to work, scooping up items and putting them in a compartment underneath her thorax.

Taking what she's collected to Nectar, they're added to her stores. Then the mechanical bee goes to Chase and lifts him from the ground with her front legs, walking quickly back in the direction of the bunker.

"Come on!" Flora calls, not waiting for them to follow before she runs after them.

Echo adjusts her cap, even though so far, it's proven to be a terrible disguise. River does the same with his scarf.

"Bye, bye, Alphadome," says Makk, looking back at the gaping crater in the earth where Oren's underground torture chamber used to be. Dust continues to rise as thick, dark smoke. Whatever was left in there will be destroyed. Echo doesn't even want to think about the bodies that are now buried under even more layers of earth, including Reed's cousin, Prairie. At least it's preferable to having your remains stored in the Sovereign graveyard, she supposes.

They get moving, keeping their heads down as they retrace their steps from earlier. River keeps his arm firmly around Echo's shoulders while Makk darts around with no hope of ever using up his endless energy supplies.

"So, what happens next?" Makk asks when they reach the scoring grounds.

"We're not sure," says River.

Makk seems to find this amusing. "But you're always sure."

"Well, we have one possibility left for the Sovereign," says Echo. "Which means the next step is getting her tested."

"That should be easy." Makk swivels around with all the blind confidence of youth in both his words and his actions.

Echo pulls in closer to River's side. "Yeah, real easy," she mutters.

"It's okay," says River. "Flora sounded like she had a plan when we asked her about it yesterday."

Echo nods, not feeling as confident as he is. After all, Flora's most recent plan to get her equipment from the Alphadome very nearly just killed them all. But River has total faith in his twin, which means so does Echo. When Makk gets to know her better, he will too.

She draws in a deep breath, steeling herself for what's ahead.

Because something tells her that an Alphadome filled with explosives is going to be nothing compared to Daphne.

CHAPTER

TEN

RIVER

The walk back to the bunker takes longer than River would like. Now they've discovered their disguises aren't terribly effective, the need to be out of sight is stronger than ever. It means they circle the village just like Nectar would have, River keeping his face tucked deep in his scarf while Echo pulls her cap low over her eyes.

"You know you look even more suspicious when you do that," Makk says, looking back over his shoulder as he permanently skips two steps ahead. "Like a turtle trying to hide."

River sighs, the dust caking every inch of his body catching at the back of his throat. They don't have a choice. The more they walk away from the Alphadome and toward the scoring grounds, the more the dust thins. Exposing their faces is even more dangerous.

And people are now moving around the village, trying to understand what's happened. Several are coughing, their frail bodies unable to cope with dust as the information that the Alphadome has been annihilated makes its way around.

Their voices occasionally reach River and Echo as they ring

the village, trying not to stray too close that they'll be recognized, but not too far, which will raise suspicion.

"Good riddance. The less reason for Oren to come to the Dead Zone, the better."

"That man is a menace. Someone needs to stop him before the whole village is next."

"Mama, why does he hate us so much?"

The final comment has both River and Echo flinching, drawing them deeper into their disguises. No child should have to ask that question. No child should wonder why one man wants them wiped from the face of the earth.

Except their instinctive motion catches someone's attention.

"Hey," a man calls out and River almost freezes.

He knows that voice.

Roark, Trid's brother and the man who took Makk hostage, the man River saved from Sledge, is striding toward them, scowling.

"We need to run," Echo says in a low voice.

Which will only draw more attention, yet what choice do they have?

Ahead, Makk has stopped, his endless energy brought to a standstill by the man who held a knife to his throat. Protectiveness flashes through River. Little scares his young cousin, but this man did.

Except defending Makk means exposing them.

And Roark is the last person River and Echo want to know they're alive.

River's muscles coil, ready to scoop Makk up and get the heck out of here. All he can hope is they'll figure out what to do if they're followed.

The sounds of crashing and crumbling steal everyone's focus. One of the huts crumbles as if the extra layer of dust was all that was needed to bring it to its knees. A plume of brown-red billows up and out, reaching toward Roark.

He lifts his arm to cover the lower half of his face as his scowl is now directed at the pile of timber and plastic.

"Quick," River whispers.

He and Echo break into a light jog, scooping Makk up as they go along. The moment River's hand brushes his back, Makk launches forward. River glances over his shoulder, registering two things.

Roark is now beside the crumpled hut, kicking at the fractured debris. Thankfully, it looks like it was abandoned.

And someone else is walking away, shaking his hand as if he just hurt it.

As if he just hit the side of a hut, making it collapse.

River turns his focus ahead, sending out a silent thanks. Sledge just created a distraction, saving them once again.

"Hurry up," Makk hisses, now looking as if he has too much energy twitching through his muscles. He's no doubt keen to get away.

"You go ahead," River tells him. They can't afford to be dashing around, bringing attention to themselves. "We'll see you in the bunker."

Makk doesn't need to be told twice. He disappears among the huts, taking a short cut. River and Echo slow once they're alone and out of sight of Roark and the others, keeping their heads down as they continue skirting the village.

By the time they reach scoring grounds, the sun is already high in the sky, once again merciless in its heat. A trickle of sweat runs down River's temple and he can only wonder how he looks with all the dust caked on him. He glances at Echo as she wipes away at her forehead, leaving a streak of mud. They're walking dirt figurines, which may actually be a better disguise than their scarf and cap.

They've just reached the bunker when the hatch flies open. Makk leaps out and almost crashes straight into Echo.

"Sorry," he says cheerfully, clearly recovered from his brush with Roark. "Gotta go. Things to do."

River frowns. "What things—"

Makk slaps his hand on River's stomach, sending up a puff of dust. "Don't talk too much while I'm gone."

With another flashing grin in his dirty face, he's gone.

River and Echo glance at each other, wondering what's going on. They enter the bunker, closing the hatch behind them. The solar torches hanging on the walls reveal the main room is empty. Movement through the doorway to the LaB has them entering it, only to stop once they're inside.

River looks around in wonder. It seems Flora and Nectar have been busy creating a LaB carved from rock and soil. Dirt shelves line the wall, solid benches below them. There are even stools jutting up from the ground beside them. It's almost identical, except it's shades of brown rather than stark white.

Flora is tending to Chase, who's lying on a bed of rock in the back corner. "I'm fine," he grumbles. "I've certainly been worse."

"Thanks to Daphne," she mutters quietly, stepping back and dropping a cloth into a bucket full of water.

River and Echo slip back out, wanting to give them privacy. They stand and wait, content to be holding each other as the minutes pass. In fact, River could stay here like this for hours if given the chance.

It's probably not been longer than fifteen minutes before Chase can be heard grumbling. "Okay, that's enough. We have a Sovereign to find."

River and Echo take that as their cue and they enter the LaB, finding Flora with her hands on her hips.

She startles when she sees River and Echo in the doorway, then smiles. "Good to see you got back okay."

River nods, not bothering with the story of Roark and Sledge. There are more pressing issues. "Why is Makk running off like he's been given a task?"

Chase sits up, swinging his legs down and resting his hands beside him. Flora's cleaned him up, revealing the scrapes and patches of angry red after he was thrown by the explosion. "Our next step is to find Daphne."

"So we can test her," Flora adds, her voice hard.

"And what does that have to do with Makk?" Echo asks.

Flora walks over to a nearby bench where her computer is set up. "Bringing Daphne in isn't going to be easy. We needed to find her weak point. A reason for her to come to us."

River joins her, trying to understand what his twin is telling him. "And you've found one?"

"I did." Flora looks up at him. "In fact, we've met her."

Her? What is his sister talking about? How could he have met Daphne's weakness?

River's eyes widen as he realizes. "Iris."

"Iris?" Echo asks, moving closer as her gaze moves between River and Flora. "Who's Iris?"

It's Chase who answers. "Daphne's daughter," he says, standing up with a wince and joining them. "Iris Confirmed the same year I did. She was found to be Vulnerable."

Echo's eyes widen just like River's did. She looks at him. "That's why you know her." She turns back to Chase. "And that means Iris is in the Dead Zone."

River blinks as his mind scrambles to connect it all. He has vague memories of the brown-haired Iris in the Sting. Being older than him, they didn't have classes together. And he and Flora tended to stick to themselves. No wonder he didn't think of her.

Not to mention, it's hard to imagine the Daphne he knows as being anything close to maternal. She'd barely mentioned Iris, even before she was sent to live in the Dead Zone.

But now they have a way to bring her to them. Surely even a cold-hearted woman like her would want to see her daughter again.

Except Chase is shaking his head. "As far as I know, Iris hasn't been seen since Confirmation."

"She's disappeared," Flora says.

"She has to be somewhere," Echo says, then frowns. "Unless she's..."

Dead. River's own brow contracts. Without Iris, going back into the Green Zone is inevitable. Which feels like a suicide mission...

"There's only one way to find out," Chase says. "Which is why we've sent Makk out to ask around."

Flora sits on a dirt stool. "So now we wait." Her gaze roams over River and Echo. "I've left a bucket with water and cloths in the crypt room so you can clean yourself up."

"Good idea," Echo says, moving her shoulders as if she's uncomfortable with the amount of grit coating her skin. "Thanks."

Flora grins. "It's also Nectar's bedroom."

"Great," River mutters. "Just who I want to share a room with."

"She's powered down," Flora says, rolling her eyes. "But the disc on her back will give you enough light to see what you're doing."

The same grin climbs up Chase's face. "We need the remaining torches in here."

Echo sits down on a nearby stool, communicating she's not going anywhere just yet. "So we find Iris, then what?"

"We send Daphne a message saying we have her," Chase

90

answers. "The minute the witch steps into the Dead Zone, we grab her."

"And bring her here to the bunker," Flora continues. "Where we test her."

River tenses. "And if she doesn't want to? We'll do it anyway?"

Although Daphne has done some heinous things, River can't be okay with what's being proposed. Testing people against their will is what his father has done, irrespective of who they were.

Chase's lips thin as he crosses his arms, not this again stamped on his face, but Flora quickly jumps in. "We'll talk to her first. Explain what needs to happen, just like we did with Clover. I'm sure even Daphne will agree seeing as we're confirming what we already know."

That she's the Sovereign.

The woman who's most closely aligned to Oren and his vision. Who's killed as easily as he has. Even seemed to enjoy it.

River shoves the unsettling thoughts away. They have to capture Daphne first, then convince her to be tested. Which means finding Iris.

The sound of the hatch opening has everyone turning in surprise. Makk appears in the LaB, breathing hard.

Echo goes to him, putting a hand around his shoulder. "Are you okay? You're back so soon."

Makk grins up at her, then wrinkles his nose. "You're super dirty."

Echo knocks some dust off her shoulder. "Keep that up and you will be, too."

Makk squeals and squirms away from her. He takes two steps toward River, then stops, realizing he's just as dirty as Echo is.

"Makk," Chase says, his voice sharper than it needs to be. "Why are you back so quickly?"

Makk straightens as if he's just snapped to attention. "Because I've already asked around. No one's heard of an Iris, let alone seen one."

Flora's eyebrows pull low. "Are you sure? You weren't gone very long."

River walks over to his cousin, not liking the way he's tensed even more. "You ran so fast you knocked all that dust straight off you."

Makk's back to grinning. "Figured it made me lighter."

River can't help but chuckle. "So, who did you talk to?"

"I started with Mom, but that was silly, because she doesn't get out much." Makk takes a deep breath. "So then I spoke to Sledge and Fray. They've moved into Ruff's hut, by the way. Say they want somewhere sturdy for their family. But they've never heard of a stupid name like Iris. So then I spoke to some of the other Razers, and anyone else who did Confirmation with her and Chase. Then I asked Cascade as I thought she might remember her from the Green Zone, but she hasn't seen her. So I asked Jupiter, who actually knows all the people no one else knows. But no one's heard of no Iris." Makk huffs out the last of his air. "Which is what I expected. Chase knows everyone, and if he doesn't know of an Iris, then no one else will."

River blinks as his mind catches up with the words that felt like they were one long sentence.

Makk shrugs. "Which probably means Iris is plain old dead."

River has to stop his hand from tightening on his cousin's shoulder. Not because of Makk's matter of fact attitude to death. That's expected from a child who's grown up in the Dead Zone. Because if Iris is dead...

Flora stalks to another bench and picks up some paper and a pen. "We'll send a note to Daphne."

"Yes," Chase hisses, his eyes lighting up. "From Iris, saying she's in trouble."

Flora scrawls across the page and River reads it aloud, knowing Echo's never had the chance to learn to read properly.

"Help, Mom. I'm in danger. Please come tonight. Iris."

Flora tears the paper off, rubs it on the bench surface to dirty it, then passes it to Makk. "Get this to Tuff."

"On it," Makk says, zipping out of the LaB and through the hatch before River's had a chance to draw a breath, let alone speak.

He leaves behind a heavy silence. River feels a little like Flora and Chase keep making decisions without any discussion, but he also knows that sending a note to Daphne was the next logical step. Still, he can't help but feel like Flora could've talked it over first. It's as if she's doing this and they're just coming along for the ride.

She turns to him, smiling. "Now you really do have time to clean up. We'll head out at twilight."

"To meet Daphne at the Betadome," Chase says grimly.

Echo tugs at River's hand. "Come on. Some clean clothes and a rest sounds good."

Although losing this layer of dirt is something he's looking forward to, River can't imagine he'll be able to sleep. Wondering if Daphne is going to arrive at the Betadome to meet her daughter will be heavy on his mind. If she does, then they have a fight on their hands.

If she doesn't, they still have a fight on their hands. Possibly a war...

But if Echo needs to rest, then he's more than willing to be beside her as she does. Listening to her even breaths is the most calming sound in the world, and he could use that right now.

He follows her down the corridor and into the large room that would've been a crypt in the Alphadome. Nectar is crouched at the back, just like Flora said she would be, her silver disc illuminating the space with a soft light. Although the sight of the robotic bee doesn't bother River. In fact, it's almost comforting.

He shakes his head ruefully. So many things have changed in ways he could never have imagined.

A bucket of water sits not far from their sleeping mat and Echo kneels beside it. She reaches in and grabs one of the cloths, the sound of water swirling and splashing filling the room. "This is what I was hoping for," she says.

River stills. There's a husky tone to Echo's voice that he wasn't expecting.

Yet fires him awake as awareness crackles through his veins.

It draws him closer until he's kneeling on the other side of the bucket. "You were?"

"Take your shirt off, River," she says, her voice almost a whisper. "I want to clean you."

River does as he's told, his gaze never leaving the beautiful, equally dust-caked girl across from him. Cool air brushes his skin, but that's not what has goosebumps prickling all over. It's the tender, heated way Echo's looking at him.

This is what she had in mind all along.

And right now, he wishes he'd thought of it first. They would've got here sooner.

Echo lifts the cloth from the water as she scoots around, her dark gaze roaming over his exposed chest. She draws her bottom lip in as she presses the cloth to his shoulder, then

94

strokes down toward his clenched stomach, water sluicing down his skin.

River sucks in a sharp breath. The water is cool. But Echo's touch is like wildfire.

Her lip stays tucked under her teeth as she focuses on washing away the dust of the explosion. River can't help but feel she's washing away the taint the Alphadome carried with it. She tenderly strokes the wet cloth over his face, his shoulders, his heaving ribcage.

When she's done, he's tingling everywhere. Images of their first night together in Nola's hut are swirling through his mind, elevating his body temperature.

"My turn," he murmurs, his voice thick with everything he feels for Echo.

Echo's answer is to remove her top, her pale skin glowing in the soft light. River's pulse is a bass drum in his chest. His lungs seem to be throbbing with it. He picks up the second cloth, his hand trembling a little as he tenderly wipes one side of her face, then the other. Echo's gaze seems to darken with every sweep of the cloth over her skin. River looks lower, his mouth going dry. He starts at her collarbone then strokes down. Echo's eyes close as she lets out a low moan.

Swallowing hard, River works to keep his raging passion under control. Washing Echo is a service of love. A way to communicate how much she means to him. Even if each layer of dust that's washed away exposes more tantalizing skin. Even if Echo, glistening in the soft light, is the most beautiful sight he's ever seen.

He should take this slow—

Echo groans as her eyes snap open. "Protect me later, River," she growls.

She launches at him and he tumbles back with a gasp. Then a chuckle. Then a groan of his own as Echo's soft curves mold to his hard planes. They fall onto the mat, the water making their skin slick as their mouths find the other, kissing ravenously.

Hands stroke. Breaths catch. Bodies find the solace and connection and pleasure they've been craving. River allows the rest of reality to fall away, losing himself to the passion and wonder of these stolen hours.

Very soon, they'll be once again searching for the Sovereign. Hunting her, knowing they have to succeed.

Right now, this moment is about him and Echo.

And the love that sparked the dream of Immunity for all.

The love that right now, is the only thing that makes that dream feel possible.

CHAPTER

ELEVEN

ECHO

E cho stirs, aware they need to head out to capture Daphne. The world just feels so perfect lying here in River's arms. Like nothing can hurt them. Like all that matters is the two of them. It proves that beauty can still exist within a world that's proven itself to be so full of hate. And if they succeed in bringing Immunity to all, that's when the beauty will truly blossom. Which is why they must drag themselves out of this haven.

In a minute.

Maybe two...

"River!" Flora calls from the main chamber of the bunker. "Echo! Get up! It's time to go."

"Urgh," Echo groans, snuggling in closer, her eyes still closed. "Your sister is so annoying."

River laughs as he kisses her forehead. "She's dedicated."

"River!" Flora calls again. "Echo! You have ten seconds until I wake up Nectar."

"We're coming!" River shouts back. "Soon," he adds in a rebellious whisper.

97

The gentle glow of the disc on Nectar's back grows brighter and a humming starts up.

"Do we really have to share a room with that thing?" Echo asks, blinking her eyes open.

"I quite enjoyed the light she emitted last night," he says. "Especially when—"

"River!" Flora appears in the entrance to the crypt with her hands on her hips. "You said you were coming out. We don't have all night. We can't afford to miss Daphne."

River releases Echo from his grasp and they sit up, straightening out the clean clothes they'd changed into after their... bath.

Nectar stands on her strong but spindly legs and walks toward Flora. She dips her enormous head so Flora can pat her. If Echo didn't know better, she'd think that metallic beast actually had feelings.

"Are we taking her with us?" River asks.

"Of course." Flora smiles at her twin. "She's very useful, in case you hadn't already noticed."

"We noticed," says Echo, answering for River. "And it's a good idea. We don't know what Daphne's capable of. Especially once she finds out Iris didn't send that note."

Chase appears from the dim light of the corridor. "At the risk of sounding like Makk, are you still talking in here? We need to get moving."

"Makk would already be moving," River points out.

"I know you all love him," says Flora as they head down the corridor. "But that kid can be a little annoying at times."

"Flora..." River seems to lose the courage to say what Echo knows he needs to tell her. Or maybe it's just the wrong time. "After we're finished with Daphne, we need to talk."

"Sounds intriguing." Flora laughs. "I'll make more effort with Makk if that's what's bothering you."

"It's not that." River runs a hand through his hair. "Well, it's to do with Makk, but—"

"River." Chase sighs. "Any chance this can wait? We really have to focus on what we're doing here. Getting Daphne to come back here with us isn't going to be easy."

"Sure." River nods. "You're right. It's waited this long. I can talk to Flora later."

Echo slips her hand into River's to show him her support. "There'll be time," she whispers. "We'll make sure of it."

In reality, there had been plenty of time earlier in the night. It was just that they had other things on their mind. Things that Echo is already thinking about doing again.

And again.

They leave the bunker and head through the scoring grounds. The night is pitch dark, but Nectar lights the way, and Echo notices Chase shiver as they pass where his family's stones have been laid.

Flora puts her hand on his back and whispers something. Once again, Echo is glad Chase has someone who cares about him so much.

"So, what's our plan?" Echo asks, assuming Flora and Chase have already worked something out, just like it was their idea to send Daphne the note. "Are we going to ask her nicely to come with us?"

"We're going to tell her we have Iris captive," says Chase. "And if she doesn't come with us, we'll kill her."

Echo gasps. "We can't do that!"

"We totally can do that." Flora laughs.

River walks silently beside Echo, and she tugs on his hand, wanting to know how he feels about this kind of dirty tactic.

"I don't like it either," River eventually says. "But I'm not sure we have any other choice."

Echo nods, finding herself agreeing against her will. "But

how do we even know she'll come? You said yourselves that she was a distant mother. Maybe she won't care enough to come."

"She'll be curious," says River. "Even if she doesn't care about Iris, she'll want to know what's so urgent."

"Or she'll want to punish Iris for breaking the rules," growls Chase. "Green Born Vulnerables aren't supposed to make contact with their families after Confirmation."

"Will she even know to come to the Betadome?" Echo asks. "You never said where to meet in your note."

"Echo!" Chase throws out his hands. "Are you being like this on purpose?"

River bristles at Chase's tone.

"Like what?" Echo shrugs. "Am I not allowed to ask questions? Would you prefer if we just follow along blindly with the plans you and Flora make?"

"Ah, so that's it," says Flora gently. "Echo, we didn't mean to make you feel threatened by making decisions without you. We were just giving you time to recover after everything you went through."

"We're fine now," says River. "And we'd like to be included in what's decided moving forward. Four heads are better than two."

"But you just said it was a good plan," Flora reminds him.

River groans. "It is a good plan."

"Great," Flora says brightly. "We're all in agreement then. And to answer Echo's earlier question, we didn't need to tell Daphne where to meet. The Betadome was obvious. It's the only place that connects the two zones. Plus, it was the last place she ever saw Iris."

Echo has to admit this makes sense.

The smell of ash is heavy in the air as they pass the crater that was once the Alphadome. They keep close to the net and continue toward the Betadome. With each step, the anticipation builds in Echo's gut, the nerves making her feel nauseous. There's so much risk associated with this.

Firstly, they're relying on Daphne coming. And coming alone. Then they need her to buy into their empty threat of killing Iris, when she knows they value peace over bloodshed. And even if they manage all that, they still haven't figured out how to get her to agree to the test. Perhaps Flora and Chase have that covered and just haven't bothered to inform them yet.

She lets out a breath, trying to dispel some of the resentment she's feeling. Flora and Chase were forced to continue without them when Echo and River chose to hand themselves in to Oren. It's not their fault. And they've been making good decisions so far. She needs to try to be more understanding.

They approach the Betadome cautiously, all eyes scanning for any sign of movement. Even Nectar is turning her head and searching the shadows.

"What if she doesn't come?" Echo whispers.

"She'll come," says Flora, sounding annoyed.

They find a place in the shadows to keep watch and Flora powers down Nectar's light.

Echo lies down on her stomach beside River, propping herself up on her elbows so she can see the giant net looming before them.

"Do you think she's already here?" Chase asks, keeping his voice low.

"Not a chance," says Flora.

"How can you be so sure?" Echo can't help but ask, even though Flora's made it clear she's used up her quota of questions already.

"Because I programmed Nectar with Daphne's genetic

sequence," says Flora. "Just like when I programmed her to find you in the Extinction Zone."

"You think of everything," Chase breathes, clearly impressed.

"So clever," River adds.

"As soon as she gets anywhere close, Nectar will alert us." Flora flips to her back to stare at the stars, demonstrating her confidence in her mechanical bee.

The night draws on as clouds cross the moon and more stars join the sparkling display in the sky. Just as Echo's beginning to doubt Daphne is coming at all, Nectar rises to her full height and scurries silently toward the net.

"She's here," Flora hisses.

The four of them follow Nectar and the sick feeling returns to Echo's stomach. This is it. Daphne's proven just how capable she is as a fighter. Surely four of them will be able to overpower her if needed? Especially given they have Nectar on their team.

But Nectar walks straight past the black door to the Betadome.

"What's going on?" Echo whispers to River.

"No idea." He takes her hand and they follow the net until they've passed the Betadome and are left staring out into the pitch black nothingness of the Extinction Zone.

Nectar gets busy unraveling a section of the net, her pincers working quickly to open up a large hole.

"She went into the Extinction Zone?" Chase asks, seeming just as confused as the rest of them.

"She must have," says Flora. "Although, I have no idea why."

"It's a trap." Echo takes a small step back. "This makes no sense. You said Iris was sent to the Dead Zone after Confirmation. She wasn't Forgotten."

"I can't explain it." Flora steps through the hole in the net. "All I know is that if Nectar says Daphne's gone this way, then that's what she's done."

Chase follows her through the net, and Echo and River climb out. Nectar sews up the net and they trail behind her into the darkness. Flora keeps Nectar's light off, so Echo listens for her low humming noise and uses that as her guide.

They get further away from the net and a shiver runs down Echo's spine as she remembers the last time she walked out here.

"It's not like then," River whispers, sensing her unease. "There's no sun. And we have Nectar to take us back if we need her."

"Quiet," Flora hushes. "She's close."

Echo swallows as they all slow their pace. It's impossible to see anything in this light. She can barely make out her hand if she holds it up in front of her face.

Nectar lights up, forcing them to shield their eyes from the sudden brightness. Her wings flip out as her whirring sound builds, and finally, she leaps.

"Pax!" a voice rings out from the darkness.

There's a huge crash and the Extinction Zone is plunged into darkness as the whirring falls instantly silent.

"Nectar?" Flora says on a gasp.

"What—" Chase's words are cut off by a loud *oomph* and there's the sound of a tussle.

Echo lets go of River's hand as they surge forward, wanting to help but it's impossible to know how. She connects with a body that she thinks is Chase but when a sharp blow collides with her shin, she realizes it must be Daphne.

She kicks back, hearing Chase moan when she makes contact.

"Sorry," she pants, as another blow lands on her chest and she falls to the ground.

"Echo!" River calls. "Are you okay?"

She scrambles back to her feet, pushing down any pain and waving her hands blindly in front of her. "I'm fine."

Flora curses as Echo hears her crashing to the ground beside her.

It might be four against one, but Daphne is mopping them up. It's almost like she can see in the dark.

Chase grunts and River lets out a howl of pain that morphs into one of anger.

"We just want to talk!" Echo shouts desperately. "Daphne. Please!"

Flora gets to her feet beside Echo. "It's about Iris. You need to listen."

The assault pauses and silence merges with the darkness.

"What?" snaps a voice that's instantly recognizable as Daphne's. "Tell me. But I warn you, if you don't have anything interesting to say, I'll kill you all right now with my bare hands. And I'll enjoy it."

"We have Iris hostage," growls Chase. "She's tied up where nobody can find her. Which means if you kill us, she'll die."

"Then I might start by only killing three of you." Daphne laughs in that uniquely tinkling way of hers. "Which shouldn't take more than a minute."

"What makes you think there's only four of us," Flora bluffs.

"You know something, Flora," says Daphne. "Ever since you were a small girl, I always thought you were irritating. You're nothing like your father."

There's a flurry of movement and a sharp crack as someone crumples to the ground.

"What have you done?" Chase shouts. "Flora, where are you?"

"Flora!" River breaks away from Echo's side as he scrambles in the darkness to find his twin.

"She can't hear you," sneers Daphne. "Now, who'd like to be next?"

Echo clenches her fists, contemplating her best move.

"Excellent," says Daphne. "The Dead Born looks like she's ready. I never did like too much female competition."

Echo's jaw drops. Somehow, Daphne *can* see them. Which means this evil fighting machine is at an even greater advantage.

They won't be taking her back to the bunker.

They won't be testing to see if she's the Sovereign.

They won't be bringing Immunity to all.

They'll be dying here in the dirt, just like she was worried they would the last time they stepped into the Extinction Zone.

Echo braces herself.

And Daphne makes her move.

CHAPTER
TWELVE

RIVER

Chase's pained groan rips through the night air, followed by a sickening thump.

"I'm looking forward to finishing what I started," Daphne snarls.

Then silence.

Panic is shredding River's ability to think. Nectar has somehow been disabled—all Daphne had to use was the Latin word for 'peace.' Flora and Chase are...

Unconscious! He frantically tells himself.

And Daphne must be wearing those night vision goggles the Green Borns use when they want to move around at night.

There's a sickening thud of flesh against flesh, but no corresponding groan from Chase. Then another thud. Daphne is beating him to death.

"You're the Sovereign!" River cries out, eyes desperately scanning the darkness in the direction the sounds are coming from.

Daphne bursts into laughter, the sound as empty as the night they're surrounded by. "You think *I'm* the Sovereign?"

"We know you are," Echo answers, now beside River. She must've followed his voice. "One test and we'll confirm it."

"You're not bringing queen bee venom anywhere near me," Daphne snarls, now sounding a little closer.

River's heart is a battering ram against his ribs as he works to bring his breathing under control. Daphne's stopped hurting Chase. They have an opening.

Echo moves so that her back is pressed against his, which is clever. They're now protecting each other's vulnerable side. River raises his fists, feeling Echo do the same.

They're ready to fight.

Even if they can't see the opponent who is a deadly fighting machine.

"Oren will be interested to know you two are still alive," Daphne purrs, now more to River's right.

He and Echo shuffle around so their shoulders are facing the same direction, along with their ears.

"You'll have to bring us in alive for that," Echo says.

Daphne chuckles, sending ice crackling down River's spine. "It's only River he'll actually want to see."

Echo stiffens, no doubt realizing Daphne's right. Oren won't care about Echo or Chase. And even Flora is well aware her own father already sees her as dead.

There's a faint sound of dirt crunching and Echo's forcefully ripped away from behind River. Her cry is cut short as she lands heavily on the ground, followed by the sounds of a scuffle.

"Echo!" River shouts.

He leaps, unable to see what he's doing, but also unable to stand by and do nothing. He collides with a body and he instantly recognizes the smooth suit of the Green Zone. Grabbing the material, he yanks with all his strength, rewarded by a grunt from Daphne as her body jerks backward.

Not willing to lose the advantage, River shoves her away, pushing through his feet so he can follow. Daphne lands on the ground with a thump and he crashes on top of her. He scrambles to grab her arms as he simultaneously pins her legs with his. But each time he gets a grip, Daphne expertly slips his grasp. Growling with frustration, River tenses his muscles, ready to hold on and not let go the next moment he wraps his fingers around anything.

Except Daphne's hands are gone. He clutches at nothing but air.

"River!" Echo calls out, no doubt trying to locate him.

Yet River doesn't answer. He can't.

The unmistakable point of a knife rests against his throat.

Despite being at a disadvantage, Daphne has won.

"Stay back, Echo," River says, keeping his voice low and even as he doesn't twitch a muscle. "She has a knife."

"I most certainly do," Daphne sneers, pressing the tip in a little harder. "And it's about to be dripping in blood."

"My father wants me alive," River warns, grasping at the last straw he has.

"This is a fight to the death. Do you really think Oren would choose you over me?"

River stills. Daphne is Oren's most loyal follower. He's nothing but the son who's turned his back on him. Of course Oren would understand that Daphne killed River in self-defense.

The part River can't stomach is that the thought hurts.

Some part of him still wishes his father loved him.

There's a low moan. "Oren...is using you just like everyone else, Daphne," Flora gasps.

River's pulse leaps. His twin is alive!

"Proelium!" Flora cries out.

The area bursts alive with light as the sweetest sound River has ever heard fills the air—whirring.

Daphne's free arm shoots to cover her night-vision goggles. River moves quickly, rearing back as he knocks the knife away from his throat. He leaps to the side, first hearing then seeing Nectar coming past his shoulder. He rolls over the dirt, seeing flashes of Nectar standing over Daphne as the two fight. Metal legs meet human limbs, the knife clangs against the robotic bee's body, Daphne snarls with venomous intent.

"Pax!" she screams over and over, her flailing arms knocking off her goggles. "Pax, you stupid machine!"

But Nectar's six legs work in perfect unison to block her wild strikes as she simultaneously immobilizes her.

River comes to a stop, breathing hard as he watches Nectar pin Daphne to the dirt like she's the bug. Daphne instantly goes limp, glaring up at the metallic head gazing impassively down at her. River would like to think she's admitted defeat, but he knows better. Daphne is saving her energy.

For when she next attacks.

A sob draws his attention to his right. Flora is crouching over Chase, tears streaming down her dusty cheeks. River's gut tightens so hard it hurts.

Chase would've been the first person Daphne killed.

"He's alive," Flora whispers, her lips climbing up even as the tears of relief continue to pour down. "He's breathing."

As if to confirm her words, Chase moans as he rolls over. "That bitch is going to pay for this."

Echo comes to River's side, wrapping one arm around his waist and resting the other on his chest, as if she's confirming his heart's beating. "But how?" she asks. "Nectar was powered down."

"When I was reprogramming her, I discovered she had an override word," Flora says as she brings Chase to his feet.

"Pax is Latin for peace," River says, his lips twisting.

Echo's face also contorts at Oren's choice of wording to have ultimate control over the robot bees.

Flora's features harden. "So I included one of my own."

"What does proelium mean?" Echo asks when Flora doesn't elaborate. She glances at Nectar as she continues to pin down a silent Daphne.

"Attack," Flora answers, slipping herself under Chase's arm. "It seemed fitting."

River frowns but doesn't say anything. He and Flora studied Latin because it's used in the nomenclature of plants. She knows as well as he does that attack isn't the only meaning of proelium.

Flora looks to Nectar as she keeps Daphne pinned. "Nectar, take her to the bunker."

Nectar scoops Daphne up with her front legs and clamps her to the underside of her thorax. Daphne acts like a limp doll and River wonders if she's even conscious, but then he sees her glacial eyes staring out from the hair falling over her face. He instinctively draws Echo closer to him, as if he can shield her from the hate.

Daphne's smart. She knows she doesn't have the strength to win against Nectar. She knows to bide her time. To wait for the right moment.

The walk back to the Dead Zone is thick with silence. Occasionally Nectar whirrs or clacks her jaws, but no one speaks. Chase's footsteps shuffle less and less, until he's walking beside Flora, rather than leaning on her. Periodically, he glares at Daphne held immobile against Nectar's black body, his gaze full of promise. She simply glares back in challenge.

River rubs the sore spot on his neck where Daphne held the knife. She'll reap the fruits of her heartless actions against Chase if she's not careful.

They slip through the net once more thanks to Nectar, then silently make their way through the scoring grounds and into the bunker. There, Flora commands Nectar to place Daphne on an earthen stool in the middle of the LaB. As Nectar does as she's told, Chase moves in and straps Daphne's hands behind her back and her feet together with twine he clearly had ready for this. His face is hard and impassive as he yanks the orange lengths tight, almost looking satisfied when they dig into Daphne's skin.

Flora pats the side of Nectar's head. "Go stand by the door, Nectar," she croons. "You've done good."

Nectar leaves and Daphne quickly straightens, her eyes darting around and scanning the dirt walls.

"There's only one door in and out," Chase growls. "And you won't be getting anywhere near it."

Daphne ignores him, her gaze falling on River. "Who told you I'm the Sovereign?"

River stops his eyes from slipping to his twin. "It doesn't matter. What does is confirming that you are."

"Was it that Dead Born scum who I had a little...chat with?" It's clear she's talking about Chase, even as she acts as if he's not in the room. "Of course it was. He wants to see me dead."

Chase moves faster than River expected considering he was only recently injured. He launches forward, striking his hand across Daphne's face so hard the crack sounds like a whip. "I don't need to lie to get even."

Echo darts to him, turning so she's facing him and pushes him back. "We agreed that we'd give her a chance to do this," she hisses.

Chase's shoulders heave up and down, and it's not the single strike that's got him worked up. It's Daphne herself.

And his drive to make her pay for all the pain she put him through.

River moves so he gets Daphne's attention. "We're fighting for Immunity for all, Daphne," he says, hoping that there's some shred of decency inside her. "No one deserves it more than anyone else."

"You have no idea what you're talking about," she spits, blood streaked across her teeth. "Everyone will die."

Echo shakes her head. "We've been to the Moon Zone. We know it was tried once before."

"Liars," Daphne shoots back. "The Moon Zone is nothing but rumors."

Flora steps forward. "We have proof." She looks to Nectar. "Play the footage, Nectar."

The small camera in Nectar's forehead appears again as she turns toward the side wall. Just like when they were on the roof of the building in the Moon Zone, beams of light shoot out. The image that appears is dark on the earthen wall, but it's visible enough to see.

They're about to watch the final moments on the rooftop when Nectar arrived to save River and Echo.

"There's no building like this in the Dead or Green Zone," River says, his gaze on the scene unfolding on the wall. "The Moon Zone is most definitely real."

He watches as he and Echo run to Nectar, Manu behind them with his scythe, the Moon Workers further back. The rain makes the image blurry and gray as Ruff jumps on, then Echo. River clamps her hand so he can join them, but Nectar dips as she struggles under the weight of three people. The panic on Echo's face is unmistakable, even in the grainy footage. The same fear is once more living inside River as he remembers how close he was to being left behind.

Then Manu strikes River across the back of his head with his scythe. He stumbles as Nectar rises.

River stares, unblinking, as he watches Ruff leap off the robotic bee and run straight toward Manu. He lifts him and throws him over the edge of the building. The moment is horrific, yet River knows it's also the start of something new.

Ruff thumps his chest, his lips moving as he makes his promise that he will not be Forgotten. Lyra steps forward, and even without sound, River can hear her words, remembering the hope that accompanied them.

"We could see where we're—"

Daphne makes a strangled sound.

River spins around, seeing a surprising emotion flash across Daphne's face. She's watching with far too much intensity.

But that's not what has him frozen to the spot. Daphne doesn't look shocked at the existence of the Moon Zone. In fact, she just recognized someone...

"River, look," Flora gasps. "That girl in the footage. It's Iris."

River blinks, just as shocked. He thought Lyra seemed familiar but he'd never known Iris well enough to be able to recognize her. And she always had that tangle of hair covering her face. No wonder Daphne was heading out to the Extinction Zone. Lyra is her daughter. She knew about the Moon Zone all along.

Chase snorts. "You sent her there when she was found to be Vulnerable. So she didn't have to suffer a slow death in the Dead Zone like every other soul here."

Daphne cuts him a glare. "She's Green Born, not Dead Born scum."

Chase lurches forward, but both River and Echo stop him. "We need to give her a chance to do the right thing," River says.

Chase glares at him but steps back. "I can wait." He stretches his neck one way then the other. "Because she won't."

River turns back to Daphne. "Immunity for all is the only way forward. Surely you understand that."

"You've seen it," Daphne says, her gaze flicking to where the scene played out on the wall. "Our ancestors tried to feed the Vulnerables, and we almost went extinct."

Echo shakes her head, unwilling to hear the same, tired old excuses. "That was before we knew Immunity was possible."

"There will be no Vulnerables anymore," River adds. "No Dead Born or Green Born. Just Immunes."

Echo takes a step forward. "To do that, we need the Sovereign."

"I told you, that's not me," Daphne spits. "Someone is feeding you lies."

"We need to find out," River says. "We need to test you." He doesn't bother explaining the process. Daphne would already know. "We know a way to do it that's safer. Micro dosing means you're less likely to react if we're wrong."

"Which we're not," Flora adds, crossing her arms.

River watches Daphne as he waits, holding his breath. He doesn't want to consider what it might look like if she says no.

If they force Daphne, he'll be one step closer to being like his father.

Yet they need the Sovereign...

Daphne's gaze goes to Echo, then River. Once again, she doesn't acknowledge Chase or Flora.

Her face hardens as she lifts her chin. "Never."

CHAPTER

THIRTEEN

ECHO

Daphne looks harmless tied to the chair in the LaB. She seems frailer, older, thinner. But Echo isn't going to be fooled. This woman is a coldblooded killer. She wasn't heading to the Moon Zone to find out if her daughter needed help. Most likely, she was going there to make sure Lyra never bothered her again.

It all makes sense now. Lyra hadn't been like the others. She'd been fascinated by their arrival. And the way she kept covering her face with her hair wasn't shyness. She was worried River would recognize her.

"We're going to need to test her against her will," says Chase. "She hasn't earned the right to have a choice."

"We can't do that," River says firmly. "That would make us just like Oren."

Daphne snorts. "You'll never be as great as your father. You don't have the backbone."

"Chase is right," says Flora, ignoring Daphne. "Oren doesn't micro dose. We do. Which is why we don't need her permission. It's completely safe."

"I'm not sure Rose would agree with that." Echo crosses her arms. "I'm with River on this. We can't test Daphne unless she agrees to it."

Flora turns to the workbench that Nectar's carved into the solid earth and begins setting up her equipment.

River goes to her side. "Flora?"

"Not now, River." She doesn't lift her eyes from her bench.

"Flora, we agreed to make decisions as a four moving forward," he reminds her.

"You agreed to that," Flora snaps, lifting a syringe from her tray. "I don't recall either Chase or me confirming that was a good idea."

"We're a team. We always have been." River puts a hand on each of Flora's forearms, forcing her to look him in the eye. "You're better than this. You're better than *him*. Don't do this."

Flora looks at River for several beats of their hearts before letting out a long sigh.

"Fine," she says. "Then we'll convince her."

Daphne stiffens. "I. Said. Never."

Chase steps forward and lands a punch square on Daphne's nose. There's a sickening crack and her head flies back. When she lifts it, there's blood rushing from her nose, which is crooked and clearly broken.

"Chase!" Echo gasps.

Daphne smiles at Echo like nothing happened as she continues to pretend Chase isn't in the room.

"I'm right here," Chase growls. "Look at me."

Daphne keeps her steely gaze on Echo.

Chase slams his foot into Daphne's shin, then brings up his knee, connecting it with her chin. With more anger brimming inside him, Chase doesn't wait for her to speak before pummeling her chest with a series of punches.

"That's enough, Chase!" River rushes forward and with Echo's help, they pull him back.

Daphne looks in terrible shape, but she refuses to give into the pain, keeping the grin plastered to her blood-soaked face. "What part of never don't you understand?"

"Violence won't work," Echo says to Chase. "She thrives on it."

"She's right," says Flora. "Let me talk to her."

Daphne seems to find this amusing. "It will be like old times. Like when you came crying to me after your mommy died."

Flora draws in a breath. "I'd like to talk to her alone. We have unfinished business."

"That's not safe," says Chase, clenching his fists. "We're not leaving you with her."

"She's strapped to a chair!" Flora throws out her hands. "And I have Nectar."

"Oh, Nectar," says Daphne. "How sweet. You gave the cute little Worker a name."

"Leave us." Flora sets down the syringe and puts her hands on her hips. "I'll be fine. I promise I won't test her."

"Yeah, she'll be just fine," Daphne taunts.

Chase moves forward and slaps Daphne hard across the side of her face. "Don't speak unless you're spoken to. Understand?"

Echo decides that maybe Flora talking to Daphne isn't such a bad idea. Chase isn't letting up. Maybe if he has a few minutes to cool down, he'll get a handle on himself.

"Come on, Chase," says River, seeming to decide the same thing. "Let's step out for a minute."

"I'm not leaving Flora," he says, launching at Daphne again like a man possessed, and punching her again, this time in the ribs.

River grabs Chase forcefully by the arm, while Echo takes his other.

"It's just for a few minutes," says Echo, well aware if they don't remove Chase, Daphne won't live to be tested for anything, let alone be able to agree to it.

"Come on," says River, dragging Chase away. "Flora has Nectar here. Daphne's tied up tight."

"Just go already!" Flora snaps. "Chase, I said I need a moment."

Chase allows himself to be dragged from the room, clearly not happy with this plan. They get him into the main chamber where it's dark but given there's no door to the LaB there's a gentle light filtering through from Nectar's glowing disc.

Chase paces, while Echo and River hover nearby, making sure he doesn't go back in. However this plays out, it's going to be a long night.

"Can you hear what they're saying?" Echo asks, trying to see what's happening inside. But Flora and Daphne are around a corner and all she can see are some carved out shelves.

"Flora's whispering something," says River.

"Chase..." Echo loses her courage to say what she wants to, then sucks in a breath to try again. "You can't stoop to Daphne's level. I saw a side of you in there that I've never seen before. And it wasn't good. Your parents—"

"Would be proud of me," he finishes. "Because I'm doing this for them. I'm doing this for everyone like them. For all the Vulnerables who've died because of people like Daphne. She's evil. And if you can't see that, you're blind."

River opens his mouth to defend Echo, but Chase jumps back in before he gets the chance.

"Don't waste your breath, River," he snaps. "It's great that you're so protective of Echo, but you're being just as naïve. Daphne isn't going to agree to be tested. Not by us, anyway.

And we're not like Oren if we test her against her will. He doesn't have micro dosing. Our test isn't deadly. We have Flora."

There's a deep muffled moan from the LaB and Chase holds up a hand. "I'll check on it."

He disappears, thankfully returning moments later, nodding. "They're fine. Daphne's close to agreeing."

"Who was moaning then?" Echo asks, trying to get around him.

"Daphne." Chase plants his feet in the entrance to the LaB. "Seems the incentives I gave her to cooperate are starting to sting."

"I'd like to see for myself." Echo tries again to move past him, but Chase is like an immovable wall.

River takes hold of her arm. "You can trust Flora. She won't be testing her. She promised."

Echo wrenches herself free, regretting taking Chase out of the room now that she can't get back in.

"Let me through," she says. "If they're just talking, I'll come straight out."

"Flora's got this." Chase's teeth are gritted, and he holds her back like she's nothing more than an annoying fly.

Another muffled moan floats from the room and Echo looks at River, exasperated. "We need to get in there."

"Flora always keeps her promises." River's voice breaks. Perhaps he's convincing himself as much as her.

"Then it won't be a problem for us to check." Echo beats on Chase's chest, but still, he doesn't move. "Please."

There's a screech from inside the LaB that sounds very much like Flora, and Chase seems to forget they exist and runs inside.

Echo dashes after him. It takes her a few moments to process what she's seeing. Daphne is still in the chair except she has a hessian bag over her head. Flora is beside her with a bleeding wound on her hand that she's clutching to her chest. And there's a strange chemical smell in the room.

"Flora!" River pants. "What's going on?"

"Are you hurt?" Chase asks.

"She bit me," Flora growls. "And she's going to be sorry for it."

Flora uses her good hand to grab at the string securing the bag around Daphne's neck and pulls it tighter. Daphne moans. It's an awful sound that seems to be erupting from her chest against her will.

"She can't breathe." Echo tries to get closer. "Get that thing off her head."

River physically shoves his twin out of the way and tears the bag off Daphne, while Echo tries to hold back Chase.

Spinning around, Echo is horrified to see Daphne's face is swollen and purple. Her eyes are bloodshot and her breath is coming in crackling gasps.

River holds the bag to his nose, a look of realization crossing his eyes. "Flora, this has been soaked in insecticide, hasn't it? I recognize the smell from Eden."

"We don't use insecticides in the Green Zone," Flora snaps. "It's dangerous for bees."

"Unless it's an emergency," says River. "To save an endangered plant species. Clover showed me once. And it smelled exactly like this."

Echo shakes her head, looking at the damage the chemicals have done. "You're lucky you didn't kill her!"

"She's the lucky one," says Chase. "But maybe not for long."

"She needed an incentive." Flora pouts. "She wasn't responding to chitty chat."

"Daphne." Echo goes to her side. "Please. You need to agree

to get tested. It can't be worse than this. We need to move on so we can get you out of this chair and feeling better."

Daphne opens her swollen lips and blinks up at her. "Never," she croaks.

"Put the bag back on." Flora strides over and clutches it out of River's hands.

But before she can open it, Echo throws herself on top of Daphne, sitting on her lap and putting out her hands. "Enough, Flora."

Daphne struggles beneath her, but Echo holds her position, knowing it's the only way to keep her safe.

A sharp pain shoots across the back of Echo's head and she's thrown forward, landing hard on the ground in front of the chair. River immediately scoops her up and drags her backward.

Rubbing her head, Echo looks across the room to see a dark pink splotch spreading across Daphne's forehead. "She head-butted me?"

"Don't touch me again," sneers Daphne. "Dead Born scum."

"At least she's acknowledging your existence," Chase grumbles.

Flora slides the bag over Daphne's head and pulls on the string, tightening it around her neck. "I'm leaving this on for one minute this time. And when it comes off, you're going to agree to be tested. If not, it stays on permanently."

"Flora!" River makes sure Echo is steady on her feet and rushes to his twin. "She can't breathe."

"That's the idea, River." Flora rolls her eyes. "Don't go feeling sorry for her. You saw what she did to Chase in the Betadome. And then again tonight in the Extinction Zone. And what she did to Echo just now. She's ruthless. It's time for us to be the same."

Echo thinks she understands what's happening here. Nothing about this is getting Daphne to agree to be tested. This is about Flora getting revenge on Daphne for hurting the guy she loves.

"Okay, we'll test her!" Echo steps forward. "Take the bag off. We'll test her without her consent."

"Echo?" River looks at her, confused.

"It's better than this," Echo squeaks out. "Anything is better than this."

"Flora, take the bag off," says River, clearly hating what he's agreeing to. "We'll test her."

Flora hesitates, and once again River pushes her out of the way and removes the bag himself.

Daphne heaves for clean air, and Echo grimaces wondering if it's already too late to change tactics. It's very possible Flora's already killed her and they'll never find out if she's the Sovereign.

Echo rushes from the room and fetches a glass of water from a jug outside and brings it in. She holds it to Daphne's lips. "Drink. You need water."

Daphne takes a large sip and tilts her head up at Echo, gratitude in her eyes. Then she spits the entire mouthful in Echo's face and a laugh erupts from her chest that sounds more like a hacking cough.

Echo blinks as the diluted chemicals sting her eyes. She's too shocked to say anything and instead stumbles back while Flora readies her syringe and picks up a scalpel. River steadies Echo as she wipes her face with her shirt.

"Give Flora space," Chase says from behind Daphne's chair. "She needs to concentrate."

Flora scratches at Daphne's arm with her scalpel and uses the syringe to squeeze a drop of venom onto the wound, just like she did with Clover. Except Clover had held still. Daphne is thrashing around in her chair, tugging on the ropes that are binding her in place, while Chase holds her head still so she can't spit at Flora.

"We're not going to know if she's reacting," River points out. "She already can't breathe."

"Good point," says Echo, desperately wishing Flora had chosen a more humane way to go about this whole thing.

"She's fine," says Flora. "I'm moving to Stage Two."

"Wait!" Echo steps forward, trying to get a better look at Daphne's arm. "We need to have the adrenacure ready. Where is it?"

"It's on the bench." Flora jams the syringe into Daphne's arm and squeezes.

Echo dives for the adrenacure, certain that Daphne's arm turned purple after the scratch test. But everything's happening so quickly, it's hard to tell exactly what's going on.

"She's reacting!" River shouts. "Hurry, Echo!"

Echo throws the canister at River, who drives it immediately into Daphne's thigh. Daphne has gone from purple to blue as her swelling intensifies. It doesn't look like any air is making it into her lungs now.

"We need another one!" River shouts. "Quickly!"

Echo returns to the bench and looks around. "There isn't another. Flora! Where do you keep them?"

"They're in that box somewhere." Aside from pointing, Flora makes no move to help her. "But we already have our answer. She's not the Sovereign."

"Flora!" Echo calls, scrambling around in the box Flora had indicated. "We need your help!"

"Daphne," River says, slapping her gently across her swollen cheeks. "Hold on. We're getting more adrenacure. It's going to be okay."

Echo's fingertips land on a second canister of adrenacure. "River! Catch!"

He puts out a hand and swipes the life-saving concoction out of the air. But instead of injecting Daphne with it, he slides it into his pocket.

"Echo, it's too late," he says somberly. "She's dead."

"She can't be," Echo whimpers. "It was a micro dose. It *was* a micro dose, wasn't it?"

River looks at Echo, his eyes filling with tears. "Of course, it was."

Echo glances at the empty syringe lying on the floor, certain the dose Flora administered was larger than what she'd given Clover.

Which means...

She shudders, not wanting to face what it means.

Because there's no getting around the fact that Daphne is dead. Which means she's not the Sovereign, and they're back to where they started.

Again.

"We're missing something obvious," says River, dragging his fingers through his hair. "We have to be."

Pieces of the puzzle fly together in Echo's mind and she whimpers as they begin to form an unwanted picture.

She's not sure what she just took part in here but she's certain it was all kinds of wrong. Which means they need to do something different, instead of making the same mistakes over and over.

Because there's no way she's ever going through anything like that ever again.

It's time to take a different path. Even if it means that she and River will need to walk alone.

FOURTEEN

RIVER

River's gaze keeps coming back to Daphne's bloated, still form. Even though her skin is swollen and tight from the venom, the bruises from Chase's strikes and the mottling from Flora's poison are just as glaring. Just as gut churning.

Daphne died the most painful and tortuous death of all the possible Sovereigns so far.

And once again, they were wrong.

Echo plants her hands on her hips as she glares at Flora. "Well, that was all levels of wrong."

Flora stiffens, then raises her chin. "We did everything right."

"How can you say that?" Echo shoots back, almost shouting. "You tortured Daphne!"

Chase steps so he's next to Flora. "You and River were the ones who insisted we have Daphne agree to being tested. If it weren't for you, we could've avoided all that."

Indignation shoots through River, but it looks like it cannonballs through Echo. She pulls in a sharp breath, turning her narrowed eyes on Chase.

"I *never* agreed to this. In fact, I think you planned on doing this all along and deliberately kept us in the dark."

Chase's chest inflates. "What are you saying, Echo?"

She draws away, her gaze snapping to Flora. "How far back does this go?" she asks, suspicion lowering her tone.

Challenge flares in Flora's eyes. "What are you talking about?"

"How far back, Flora?" Echo throws her arms out. "You're the one who gave us the names of the three women you believed could be the Sovereign. Now every one of them is dead."

It's Chase's turn to look indignant. His spine stiffens as he cuts his hand through the air. "That's enough, Echo! I get that you're angry, but you can't go around accusing—"

"All I did was ask a question," Echo says, the control in her voice belying the way her clenched hands tremble. "One I want Flora to answer."

River's frozen, watching the two women he loves fight. He can understand Echo's anger. He's just as uncomfortable with how everything has unfolded. Guilt and regret are like acid in his stomach.

But he also knows how fragile Flora is, whether others see it or not. These accusations would be cutting her deep. He takes a step forward, wanting to defuse the situation. Maybe they need to talk about this later, when everyone's calmer.

When Daphne's dead body isn't staring at them in accusation.

Flora's gaze flies to River and he stops. Her lower lip trembles ever so slightly as she silently implores him, although he's not entirely sure for what. He loves her with all his heart, but he can't condone what she just did.

"Echo," he says softly. "I—"

"No, River," she says, sounding angry and sad at the same

time. "I don't need you to back me up. You don't have to choose."

He can't help the gratitude that flows through him. Even in her anger, she understands the position he's in. "Could I talk to Flora alone for a moment?"

Echo hesitates, but then nods. She flashes a look at Chase. "A circuit breaker is a good idea. Let's get some fresh air."

Chase looks from River, then to Flora, who nods her agreement. Brushing his hand over hers, he exits the LaB and Echo follows. She pauses as she passes River, her dark gaze finding his. His stomach tightens as he registers the storm of emotions brewing in there.

Pain.

Sadness.

And suspicion.

River almost can't hold her gaze. He understands why Echo's feeling like that. Rose died instantly. Clover passed the Sovereign test, then died when stung. And now Daphne.

But allowing those doubts to flourish leads him down a path that makes his chest hurt. So much has been taken from him in the fight to find the Sovereign. Losing faith in his twin isn't something he wants to add to the list.

Echo must see something that doesn't comfort her because she looks away, her mouth tightening. She exits the LaB, her soft footsteps trailing up the stairs after Chase. The hatch opens, then closes, leaving River alone with Flora.

He glances at Daphne, nausea stinging the back of his throat. Her bloating is worse as the venom continues its devastating impact on her body, even though she's dead. It seems to highlight the bruises and her eyes are swelling in ways none of the others did.

Because of Flora's chemical attack.

"Let's talk out there," he says quietly, then turns without

waiting for a response. He needs a circuit breaker as much as Echo does.

Flora follows quietly and he turns to face her once he's in the main room, registering that Nectar has followed her.

Flora shrugs sheepishly. "She's programmed to stay close unless I tell her otherwise." She looks back at the robotic bee. "Pax."

Nectar instantly powers down, just like she did when they were in the Extinction Zone and Daphne used the word. It's a harsh reminder that Flora certainly holds a lot of information he hasn't been privy to.

"What just happened, Flora?" he asks quietly, his confusion weighing his words.

She turns to him, her chin rising just like it did with Echo. But then it stops. Her shoulders drop. "I keep trying, River. I keep hoping I'll figure it all out."

River's first instinct is to comfort her, but he stops himself. He needs answers and he's made too many assumptions. "Figure what out, Flora? We need to find the Sovereign."

Flora raises her green eyes to his and he has to stop himself from drawing in a sharp breath. Pools of misery stare back at him. "Maybe there is no Sovereign," she whispers. "Maybe Mother Nature knows we're not worth saving."

River strides to her, clamping his hands around her arms. "What? How can you say that? We have everything to fight for."

"A father who doesn't love me?" she asks bitterly, her mouth twisting. "A mother who turned her back on us without once looking back?"

River realizes the opportunity he was looking for has shown itself. His sister doesn't know about their mother being in the Hive. But Flora speaks again before he can tell her.

"If my own father couldn't love me, what does that say about me?"

River's hands tighten on Flora's arms. "He doesn't love me either." Daphne's words ring in his ears, still holding the power to hurt.

Do you really think Oren would choose you over me?

"Does that make me a bad person?"

Flora sighs. "Oren loved you. He probably still does. He wouldn't have done all of this if he didn't want to punish you." Her body seems to sag. "When I was found Vulnerable, he turned away and never looked back."

River blinks. Turns out indifference is worse than hate.

He draws her to him, wrapping his arms tightly around his twin. He knew Oren's rejection had created a wound, but it's far deeper than he thought. As if to confirm his thoughts, Flora crumples against him, burying her face in his chest as her shoulders tremble.

"And our mom didn't turn her back on us," he says softly, glad he can give her this—proof that she's worthy of love.

Because somehow, it feels as if that proves to her the rest of the world is also worthy.

Flora looks up at him, her face tear streaked and pale. "Am I going to have to shut that down with a few home truths, too?"

His lips twitch, appreciating her sharp mouth is a product of a sharp mind. "You were right. Mom came to the Dead Zone. She became Nola, Echo's friend."

Flora's eyes widen. "But how..."

"Echo had a hunch when she met Makk's mother." River smiles. "Who is our aunt Marigold."

"Makk's our cousin?" she asks, astounded.

River nods. "Although the two sisters didn't know they were in the same village. They've both been prisoners in their own huts, too scared of Oren finding them."

Flora pulls away, her mouth still agape. She glances over her shoulder toward the hatch, as if she's considering running out to find their mother right now. She frowns, looking back at him. "But Nola's…"

"In the Hive," he finishes for her. "She sacrificed herself so I could get out. She never stopped loving us, Flora. Some days I wonder if she's been waiting for us. That's why she took the Code with her."

Flora blinks. Then blinks again. "She's been waiting for us…"

River grins, glad to see the painful ghosts that were haunting his twin's eyes are being chased away by the knowledge that she matters. But the action quickly dims as he realizes those ghosts are more like demons.

And that they've been influencing Flora.

He takes a step toward her, needing to know. "Why did you do that to Daphne?"

"To make her hurt," Flora says simply. She looks up at him. "Because I hurt." A tear glistens in her eye. "And I don't know how to stop it."

He reaches out and takes her hand, finding it cool and trembling. "We stop it when we make this right," he says. "When people are no longer defined as Vulnerable or Immune."

Flora's gaze drifts to the earthen floor as she looks thoughtful, and he can't help but add one more statement. One final truth.

"When people stop doing selfish things under the guise of being selfless."

Her gaze shoots to his and he almost takes the words back. The pain that flashes in Flora's eyes is unmistakable, and he's not here to add to her wounds. But she needs to realize they need to be healed.

Because what happened to Daphne can never happen again.

Her brows contract. "You still love me, don't you, River?"

He has her back in his arms before the question is finished. "Of course," he says, pressing a kiss to her dark hair. "I'll always love you, Flora. Never doubt that."

She sighs, sinking into his chest and he simply holds her tighter. With every shred of his being, he wishes that this could be enough to heal the hurt their father has wrought. That the world they live in has fed. The divide that exists within Flora is as undeniable as the chasm between the Dead Zone and Green Zone.

A sound from the stairs has them both looking over, seeing Echo and Chase standing there. Chase is looking relieved.

While Echo is frowning.

"Sorry," Chase says. "We have to get rid of Daphne's body before dawn."

River and Flora pull away. He hadn't realized day was so close.

"Nectar can drop her in the Extinction Zone, somewhere away from the Moon Zone," Echo adds. "All Oren will know is that Daphne disappeared without a trace."

River nods, knowing it's their best course of action. Oren will still be suspicious, probably blame them, but he won't have any proof.

Flora goes to Nectar and presses a hand on her smooth thorax, whispering, "Proelium."

River can't help the small frown as he hears the word again, but he quickly smooths it away as Nectar whirrs and comes to life. She goes back into the LaB and returns with Daphne's limp, bloated body and carries her toward the hatch. Chase follows, his jaw tight.

Flora joins him, offering River a small smile. "I'll help him."

River watches as they exit the bunker, unsure how he's feeling. Even less sure how he's supposed to be feeling. He has no idea if anything's been resolved with Flora. All that's been confirmed is his worry that she's hurting and fragile.

He turns to Echo, wondering if there's any way to lighten the heaviness that's creeping into his chest. He lets out a breath as she steps toward him, her eyes are soft with compassion as if she understands what he's going through.

But then she asks a question that has the tension snapping right back. "What does proelium really mean, River?"

CHAPTER
FIFTEEN
ECHO

Echo waits while River's words seem to be trying to catch up to his racing mind.

"Flora told you what proelium means," he eventually says. "It means attack."

"She did say that." Echo crosses her arms. "And you frowned when she said it. Twice. So, what does it really mean?"

River lets out a sigh. "It *does* mean attack. It's just that… well, it also means something else."

Echo nods. "And that would be what exactly?"

"It means war." River winces. "But I'm sure Flora was thinking of attack when she programmed Nectar."

"War is an odd word for someone who claims to want peace, don't you think?" Echo hates that she can't let this go.

River shrugs. "Perhaps she thinks there needs to be war in order to find peace."

"And you're okay with that?" Echo tilts her head.

"Of course, I'm not!" River shouts. "I don't want a war any more than you do. But I'm coming to accept it might be inevitable. And if that's the case, then we'll be glad we have Nectar on our side."

"On Flora's side," Echo corrects, feeling the need to make the distinction.

River's eyes flare. It's the first time she's seen him direct anger at her since she first arrived in the Green Zone. And that was because of Flora, too.

"Flora is on our side," River grinds out. "I spoke to her just now. I'm more certain of it than ever."

Echo pauses, unsure how to approach this. How does she get River to see what's becoming so clear to her?

"What did she say?" Echo asks, needing more information before she makes her next move. "What possible excuse did she have for the way she treated Daphne? No matter how evil Daphne was, she was still a human being. Flora not only stooped to her level, she went far lower."

River takes a step back from Echo. "That's not true. The only reason we didn't see Daphne kill anyone was because we never gave her the chance. Flora isn't like her. She's just hurting. You've got no idea what it feels like for your parent to turn their back on you."

"That's true." Echo manages to keep her voice level. "Dead Borns generally don't live long enough to get the chance to abandon anyone. Unless you're talking about death, of course. Seems like the remainder of the civilized world has turned their back on us instead."

"The Green Zone turned its back on me, too," River huffs. "You can't claim that for yourself anymore."

Tears sting at Echo's eyes. "I don't want to argue, River."

"Neither do I." He reaches for her, then thinks again and withdraws his hand.

"I just want you to see what's happening," she says. "We've been trying to find the Sovereign for a while now.

And every time something has gone wrong, who's been there?"

"We've all been there," he says, avoiding the question. "Including Chase, and I don't see you blaming him. He was the one who beat Daphne to a pulp."

"I don't condone what Chase did." Echo's shoulders slump. "But I can also see that he was giving her back some of what she's given him. Are you forgetting she tried to set him on fire? Flora's different. She took things to a whole new level."

"She's not thinking clearly," he says. "That's all it is."

Echo shakes her head. "I disagree. She's thinking very clearly. More clearly than we've been. She was the one who came up with that list of three possible Sovereigns. And coincidentally, all three were people she had a score to settle with."

River's jaw drops. "That's not—"

"Rose saw Flora with Chase in the Green Zone," Echo reminds him. "And Flora wanted to make sure she didn't tell anyone."

"That's speculation," River shakes his head, not seeming at all convinced.

"Daphne's more obvious," she presses on. "She beat up Chase and nearly killed him. Flora needed to pay her back for that. Then Clover..."

"Then Clover what?" he snaps.

"Clover was in love with you." These words still leave a bitter taste in her mouth. "I think Flora wanted to pretend Clover was the Sovereign to tear us apart."

River grunts. "And why would she want to do that?"

"Because she's never liked me," says Echo on a sigh. "Not really. I came between the two of you. I changed you as a person. I brought you here to the Dead Zone. She wasn't counting on that."

"She does like you!" River begins to pace, not accepting any of this. "And the test clearly showed Clover was Immune. She didn't react at all to that sting from the queen."

"Flora could easily have faked it," says Echo. "We don't really know what she injected her with. She made it look like Clover was Immune. Then when Clover went back to the Green Zone, she found out she was Vulnerable. That's why Oren was so happy to return her here. She was useless to him. And it's why she didn't want to go into the Betadome to help me pick the fruit. She was petrified. And for good reason. It killed her. *Flora* killed her."

River's face turns pink, and Echo knows she's treading a fine line. But she has to get these thoughts out. And now that she's spoken them aloud, they're starting to make even more sense than when they were swirling around in her mind.

"And what about you?" River asks. "If Flora hates you so much, why did you survive the queen bee sting if Flora's really controlling all of this?"

"Because maybe I really am the Sovereign." Echo jams her hands on her hips as she lets this sink in.

River opens his mouth a few times, but words fail him once more.

"Flora thought the test would kill me," says Echo. "That's why the first queen died before she could sting me. Flora chickened out when she realized how much you care about me. She was the one holding the queen. It was perfectly healthy in that little prism one minute, and dead the next. I think she shook it up when nobody was watching."

"Then why didn't she stop you from collecting another queen?" River smiles as he thinks he's found a hole in her theory.

"She couldn't stop me without it being obvious what she was up to," says Echo. "Plus the chance of me successfully collecting a queen from the Betadome was very slim."

"But you did collect one." River nods at the memory. "And Flora allowed you to be tested."

"And she was more shocked than anyone when I survived," says Echo. "Don't you remember? Her reaction was downright strange."

"But you're not the Sovereign, Echo." The gentle tone returns to River's voice. "We couldn't produce immunity from your spinal fluid."

"You mean Flora couldn't," she corrects, not willing to let this go. "Because she didn't want it to be me. She took my spinal fluid so she could experiment with it. She had no intention of letting us continue to think I was the Sovereign. But it's me, River. I'm the Sovereign. I know it."

"There has to be another explanation." River shakes his head, refusing to see any shades of gray in his sparkly gold twin.

"Then I'd love to hear it." Echo does her best to show the sadness she's feeling deep in her soul. She knows it hurts River to hear this, but it has to be said. Everything that's happened so far can be explained by her theory. Flora's been messing with them this whole time.

"Maybe the queen we tested you with wasn't really a queen," says River. "That's why Flora couldn't produce immunity."

"She was a queen, River." Echo rolls her eyes. "You saw her. I saw her. We all saw her. You're going to need a better explanation than that."

"I can come up with one." River smooths a wrinkle from his trousers, avoiding Echo's eye. "One that doesn't involve you turning on my sister. My *innocent* sister. I just need a little time."

"Time!" Echo laughs. "Our time ran out ages ago. More and more people die every day it takes us to figure this out. Your own mother is in the Hive, for crying out loud. If that's not an incentive to get moving, then I don't know what is."

"We are moving." River sounds angry again. "But we need to move as a team. The four of us can do this if we work together."

Echo lets out a whimper. "Except we're not working together. Only three of us are. Or two if Chase has already figured this out and has chosen Flora over the cause."

"Chase wouldn't choose anything over the cause," River snaps. "Not even Flora."

"We could have solved all this if Flora hadn't been getting in our way."

Echo marches toward the LaB. If River can't be convinced by her words, then it's time for her to prove it to him. To show him she really is the Sovereign. Maybe then he'll believe her and they can get on with what they need to do. They've been wasting time looking for the Sovereign, instead of looking for the Code, when they've known who she is this whole time.

It's Echo. She's never been more certain of anything in her life.

"Where are you going?" River asks.

Echo doesn't answer. She enters the LaB and turns on a torch to light up the room. She goes to Flora's box of supplies, looking for something she'd noticed when she'd been frantically searching for more adrenacure for Daphne.

Her fingers land on the canister she needs, and she takes it out with shaking hands, knowing what she needs to do.

River appears in the doorway and his eyes widen as he registers what she has. "Put that down, Echo."

She shakes her head, clutching the queen bee venom like her life depends on it. Which to be fair, it does. All their lives do.

"Echo, don't," says River, holding up his palms as he

approaches her slowly. "You're not the Sovereign. Put that down."

She looks into his beautiful green eyes, adrenaline coursing through her body as she prepares to do what she knows she must.

"Talk to me, Echo." River continues to advance, forgetting how well she knows him. He's going to pounce on her. To prevent what's already too late for her to stop.

"Makk is right," says Echo. "We talk too much."

She slams the canister into her thigh and feels the sharp sting as the queen bee venom enters her bloodstream.

"Echo!" River shouts. "What have you done? No!"

She collapses on the floor, both surprised and relieved that he still cares about her after what she just accused his sister of doing.

Blinking up at him, she finds those green eyes again, and waits to see if her body's going to react. She's gambled everything on this moment.

River is either looking at her for the last time.

Or he'll soon be looking at the irrefutable truth.

CHAPTER
SIXTEEN
RIVER

R iver's heart stopped the second Echo injected herself with the queen bee venom.

Now, with each moment that draws out, it convulses. Constricts. Chokes on the grief that's trying to drown it.

Echo's eyes flutter closed as a shuddering breath falls from her lips.

"Echo! No!" he cries, turning away even though all he wants to do is hold her, somehow shielding her from fate. She needs adrenacure. Now!

Her hand grips his arm before he can get up, shocking him with her strength. He spins back, expecting to see her face bloated, her skin turning that awful shade of bruise, her gaze full of goodbye.

Except Echo smiles at him. Draws in a deep, peace-filled breath. And smiles wider.

She's not swollen. Not wheezing.

She's downright beautiful as she glows, the truth shining from her eyes.

River's frozen to the spot, astounded. Yet, somehow, not surprised at all. After everything they've been through, after the unimaginable price others have had to pay, it was Echo all along.

She's the Sovereign.

River shakes his head, a rueful smile climbing up his lips. "I can't believe I didn't see that coming."

Echo huffs out a laugh. Then she's launching herself into his arms as he simultaneously yanks her against his chest, holding each other tightly. They pull apart long enough to press their lips together in a fierce kiss. Relief, shock, and joy are whirling inside him.

He can't believe their frustrations with all the lies overflowed, bringing about the ultimate truth.

Echo pulls back enough to clasp his face, her dark eyes full of love. "Sorry, that probably wasn't the best way to confirm a hunch."

River chuckles, pressing a tender kiss on her mouth. "Effective, but my heart just aged a century or two."

Her smile is so sweet it makes his gut ache. "Sorry." She presses a hand on his chest. "I want this in my life forever."

"Always, Echo," he says, his smile falling away under the weight of the truth.

This kiss is longer, deeper, sweeter. One that awakens the passion that's never far away. It quickly becomes hotter, wilder, freer. River's arms move down to mold Echo to him, while her hands come up to grip his hair, locking him into place.

They taste, touch, devour the new reality they just uncovered. One with an answer. A future.

A testament to what their love has made possible.

Except they both pull away, hearts hammering as they smile at each other ruefully.

"I don't think this is the time to make out with the Sovereign," River says, his eyes still drawn to her moist lips.

Echo releases her hold with a disgruntled sigh. "My new title is already getting in the way."

River laughs, and they hug before standing up. He looks down at her, questions now having the space to be acknowledged. "How did you know?"

Echo shrugs. "It's the only thing that made sense. I'm the only one to have actually survived a queen bee sting."

River nods, his brow pulled low. They discounted that too quickly.

The fine muscles around Echo's mouth tighten. "Which raises the question of why the Immunity Flora produced from my spinal fluid didn't save Navy."

River's eyebrows pull even lower even as he remembers having to watch Echo with Chase's knife pressed against his throat, terrified, as she was harvested. That scene now seems to embody everything that defined the tumultuous search for the Sovereign.

Pain.

Confusion.

A truth that always seems to be out of reach.

"Echo..." Despite all that, he doesn't think he can rehash the argument that sparked the most terrifying, life-changing moment so far. Flora's his twin. What sort of person is he if he doesn't have faith in her?

"I don't want to fight about this either," she says, pressing her hand to his cheek. "Compromise? I'll hold my tongue if you agree to keep an open mind about what I said. We both have some thinking to do."

.   .   .

RELIEF HAS the tension melting away. He turns his head and kisses her palm. "I like that."

"Me, too," Echo says with a smile.

They hold each other tightly for long seconds, Echo tucking her head into the crook of River's neck while he savors the moment. He's holding the Sovereign.

Echo's not only his ray of hope.

She's humanity's very beacon.

Sounds from the hatch have them pulling apart to see Flora and Chase coming down the stairs, Nectar dutifully following behind them.

Chase's gaze flickers over River and Echo as they remain holding each other. "It's done. Daphne's body won't be found."

But it's Flora who River's watching. He notes the way she glances at them, but then her gaze quickly skitters away. He has to stop himself from stiffening. From suspicion trying to germinate in his mind.

Who's he kidding? It already has...just waiting to blossom. He hates that Echo's words have gotten to him. But he also promised he wouldn't discount what she said about Flora.

Flora gasps as she registers the queen bee venom canister on the ground a few feet away from them. "What happened?"

Echo tugs away from River and he lets her go, even stepping away a little so she can have her moment.

She draws in a breath, summoning the soul-deep strength that drew him to her. "I injected myself with it."

Chase almost leaps as he takes a step closer. "But you're... alive!"

"Very much so," Echo says with a nod. "I suspected I was the Sovereign, so I confirmed it."

And almost stopped River's heart in the process.

Chase lets out a low whistle. "That took some serious bal—"

"You're sure?" Flora strides over to pick up the canister, studying it as if she's trying to ascertain if it's a fake.

Echo tenses, and although she doesn't glance at River, he knows what she's thinking. Flora's acting strangely, just like the first time Echo was injected with queen bee venom. As if she can't understand how this has happened. He has to admit, it makes him feel uneasy. Her actions are like fertilizer for the suspicion...

But Flora's eyes shoot up to Echo, then River. "She really did inject herself with queen bee venom."

"I really am the Sovereign," Echo adds, as if trying to make sure Flora understands the ramifications of this.

River finds he's holding his breath. Echo's convinced his sister doesn't like her. That she's lying and manipulating, although he has no idea why Flora would want to. And right now, Flora's acting as if that theory could be plausible.

A smile explodes across Flora's face. She tucks the canister into the pocket of her trousers and launches herself at Echo, hugging her tightly. "I'm so happy for you!"

Echo blinks, then wraps her arms around River's sister. "Ah, thanks."

"This is amazing news," Flora gushes as she pulls back, holding Echo's upper arms. "Of course it was always you."

"So, after all that, we've got ourselves a Sovereign," Chase says, grinning.

Echo blushes a cute shade of pink. "It seems so."

Flora finally releases her, clasping her hands to her chest. "This is the best news ever." She turns to River. "We're one step closer to Immunity for all!"

Echo glances at River from the corner of her eyes. She wants him to ask the question.

And she's right. He's the one who should give it voice.

He's the one who wants to prove his loyalty isn't misplaced.

"Except it didn't work the first time," River points out. "When we tried to make Immunity from Echo's spinal fluid, Navy died."

Chase's brow slams down, seemingly not appreciating the accusation River isn't trying to make. Yet, he doesn't say anything. Simply waits for Flora to answer, just like River and Echo are.

Flora frowns. "I did the best I could without the Code." She hunches her shoulders. "I'm sorry I got it wrong."

Chase strides to her and slips his arm around her shoulder. "You tried, babe. We've all learned some hard lessons along this trial by fire."

River relaxes, discovering his muscles had been wound tight. "He's right. You've worked hard toward Immunity for all."

Flora nods, seeming to curl even deeper into herself. "Thanks. None of this has been easy on me."

Chase tightens his hold, pulling her in to press a kiss on her head. "No one would think you'd deliberately hurt anyone," he soothes, then grins cheekily. "Unless it was Oren."

Flora giggles, squeezing him, and River finds himself hoping she'll deny it. Even as he knows it would be a lie...

His twin looks up at Chase with a gasp. "It's time to get the Code!"

Echo's gaze flies to River and he stills. That means going to the Hive.

To free his mother.

Echo slips beside him, a soft smile gracing her lips. "She's going to be so happy to see you."

Chase snorts. "Who would've guessed that cranky old

crone was the sweet mother you wanted to find so badly," he says to Flora.

She slaps his chest painfully as River realizes she must've told him who Nola really is. "The Dead Zone has a way of killing sweet. Plus you know the scurge has a way of making people seem older than they are."

"True," Chase grunts, making a show of rubbing his chest. "Ouch, by the way."

Flora pushes out her bottom lip. "You want me to kiss it better?"

River looks away, finding Echo doing the same. At least they can agree this is one part of Flora neither of them like seeing.

"Later," Chase says in a whisper that has no chance of being unheard in the enclosed space of the bunker. "First, we have to organize the attack on the Hive."

River's gaze snaps back to him. "Attack the Hive?"

Chase nods sharply. "If we're going into the hellhole, we're blowing the place up as completely as Oren did the Alphadome."

"But..." River doesn't finish the sentence. Everyone in the bunker knows what that will mean.

Oren will no longer be able to produce the fake Immunity for the Green Borns. They'll no longer be Immune.

"It's time for the truth to be exposed," Echo says quietly, but with conviction.

River knows that at least about this, she's right.

Oren's lies are about to come to an end.

River lifts his chin. "We'll need to get a message to Tuff. To meet us tonight."

A lot of thought and planning are going to be necessary. Getting into the Sting will be dangerous, then the Hive. They'll need explosives. A block of time to release the poor souls trapped inside.

And then they'll have to escape, leaving behind the heart of the Green Zone, primed to be annihilated.

"You two will need to stay here until it's dark." Chase spins on his heel as he takes Flora by the hand. "We'll go find Makk. He can tell his father we need to meet."

Flora stops once they're at the base of the stairs, drawing Chase to a halt with her. She turns back, her green gaze falling on Echo. "When I come back, I'd love to spend some time together." She flushes as she ducks her head. "If you're not too tired."

It takes Echo a split-second to recover from her surprise. "Sure."

Flora beams, then tugs Chase toward the hatch, a skip in her step that has River smiling.

Echo was convinced Flora doesn't like her, but that part of her theory was just proven wrong. Flora is clearly trying to forge a friendship with the girl he loves.

He turns back to Echo, taking her hand, needing the grounding right now.

He's tired. He's still reeling. They've made a giant leap in a short space of time, then promptly committed to a dangerous mission so they can keep moving forward.

But one thought dominates River's mind, sitting solid and unmoving amongst the whirlwind he can barely sort through.

He's going to free his mother.

SEVENTEEN

ECHO

E cho can't sleep.

She tries lying on her back. Her side. Her stomach. Her other side.

She counts backward from ten so many times it starts to sound the right way around.

She mimics River's deep breathing. She holds her breath.

She thinks of the names of every person she's ever known.

But none of it's of any use. Her brain just won't let go of reality and give her the respite she needs. There are too many thoughts swirling and tumbling and replaying through her mind.

River. Flora. Navy. Clover. Rose. Daphne. Nola. Oren. Lyra. Makk.

It's too much. She sits up, wiping sweat from her forehead, even though the air is cool in the bunker. Her locket is twisted around her neck and she straightens the chain and presses it to her lips, thinking of her father.

Nectar emits a soft glow from the corner of the room and Echo looks down at River, glad at least one of them can sleep.

Hopefully the rest helps him to see things more clearly when he wakes. Because he still has his blinkers on when it comes to his twin.

It doesn't matter how much evidence Echo laid at his feet, he still can't see the possibility that Flora is up to something. Well, that might not be quite fair. He can see it—it's the believing part he's struggling with. Which she admits is understandable. Love has a tendency to make people blind. As does hate. They're two opposites yet have so much in common. A little like Echo and Flora...

She sighs softly, resisting the urge to stroke River's beloved face in case she wakes him.

She'd been so sure Flora was up to something when she'd driven that queen bee venom into her thigh. And surviving it only added to that. Yet Flora had a perfectly reasonable explanation. The Immunity hadn't worked on Navy because Flora didn't have the Code. Her ratios were out. Possibly an ingredient was missing. And Flora had been so nice to Echo after she'd recovered from the shock of being told she's the Sovereign. Which means Echo needs to keep her half of the deal she made with River.

She'll hold her tongue about Flora. Eventually the answer will be obvious. She's either playing them or Echo's imagined the whole thing. It wouldn't be the first time she's made something up to explain something she didn't understand.

Chase comes immediately to mind. She'd imagined a whole relationship with him before Confirmation, when it had never been anything more than a friendship. Perhaps Flora is the same. If there's one thing Echo's learned recently, it's never to jump to conclusions.

There's a noise in the main chamber of the bunker. Chase and Flora returned earlier after talking to Makk. Flora stuck her head into their room and Echo had shamefully pretended to be asleep. She's not ready to spend time alone bonding with River's twin just yet, no matter how happy it makes him.

Hearing light footsteps, Echo glances down at River again. She presses her fingertips to her lips and kisses them, transferring the kiss as softly as she can to his forehead. Getting up, she walks quietly down the corridor, keeping close to the wall. She might be avoiding Flora, but that doesn't mean she doesn't want to know what she's up to.

There's a flash of movement as Flora heads for the stairs. Echo follows. It has to be dark outside by now. Where could Flora possibly be going? And without Chase. Or Nectar. She rarely goes anywhere without at least one of them by her side.

Flora tiptoes up the staircase and Echo waits for her to get outside before she goes after her.

It's late evening, the last of the sun's rays quickly disappearing, which makes it too early for Flora to be going to meet Tuff. Besides, she wouldn't have gone alone to do that, which makes it even more of a mystery as to where she's heading.

Flora moves quickly, and Echo scrambles to keep up with her, already regretting her decision to let River sleep. If Flora is headed somewhere she shouldn't be, then he needs to be here to see it with his own eyes.

Dread punches Echo in the gut as she faces the possibility Flora might be going to the Green Zone. What if she's meeting Oren? What if she's been working with him this whole time? Then she takes a sharp turn, and heads for the village and Echo draws in a deep breath, reminding herself of her earlier promise not to jump to conclusions.

They weave their way through the streets of the Dead Zone. Echo keeps Flora at as much distance as she dares without losing her. Flora passes Nola's hut, pausing for a few moments to study it, and Echo knows she's thinking about her mother. River had finally found the chance to tell her what he found out. He said she took it well, and it was clearly a relief for him to have it off his chest.

Flora turns a corner and passes through the center of the Dead Zone. It's not until several minutes later when they've almost reached the edge of the village, that Echo realizes where she's headed.

She's going to Makk's house. Or more accurately, to visit her aunt Goldie. It seems she does have questions, just none that she thought River would be able to answer.

Flora approaches Goldie's house and stops outside the solid door. There's a dim light burning inside, making it one of the few households to be awake at this hour. Most likely because it's the only one to have light.

Echo remains in the shadows, waiting for Flora to knock. But instead, she turns and looks in Echo's direction.

"Would you like to come in with me, Echo?" she asks.

Heat rises to Echo's cheeks as she realizes Flora had known she was behind her this whole time. She steps out into the open and bows her head.

Flora takes several steps to close the distance between them. "Why did you follow me?"

"I wanted to know where you were going," she answers honestly.

"You could have just asked me." Flora touches her lightly on the upper arm. "Instead of pretending to be asleep, then following me here. You knew I wanted to spend time with you."

"I'm sorry." She keeps her head bowed.

Flora slips her hand in Echo's. "You may as well come inside with me. You'll hear better than if you try to eavesdrop from out here."

Echo can't tell if she's joking but goes with her anyway. It's not like she has much choice. And it's true she'd like to know what Flora came here to say. Especially at this late hour.

Flora knocks gently on the door and there's a flutter at the curtain.

"Hello?" Flora calls in a loud whisper.

"Who is it?" comes a gravelly voice from the other side of the timber.

Echo's brows shoot up. "Is that Tuff?" she whispers.

Flora shrugs then presses herself closer to the door. "It's Flora and Echo."

The door opens a crack and Tuff peers out, looking them up and down.

"Get in." He opens the door wider.

Flora enters first and Echo slips inside behind her.

There's a glowing candle that's almost burned down to its wick, casting the hut in warm light. Goldie is seated at her table, and Makk rises from his bed underneath the window and stumbles over.

"Do you need me?" he asks with his eyes barely open. "Is there a message for me to run?"

"You already did a good job of that," Flora says brightly, seeming to be making an effort with Makk now that she knows he's her cousin. "We asked to see Tuff and here he is."

Makk frowns at Flora, still not seeming to have warmed to her. "Where's Chase?"

"Asleep," says Flora. "We weren't expecting to meet your father until after midnight."

"Came early," Tuff grunts from the chair he's seated himself in. Makk goes to him and crawls onto his lap. Tuff wraps one of his thick arms around his son and presses his cheek to the top of his head briefly.

It's a tender moment that takes Echo by surprise. Makk looks so small and vulnerable on his father's knee. She's also never seen him so quiet. It's clear these two have a special bond, which explains all the risks Tuff's taken to keep his son healthy and safe. And why Makk's so keen to play his role in all of this. It's not Chase who's his role model. It's his father, despite their very clear differences.

"Why are you here?" Goldie asks, directing her gaze at Flora.

"I know who you are," Flora says as she and Echo take the two remaining seats. "River told me. You're my mother's sister."

Goldie nods. "You look like her."

Echo sees no resemblance between Nola and Flora. Although, she never really had the chance to study Nola's features. She kept her hut dark and either had netting wrapped around her face or avoided looking in Echo's direction. Echo had wrongly assumed it because of the way the scurge had ravaged her, but she now knows there was a deeper reason. She hadn't wanted to be recognized, happy for people to know her as the mad old woman who never left her home for fear of bees.

Fear of Oren, more like it.

"Good to see you, Flora," says Tuff.

Echo hurts her neck she swivels so quickly to look at Tuff. She's never heard him use so many words at once. It wasn't all that long ago that she didn't think he could talk at all. Then she remembers the way Tuff had approached River with the map, showing him how to get to Flora to make sure she was safe. He seems to have some affection for her, which she can only guess comes from his knowledge that she's related to the woman he loves. It's likely one of the reasons he's been helping River as well.

"It's good to see you, too." Flora smiles brightly at Tuff. "Being away from the Restricted Area suits you."

Tuff nods, returning his attention to his son as he cuddles him into his broad chest.

"Is that why you're here?" Goldie brightens, leaning forward toward them. "Are we going to rescue Nola from that awful Hive?"

"We should get Chase and River for this," says Flora, seeming uncomfortable. "I didn't expect Tuff to be here."

Makk wriggles off his father's lap.

"Stop right there," Goldie scolds. "Makk! It's too late for one of your missions."

But Makk's already halfway out the door. He turns back to his mother, his face serious as he puts a hand on his chest. "The Razers aren't ruled by time. Our work is too important for that."

He's gone before anyone can stop him.

Tuff shoots Goldie a concerned look and she quickly takes his hand and squeezes it. "I told you I can no longer control him."

She gets a nod and a grunt in response, and Echo sees the Tuff she first met in the LaB. Gruff. Hard. Damaged. But with a layer of kindness buried underneath.

"What was Mom like growing up?" Flora asks Goldie, her eyes filling with tears.

"I really miss her."

So, that's why she came here. It seems she wants to know more about her mother.

Goldie looks at her niece. "Your mother was beautiful. And cheeky. She always made me laugh. Her mind was just so quick."

Echo laughs softly. "She's still like that. Although her jokes are probably a little less tame."

"I doubt that." Goldie chuckles. "She was positively wicked. In all the best ways, of course."

Flora purses her lips, seeming horrified. "I never once heard my mom say anything inappropriate."

"That's only because Oren was around," Goldie points out. "And besides, she was hilarious. Her jokes were never at anyone else's expense. She just called it as it was."

"Which is probably why Oren got rid of her." Flora crosses her arms, looking like a hurt little girl.

Echo studies River's twin, wondering if she misjudged her. She may not have had a tough childhood in the same way as Echo, but she's faced her share of challenges. And she clearly came here for the right reasons. Maybe River's right. Perhaps everything that's gone wrong can be explained some other way. After all, none of them really know what they're doing here. They've been making it all up as they go along since day one.

"Let me make you a drink." Goldie stands up. "I have some peppermint tea I made earlier."

She rattles around in her makeshift cupboard, fetching four cups and a jug with bright green leaves floating on the top. It's at room temperature, like all liquids consumed in the Dead Zone, but Echo's mouth waters at the sight of it. It's a rare treat to drink anything quite so fancy around here. They wait while Goldie sets it down on the table and fusses over getting everything perfect. Perhaps she finds this ritual easier than answering Flora's questions. Echo's certain she's buying herself some time.

"Tuff brings me peppermint whenever he can." Goldie smiles affectionately at him. "He knows it's my favorite."

"Mom liked it, too," says Flora, bringing the conversation back to what she came here to talk about.

"I imagine she still does." Goldie pours the tea and sets a cup down in front of each of them. "Not that she'd have had any for a while. I'd have brought her some if I knew she was so close."

"So, you really never knew?" Flora takes a sip of her tea and wraps her hands around the cup. "You could have walked to each other in minutes."

Goldie shakes her head. "I wish I could have taken care of her. Kept her from getting the scurge. Thankfully, she had Echo. Makk told me how wonderful you were to her."

Echo waves away her praise. "I didn't do much."

"You did more than anyone else," says Goldie.

"I've never said thank you, Echo." Flora rises from her chair and wraps her arms around Echo in an awkward hug. "You're such a good person. I'm so glad it's you who's the Sovereign."

Heat flushes to Echo's cheeks as Goldie lets out a gasp.

"We only just found out," she quickly explains as Flora releases her. "But we don't have the Code. We can't help anyone without it."

"It's not you." Tuff swallows his tea in one gulp and stares at her. "You're not the Sovereign."

"I've survived queen bee venom," Echo tells him. "Twice."

"Oren took your blood," says Tuff. "He tested it. It's not you."

Echo remembers when she'd been gassed until she was unconscious and woke with a puncture mark inside her elbow. The thought has her rubbing at her arm, the memory feeling no less a violation of her rights than it had at the time.

"He tested it wrong." She sits back in her chair, refusing to be swayed from her belief in who she is. They've been through this before. She's not doing it again.

The door to the hut bursts open, and Makk, River and Chase enter, all panting heavily. Chase goes directly to Flora, while River comes to stand behind Echo, putting his hands on her shoulders and squeezing gently.

"You should have woken me," he says.

"I didn't know I was coming here," she tries to explain.

She passes him the remainder of her tea, which he quickly drinks.

"She followed Flora," says Makk. "I heard them talking outside before they came in."

"I thought you were asleep." Echo raises a brow at Makk, avoiding having to witness River's reaction to this. She really hadn't done very well with her half of their bargain.

"Razers never sleep." Makk climbs back on his father's lap, which makes him look nothing like the brave soldier he claims to be. The fact he doesn't realize it has Echo's heart melting.

Chase clears his throat. "Thanks for coming, Tuff. We need to talk to you about the Hive."

Tuff nods to show he's listening.

"We're going to get everyone out," Chase says. "Then we're going to blow it up."

"How?" Tuff asks, economizing his words as usual.

"Well…" Chase pauses.

"We were hoping you'd help us." Flora bats her eyelashes at him, although Echo is certain she's wasting her time. The only reason Tuff has helped any of them is because of Goldie and Makk.

Tuff shakes his head as he opens his mouth to protest but is stopped by Goldie slapping her palms on the table. The action causes the dwindling candle to extinguish, and the hut is plunged into night as blackness wraps around them.

"He'll do it." Goldie's voice is firm and pleading in the darkness. "Won't you, Tuff?"

There's a long pause and Echo finds River's hand and holds it tightly as they wait for their answer.

"Tomorrow is Harvest Day," Tuff eventually says. "I'll help you. But we'll do it tonight."

CHAPTER
EIGHTEEN
RIVER

"As in, now?" River asks incredulously.

Tuff is saying tonight as if it's not already dark outside. It's most definitely night.

The grizzled man glances at him from the corner of his eye. "Tomorrow is Harvest Day," he grunts, repeating himself.

Which is the busiest day in the Green Zone.

And also when the prisoners in the Hive will be forced to endure another torturous extraction.

Which means Tuff's right.

"It has to be tonight," River says, a strange combination of dread and determination settling in his gut.

Echo reaches out to grip his knee. "We'll get her out." Her fingers tighten. "We'll get them all out."

Makk leaps off Tuff's lap. "It's going to be epic!"

"Oh no you don't," Goldie says, frowning fiercely. "You're not going."

Makk opens his mouth to object, a familiar tilt to his chin angling it up, but Tuff rests a hand on his son's shoulder. "She's right, Makk."

His mouth instantly snaps closed and his shoulders sag with disappointment as he nods. "Fine, then."

River blinks, surprised, yet somehow not really surprised by Makk's immediate compliance. He knows how strong the father-son bond can be, how much a young boy can be desperate to please his hero.

"Good boy," Tuff grunts, squeezing Makk's shoulder.

Goldie's face softens as she watches the two of them, her body unwinding as if she was ready to pin Makk down by force. She probably would've had to with that stubborn streak of his. Tuff's influence is a testament that the young boy's been missing the presence of a father.

All because Oren's divided people into Immune and Vulnerable, tearing families apart, robbing children of their parents. River clenches his hands. Tonight is definitely when they need to go back to the Sting.

Chase is staring out the window even though the curtain is pulled across, his gaze unfocused. "We have to think how we'll get in. Oren's doubled the number of guards in the Betadome, Green Zone, and no doubt around the Sting."

They've snuck in a few too many times.

And Oren will be wondering where Daphne is, and why she hasn't returned.

The entirety of the Green Zone will be on high alert, every camera and guard keeping an eye out for intruders. It's going to be practically impossible to find a way in when the black door is locked and the tunnel collapsed, then make their way through the Green Zone, and up to the Hive without being seen.

Chase clenches his jaw. "We can't afford to fail."

That would mean another harvest for those in the Hive. Including River's mother.

And no Code.

Flora leaps to her feet. "Nectar!"

Goldie and Tuff look at each other, confused, but Echo gasps before they can ask a question. "Yes!" She turns to River. "We can arrive in the Green Zone the same way we arrived here from the Moon Zone."

River's eyes widen as he realizes what's being suggested.

They'll fly to the top of Sting!

Makk groans. "Not fair!" He turns to his father. "They're gonna fly on a Worker! Surely you can't make me stay—"

Tuff arches a brow. "No."

Makk huffs and crosses his arms, but actually stops talking. Not only that, despite the scowl, he clearly intends on doing as he's told.

Chase presses a kiss to Flora's head. "As always, you're a genius."

She beams, even blushes a little, as she looks up at him. "I just want to see you succeed," she whispers.

A new mix of emotions swirl through River. The soft adoration on his sister's face is touching. He's glad she found someone to love so totally. But her response makes him uneasy. It implies she's doing this for Chase, not for Immunity...

Chase grins. "Come on. We've got a bee to ride."

Tuff pushes to his feet. "I'll meet you there," he says, his voice rougher than usual. "I'll have everything ready."

River swallows as he realizes what 'everything' means. The explosives.

Tuff squeezes Makk's shoulder, shares a long look with Goldie, then leaves. His wife and son simply watch, no doubt used to the goodbyes they know could be the last. Judging by the way Goldie bites her lip the instant it trembles, it hasn't got any easier.

Chase and Flora exit the hut, and River and Echo follow

them to the door. River notes that Makk goes to stand beside his mother as she also comes to her feet, wrapping an arm around him, either in comfort, or to stop him from following them. Impulsively, River walks over and hugs them both.

Makk's response is instantaneous. He throws his arms around River's waist and squeezes. Goldie hesitates, probably surprised, before relaxing and hugging both River and Makk.

"Be careful," she says quietly. "I've only just found you."

River's chest tightens. "I'll bring her back," he says, hoping it's a promise he can keep.

Pulling away, he returns to Echo, finding her watching them with soft eyes. He takes her hand and they leave the hut together, walking quickly to catch up with Flora and Chase. They have to get into the Hive and back out before dawn.

River looks up at the night sky, calculating it's probably sometime after midnight. That's certainly enough time to fly over on Nectar and get everyone out.

Also more than enough time to fail.

River moves closer to Echo, pushing the insidious thought away. If they fail, they won't come out of this alive. Which means it's not an option.

The village is dark and silent as they make their way to the scoring grounds, the air warm and still. No one talks and River wonders whether it's because they need to stay quiet, or whether the looming mission is weighing down on everyone's minds. It feels like there hasn't been enough time to prepare.

Even though there's nothing to organize. They need to get into the Sting, free the prisoners from the Hive, load it up with explosives and get out.

Nectar meets them outside the bunker, and River realizes Flora must've already called her with the controller she always carries now. The silver disc on the bee's back glows softly in the night as the lights in her large eyes flicker rhythmically.

Flora reaches up to rub her jaw. "We'll have to go two at a time."

River's already learned Nectar can't carry more weight than that when they escaped from the Moon Zone. "Echo and I can go first," he suggests.

Echo nods in agreement. "We'll make sure the way is clear while we wait for you to arrive."

Flora looks at River, chewing her lip. "Okay," she agrees, seeming reluctant.

River suspects the reality of what they're about to do is sinking in. The moment they step foot in the Sting again, every moment will be life or death.

He strides to his twin, scooping her up in a fierce hug. "We can do this," he tells her.

Flora squeezes him tightly. "I can't lose any more people, River," she whispers hoarsely.

He pulls back, holding her green gaze. "There's so much to gain from doing this," he says, his conviction keeping his voice low.

The Code.

Their mother.

Exposing the truth about Immunity.

River steps around her and leaps on Nectar, conscious that time is ticking. Echo quickly joins him, turning to look down at Chase.

"If we're not there when you arrive, then you'll know there are more guards than we were expecting."

He nods, his face stoic. "Be careful."

"You, too." River tightens his hold on the strap that's wrapped above Nectar's thorax and grips her smooth body with his thighs. Echo slips her arms around his waist, tucking in close to his back.

It's time.

"Nectar, take them to Eden," Flora instructs, her voice tight.

The mechanical bee instantly lifts off the ground, shooting toward the net, and River and Echo focus on simply holding on. Just like the other times, Nectar undoes the net, flies through, and then repairs the hole as if they were never there.

Then, they're spearing into the sky, the wind slapping their faces and tugging at their clothes. The Dead Zone grows smaller as they fly over it, the Betadome is little more than a silver blur below.

River wishes there was the opportunity to appreciate the wonder of flying on Nectar, just like he did the first time with Echo. They could marvel at how expansive the horizon is, at seeing their familiar world from a whole new angle, frown at the stark contrast between the jagged streets and alleyways of the Dead Zone and the smooth, symmetrical perfection of the Green Zone. One dark and dead, the other so full of life it practically glows.

But the Sting is fast approaching.

Impossibly tall as it tapers to a point, it's a luminous beacon in the night. Nectar circles it, her wings creating a soft hum that now feels unnaturally loud. She moves in close as they soar to the higher levels, the hexagonal tiles shimmering as the light of her disc illuminates them. It feels like River could reach out and touch the smooth, white wall.

The balcony that leads into Eden appears, and River tenses, feeling Echo do the same behind him. They're here. The dark outlines of plants come into view and River can't help but remember the last time they were here.

When Clover was threatening to jump.

River pushes away the memory, not wanting to dwell on the sacrifice and loss everyone has endured in the search for the Sovereign. Not when they're about to be one step closer to Immunity.

As long as they survive this...

Nectar lands gracefully among the shrubs and River and Echo leap off quickly, falling into a crouch and then shooting straight back, heads snapping from side to side. If they've been seen, then it's their job to remove the threat before Flora and Chase arrive.

Behind them, Nectar lifts back into the air and whirs away to pick up her next travelers. River and Echo hold still, listening intently.

There's a gentle breeze. Nectar's fading whirring. And their harsh breathing.

But nothing else.

Eden appears empty.

Simultaneously, they walk toward the glass doors as silently as possible. The interior of Eden is gently lit, illuminating the rows upon rows of seedlings in various stages of growth. The walkways are empty. The space is clear.

They're alone.

River lets out the breath he was holding, discovering his throat feels tighter than it should. He frowns. He hasn't had serpentwood in some time and he's been in the Dead Zone long enough that he'd almost forgotten about his allergies.

The sound of footsteps beyond the large doors to Eden cut the thought abruptly short.

"River," Echo hisses, grabbing his hand and jerking him toward a stand of bushy shrubs.

They both squat down just as the doors slide open, spilling light into the room. The footsteps instantly become louder, sharper. Two sets make their way down the center walkway, steady and rhythmic.

River and Echo freeze, their hands tightly clasped together. They can't afford to be found.

And if they are, they'll have to fight. They promised Flora and Chase they'd ensure everyone got to the Hive. These two guards can't leave Eden once they know there are intruders here. Right now, River's realizing what that's going to mean.

If they're found, it's kill or be killed.

River works to even out his breathing, to make it as smooth and silent as possible. Except his windpipe is steadily constricting. His lungs are progressively shrinking. The air drawing into his lungs is doing so through a tube the size of a reed. It means there's a wheeze. A slight one, but definitely a wheeze. And he's certainly not silent.

Echo's hand tightens around River's and he knows she can hear it.

All they can do is hope the guards don't.

The footsteps stop. River closes his eyes, desperately hoping they don't come any closer.

"Looks the same as it did ten minutes ago," one of them grunts.

"Nah, I reckon those plants over there have grown a couple of inches," the second man jokes.

Chuckling, they turn and the footsteps recede. The door whooshes open, then closed.

River and Echo sag against each other in relief. Luck was on their side.

Echo turns to him. "We need to get you out of Eden," she whispers, her hand coming to rest on his chest. His breathing is becoming more and more labored. "Or we need to see if there are any serpentwood plants here we can use."

River shakes his head. Now that he knows exactly how important that endangered species is, there's no way he can justify it for his own use. "We just...need to wait for..."

A flash of light on the balcony reveals Nectar landing with Flora and Chase. They leap down and run straight in, clearly ready for a fight.

River and Echo push to their feet, revealing themselves.

"The place is empty," Echo says.

Chase's shoulders drop as he lets out a breath. "Good. Guards would only complicate things."

River glances at Echo, letting her do the talking. He's going to save the limited oxygen his body is getting.

She takes his hand and tugs him toward the door, speaking over her shoulder. "Actually, there are guards patrolling the Sting. Possibly a lot of them." She pauses at the door, listening. "Which gives us ten minutes to get to the LaB."

CHAPTER
NINETEEN
ECHO

Creeping through the Sting at night is a strange feeling. It's both completely familiar and totally foreign. It wasn't all that long ago that these white corridors and shiny tiles had overwhelmed Echo with their sparkly newness. But now, they're like a favorite shirt that's become too small. Still worthy of admiration yet completely suffocating.

The fear is constricting her lungs, which makes her wonder how River is coping. He wouldn't have lasted much longer in Eden with all that pollen around. Not that they'd been able to hang around anyway. They have ten minutes to clear these corridors and get themselves into the LaB before the guards circle back on their next round.

They descend another flight of stairs with Chase and Flora in the lead. Nectar has stayed behind, crouching low in the foliage of Eden, ready and waiting for when it's time to escape. Returning two at a time may prove challenging—or even deadly—but it's not something they can worry about now. They have to get into the LaB and find out what Tuff needs from them to get the people out and blow the Hive sky high.

Echo turns to look at River, still concerned about his breathing.

"I'm fine," he says, keeping his voice low.

She listens, unable to hear a wheeze, although it's hard to hear anything over her beating heart so she's going to have to take his word for it.

"You need to tell me if you're not fine," she says sternly.

He nods. "I always do."

Echo isn't sure about that. He's very good at hiding discomfort to protect those around him. But if he says he's fine, that has to be good enough for now.

Flora reaches the landing of the floor to the LaB and cracks open the door while the rest of them crowd behind her.

"It's clear," she whispers.

They tiptoe out into the corridor, aware they have to hurry. All is quiet as the Green Borns sleep peacefully on the residential floors, just as oblivious about what's happening around them as they've been their whole lives. Soon, that will change. It has to.

The double doors to the LaB sense movement and open.

Echo draws in a deep breath. Getting inside the LaB is undoubtedly the most dangerous part of this mission. But Oren has to sleep sometime. There's no reason to think he's lurking around the LaB at this time of night. Especially when he has Harvest Day to contend with in the morning. He needs his rest.

Flora nods, indicating the coast is clear and they step into the LaB. A figure leaps out in front of them and Echo freezes as River throws himself in front of her. Chase charges forward, growling like a beast.

Echo fights dizziness as her stomach turns to lead. She tries to figure out what's going on. There's too much movement. Too much tension. And way too much at stake.

Chase collides with the figure and grunts as they fall to the floor.

"It's Reed!" Flora says, rushing over. "Chase, stop!"

Echo fights her way around River to see Chase release a terrified Reed who's curled himself into a ball, shielding his face.

"Don't hurt me," he begs.

"Then don't sneak up on people," Chase snaps, getting to his feet and dusting himself off. "I thought you were Oren."

"Thank goodness it's you." River helps Reed up.

Echo isn't as sure she trusts Reed. He's proven he's capable of working on both sides of this war. Mainly because he doesn't seem sure of which side he wants to take. He believes in the ideals Oren has fed him his whole life. But he's also seen with his own eyes the consequences of them. There's a whole war of its own raging inside him, which means they can't be certain what he'll do next. But whatever the case, he'd been the one to save them when they'd been taken to the Sovereign graveyard, so she'd far rather see him than Oren.

Reed pulls back his shoulders, keeping a safe distance away from Chase.

"What are you doing here?" Echo asks.

"Waiting for you," he says. "Tuff asked me to be the look-out. Although, now I'm not so sure I should have said yes."

Reed ushers them further inside the LaB and the doors close behind them. It's dimly lit and they quickly wind their way past the work benches to the door that leads to the Restricted Area.

"Do the guards patrol in here?" Chase asks.

"Sometimes," says Reed. "Hurry up, just in case."

Echo glances at River, wondering if this could be a trap. But he nods reassuringly at her, putting a steadying hand on her back.

"Thanks for your help, Reed," says Flora. "I knew you had a good heart."

He grunts as he taps the combination into the keypad and the door opens. The Restricted Area looms before them, and Echo draws in a breath, unsure if she's ready to step back inside this awful place that has pain and misery embedded in its walls.

Reed moves back away from the door.

"You're not coming with us?" River asks.

"I'm the lookout." Reed swallows and his Adam's apple bobs as if in agreement with his words. "I need to...look out."

River pats Reed on the back and they step into the holding area. The door behind them slides closed, cutting them off from Reed and the LaB.

"He'd better not tell Oren we're here." Chase clenches his fists.

"He saved River and Echo, remember?" Flora reminds him. "He told them which Worker to run to. Without him, they'd never have made it to the Extinction Zone."

"We can rely on him," says River, forever his trusting self.

Echo looks across at Flora, wondering if the lack of trust she has in people has come from the way she was raised. River grew up with no reason to question anybody's motives, whereas Echo's wits had been what had kept her alive on the streets of the Dead Zone. That has to explain it, surely? Although, lately, River's been let down far more than Echo has. Mostly by his father.

Flora presses the green button to open the door to the main chamber and a golden glow instantly bathes them in its deceptive warmth.

"Tuff?" Flora calls.

Echo slips her hand into River's, needing his comfort. This is the place of their nightmares. Actually, it's worse than nightmares. Because what happened to them in this room was very real.

They exit the holding area out onto the yellow tiles of the hexagonal room.

"This is the Hive?" Chase's eyes are glued to the back wall that's humming and glowing behind the sticky white goo it's coated in.

"What did you expect it to look like?" A shudder runs down Echo's spine at the hexagonal shapes lining the wall.

"I knew it looked like a Hive," Chase says. "I just didn't realize it would look...so much like a hive."

If Echo weren't so scared, she'd roll her eyes.

Ignoring Chase, River touches Flora on the arm and points. "Mom's in there."

"Not for long." Flora tucks her short hair behind her ears and marches forward.

"Don't touch it!" Echo warns, remembering how she'd become entwined in the sticky substance. "Once that stuff gets a hold of you, there's no breaking away."

Heeding the warning, Flora stops where she is and spins around. "Where's Tuff?"

The hidden panel in the wall that leads to Oren's office opens and Tuff steps out.

"Here," he grunts, having clearly been watching them from the one-way window. "Get back." He ushers them behind the dark line that crosses the floor and presses a tile on the wall.

The thick glass screen slides up and Echo tries to stop her legs from shaking. The last time she'd seen this happen, they'd been on the other side of the screen. She reminds herself they're safe on this side.

"We need to get the people out!" River lets go of Echo to run a hand through his hair. "What are you doing?"

"It's okay," Tuff grunts. "Reed fixed it."

The hatch beside the Hive opens and a long metal leg pokes out.

"He fixed what?" Flora screeches. "Tuff! What's happening?"

"The Worker." Tuff doesn't seem to feel the need to elaborate further, leaving Echo wishing they were being helped by someone who used a few more words.

Flora presses up to the glass. "Reed must have reprogrammed the Worker to get the people out safely. But it's not safe for us just yet. Is that right, Tuff?"

The grizzled man nods.

The Worker emerges from her hidden compartment and Echo concentrates on her breathing, realizing she's not as terrified as she was the first time she'd seen one of these deadly machines. Now that she knows they can be reprogrammed and used for good, she decides they're a bit like Reed. Helpful. But you never really know what side they're on.

The Worker goes straight for the Hive and gets to work on the closest cell, clearing the slime and pulling the hexagonal façade forward. A person is lying on a bench, just as Echo knew there would be. The Worker's forelegs move across their body, working efficiently to remove the slime, letting it ooze to the grates in the floor where it's sucked away.

A terrified man sits up and crawls back on the table, trying to put some space between himself and the Worker. But she isn't interested in his reaction to her. She picks him up with her pincers and carries him over to the side of the room where she sets him down. The man quickly moves back until he's pressed into a corner and looks up to see five sets of eyes staring at him from the other side of a glass wall. His face fills with even more horror.

"It's okay," Echo mouths, willing him to understand. "It's okay."

Pulling up his legs, his shaking is visible even from this distance. He glances around the room and sees there's nowhere to escape.

"We need to pull down this wall," says River, pressing his palms on the glass. "We need to get to him. He's terrified."

"Can't," says Tuff, not looking River's way.

Flora groans. "Reed must've programmed her to rescue those trapped in the Hive. If we go in there, the Worker will kill us."

"Hold on!" River shouts to the man, even though he can't possibly hear him. "We'll get to you. You're safe!"

The Worker returns to the Hive and begins work on the next cell. This time, a woman emerges and when she's set down beside the man, they stare at each other, whispering frantically as they try to figure out what's going on. The man points at the five of them behind the wall and the woman's hands fly to her mouth. She gets up and runs to the glass wall, banging on it, her lips forming the same word over and over again.

Help! Help! Help!

"We *are* helping you." Echo wipes away a tear, remembering how frightened she'd been when she'd emerged from the Hive. "Hold on. It's okay."

The Worker frees more people and soon there are at least a dozen huddled against the glass wall, begging for help, not understanding they're already safe.

"Can we lower the wall just a little bit?" River asks. "Just enough so we can talk to them?"

"Too dangerous," says Tuff.

"River!" Flora points at the Hive. "It's Vernon!"

Sure enough, Vern has emerged and is striking out at the Worker in fury. The metallic bee strikes back, sending him skittering across the room as she turns back to the Hive and gets to work on the next cell.

Vern is helped up by two people and immediately runs back at the Worker who kicks him with one of her back legs, not even so much as looking up from her task.

Backing away this time, Vern turns to face the glass wall. Echo gasps to see how healthy he is. In fact, he looks years younger than before he'd gone into the Hive, which is either the result of his detox from drinking all that kasi or the nutrition he's been fed with by the slime.

"River," Vern mouths as his eyes widen.

River nods at him, keeping one palm on the glass. Vern comes over to him and presses his hand to the other side of the wall.

Vern smiles despite the large bruise on the side of his cheek already blooming.

"He understands," says River. "He knows we're helping him."

Vern goes to the other people and says something, talking hurriedly as he explains. A sense of calm seems to wash over them as they huddle in the corner, waiting for all this to be over.

The next person to emerge is Leif, the Green Born Vulnerable who'd taken River's place in the Hive. He seems stunned to have been released and one of the women wraps her arms around him in a way that makes Echo think they know each other. He hugs her back and a wave of gratitude rolls like a wave through Echo's gut. Leif may have volunteered because he'd been afraid of his new life in the Dead Zone, but he was certain to have regretted it the instant he was placed in the Hive. But it's because of him that they've been able to achieve everything they have since they escaped.

"River," Flora breathes. "Look, River. It's Mom."

Nola is emerging from the Hive. She doesn't struggle as the Worker strips the slime from her body and sets her on the ground.

Echo lets out a gasp to see the difference in her old friend. Because, somehow, she doesn't seem old at all. Her skin is clear. Her back is straight. Her eyes are filled with light. She looks exactly like the mom Echo had imagined River to have before she knew it was Nola.

River and Flora are pressed hard against the glass now, their hands and chests molding to the wall. Both of them are weeping like the small children they were when they lost their mother.

Nola sees them and walks to the glass, her own tears trailing down her rejuvenated face.

She stands before them, only inches apart that must feel like miles.

"My children," she mouths, her fingertips reaching the glass as she looks from her son to her daughter.

Echo feels a gentle hand on her shoulder. It's Chase. He's just as moved by what he's witnessing as she is. They both know what it feels like to lose a parent. Yet neither of them can imagine what it must feel like to have one returned. She slips an arm around her old friend and holds him tight.

Everything they've done up until now has been worth it. Because it led to this.

A moment of pure happiness contained within the walls of a place built on misery.

Oren has taken so much.

But he couldn't take this.

CHAPTER
TWENTY
RIVER

R iver's vaguely aware of the Worker removing the others from the cells in the Hive. He's vaguely aware of the tears wetting his cheeks. He's vaguely aware he should move.

But he can't.

Seeing his mother on the other side of the glass has rendered him frozen, the rest of the world relegated to the background. He's known on an intellectual level that his mother is still alive. It was news he never expected to hear yet was more than willing to accept as truth. The loss and grief of the past five years would've been a nightmare that he could finally wake up from.

Except now that she's in front of him, her own tears glistening, her face so achingly familiar, it's a reality he didn't quite let himself believe. Not when it could've been another lie.

"River," Echo says softly. "Everyone's out."

He nods, not taking his eyes off his mother. His fingers curl against the thick glass. The wall between them is the last barrier, and one he wants gone. He wants to hold his mother, to confirm this isn't a dream.

Flora clears her throat. "We need to step back, River."

Blinking, he tears his gaze away to look at his twin. The same joy effervescing in his soul is shimmering in her eyes. She turns to Tuff. "Lower the wall."

Chase moves closer to Tuff, his gaze flickering to the Hive and River's about to tell them to hurry up when he realizes why Chase is hesitating.

Now that she's finished removing everyone from the cells, the Worker is standing in front of the slime-covered wall. Her jaws move, her antennae twitch. The blue light of her disc pulses softly.

What is she going to do the moment the wall is lowered?

"Do we need to be ready to run?" Echo asks, her body wired with tension.

And what about the people on the other side of the glass, including River's mother. Will they be able to get out in time?

Flora rolls her eyes. "It's fine."

Chase's eyebrows hike up to say, 'if you say so,' and he steps back as Tuff presses the button.

The wall instantly begins to move down, removing the final barrier between River and his mother. He holds his breath, feeling as if a veil is being dropped. In a handful of seconds, there will be nothing between him and the one person who loved him unconditionally throughout his childhood. The one person who showed him the definition of the word.

At first, the whirring sound doesn't alarm him. He's heard it enough from Nectar that it's becoming familiar, almost comforting. But the scream that pierces the widening gap is far from soothing.

It sends panic shooting through River.

So does the way the people in the Hive throw themselves at the lowering glass, trying to scramble over.

Because the Worker is rearing up and screeching, her front legs slashing at the air.

She launches forward, the short distance between her and the prisoners ensuring they won't have a chance to get away. Suddenly, the wall seems to be creeping down. It's moving too slowly.

River's mother will die before he can get to her.

"Pax!" Flora shouts.

The Worker stops mid stride, her legs clattering to the tiled floor. She sinks down into a crouch, tucks herself in tightly, and powers down.

River's breathing hard, even though he hasn't moved. The drive to fight is still firing down his nerves. He turns to his sister, eyes so wide they hurt. "What the..."

"I had to wait until the wall was down enough for the Worker to hear me," Flora explains. "I knew there would be enough time."

He nods, trying to get his breathing under control as his pulse feels like it won't slow anytime soon.

Echo moves closer to him, her hand brushing his back. "River," she says quietly. With meaning.

He doesn't need to look back at her to know what she's telling him. He raises his gaze slowly, the surreal feeling returning. The feeling that this is really happening, even as he wonders if it's just wishful thinking.

But it's undeniable.

The wall is down. There's nothing standing between him and his mother.

She lets out a sob and it's the impetus for him to move, to hold her, to comfort the both of them. River engulfs his mother in a hug, letting out a strangled sound when her soft body is engulfed by his. Flora slams into them and he brings her into the fold.

They hold each other for long moments, allowing the reality of the moment to sink in.

This is real. They're together. They're touching, crying, laughing.

It's more beautiful than River could ever have imagined.

Chase clears his throat and they pull apart begrudgingly, conscious this isn't the time.

River's mother clasps his face. "My clever boy." She caresses Flora's cheek. "My sweet daughter."

"Let's get you out of here, Mom," River says, the urgency of the situation sinking in.

Echo steps around them, ushering the others away from the wall and toward the door to the Restricted Area. "We'll explain everything once you're safe," she tells them. "For now, we have to get out of here as quickly and quietly as possible."

The people, mostly Green Borns who look both relieved and terrified, nod, looking around. A woman rubs her arms as if she's cold, whilst a man's gaze keeps going back to the Worker, his lips moving without saying a word. There's no telling how long some of them have been in the Hive. How many times they've been harvested...

The door to the Restricted Area opens, making several people recoil. River breaks into a run, wanting to be by Echo's side if they're about to be attacked when Tuff walks through carrying two black bags. He must've left to get the explosives.

River stops, letting out a breath. Some warning would've been nice, but then again, Tuff isn't one for talking.

A cry behind River has him spinning around. Vern runs at Tuff, fury twisting his features. "You'll never hurt us again!"

Tuff reels back, looking alarmed. His gaze darts from the black bags to Vern and River instantly knows why.

He's a walking bomb.

River and Echo reach Vern at the same time. She pushes

him from the front while River hauls him backward, his arm clamped across his chest.

"He was there every time!" Vern grunts, trying to get them off him. "He's part of this!"

"He's helping us," River says as he marvels at his friend's strength. The people in the Hive are probably the healthiest in any of the Zones. Well, physically...

"He's lying! He's a traitor! A torturer!"

River realizes that the terror of every harvest is currently coursing through Vern. That all the helpless agony is now aimed at Tuff. The only way to stop this may be to knock Vern unconscious, which then means somehow dragging him back to the Dead Zone. River steels himself, knowing there's no alternative. No one is being left behind.

He's just clenched his fist when his mother appears in front of them. "Vern," she says quietly. "We need to listen to them."

The effect of her words is instantaneous.

Vern goes limp. His breath comes out in a whoosh. "Magnolia," he chokes.

And then he's wrenching out of River's and Echo's hold. They let him go, stunned at the emotion that just ravaged the faces of the two people who fall into each other's arms.

"Vernon," says River's mother, her voice soft and tender.

River watches, astounded, as they hold each other for long seconds. The way their bodies are pressed so close, with such familiarity, with such intimacy, suggests this is more than two friends reuniting.

Surely not...

Chase clears his throat again. "If we can save this for when we're not in mortal danger, that would be appreciated."

Turning away, River knows he's right. The reunions, the questions, will have to wait. They have to get out of here first.

Tuff strides forward, giving Vern a wide berth as he

gingerly carries the bags. He carefully places them down, then turns for Flora. "The controls for each of the cells are over there," he says, indicating toward the central control panel with his chin.

She nods and walks over, skimming her fingers over the buttons. She presses one and the cell in the top right-hand corner silently slides out. Tuff reaches down and opens one of the bags, removing a small package wrapped tightly in black cloth. Attached to the front is a small square, a tiny wire sticking out from it. He places it at the rear of the empty shelf protruding from the wall, then gives it a sharp shove. The metal bed silently slides back into the wall, the opaque slime covering it protectively.

Encasing the explosives within it.

"They're going to destroy it," River's mother gasps behind them.

Vern grunts. "It should've been done a long time ago."

"We have to get out of here!" someone else cries.

Chase has moved to them before the panic can continue to grow. "The explosives are controlled remotely. We'll be well away from the Sting when it blows."

As if to prove the point, Tuff picks up a small controller that looks similar to the one Flora uses for Nectar and gives it to Flora. "We can't be too far away," he warns.

She pockets the remote carefully, nodding, then quickly presses several more buttons. More shelves slip out of the wall, waiting for the explosives.

River quickly walks to the bag. "We'll help," he says, knowing Echo is right behind him.

She lifts out a packet of explosives. "It'll be quicker."

Tuff also collects a pack, showing it to them. "Press this," he instructs, pressing a button on the side of the package.

A small, red light comes on, pulsing gently.

Waiting for the command to detonate.

Then he turns to the open cell closest to him, carefully placing the packet. "They need to be placed at the back. So the explosion is contained to the wall."

And not the rest of the Restricted Area, which would be much more of a threat to the Sting itself.

Echo nods, her eyes scanning the wall. "That's why there are lots of small packages. It will create a series of smaller explosions, rather than one big one."

River gets his own packet, ignoring the fact that Tuff probably knows so much about explosives because he's the one who rigged the Alphadome. They barely escaped that explosion alive.

They work quickly, Flora opening the cells at the control center, River, Echo and Tuff planting the explosives, Chase keeping the wide-eyed prisoners as calm as possible. They work around the silent, still Worker, each making sure not to touch her as if she could come back to life at any moment.

It doesn't take long for each cell to be planted with an explosive. In the space of less than half an hour, the Hive goes from containing helpless humans to deadly bombs.

River and Echo look at each other, a silent understanding passing between them. The moment the first explosion tears through the Hive, there will be no turning back. A statement will be made. A message will be sent.

War will be waged.

They reach out and weave their fingers together as two words pass between them.

It's time.

Tuff leans down to pick up the two empty bags. He strides to Flora, his hand hovering over a button on the control panel. "Say the word and the cameras will be disabled," he states flatly.

River nods, realizing the moment the Hive explodes Oren will know they were here. He'll assume they turned off the cameras so they can escape.

Which is exactly what they're going to do.

River turns to his mother, already anticipating what it will be like to spend time with her. They have so much to talk about. So much to say. And yet all he wants to do is hold her, look at her, sit with her in silence.

The knowledge that he's carving time out to do all of that spurs him into action. He takes Echo's hand and they rush to join the others by the door that will lead them out of here. That will lead them to freedom.

Chase's hand hovers over the panel that will open it. "Once this opens, we need to run, and run fast. No talking unless we have to."

The pale faces around him nod as a few people shift nervously. Everyone knows this is going to be dangerous. And yet hope has them all leaning forward, all willing to take the risk.

Even when they have no idea what a big step forward this will be in the fight for Immunity.

It will reveal the truth that Immunity never existed.

And that it soon will be reality.

There's a whoosh of air behind River, followed by the sound of sharp, steady clapping. Dread blooms in his gut as his blood turns to ice.

No...

He turns slowly, the dread forming a hard, jagged lump. Oren is standing in the doorway to his office, the opaque glass now clear. He possibly saw the whole thing. Watched it, knowing they were all fooling themselves.

Knowing he had no intention of letting any of them go.

CHAPTER
TWENTY-ONE
ECHO

E cho lets out a gasp that quickly dissolves into a moan.

Oren is here. And his hard gaze is zeroed in on River. "This time, you've gone too far," he snarls.

"This time?" River pulls back his shoulders. "Pretty sure you said that last time."

"Get out of our way." Vern muscles forward, only for Nola to pull him back.

"Careful," she hisses. "I'm not losing you again."

Oren's gaze snaps to Nola. "You really should've stayed dead. I liked you far better that way."

"Well, I never liked you," she retorts. "You took everything from me."

"I gave you everything." Hatred burns in his eyes. "It was your choice to throw it all away."

Chase barges forward. "As entertaining as this is, we don't have time for couples counseling. Step aside, Oren, or..."

Oren seizes his opportunity. Chase hasn't had time to think through his threat. "Or what, Dead Born? You'll blow up the

Hive, along with everyone in here? That doesn't seem very heroic."

The people who've only just been released from their sticky prisons recoil. Panic builds as they try to figure out the best place to stand. They won't go anywhere near the wall of death they just came from. They won't get close to the Worker, even if she's currently at peace. And they most definitely won't take a single step toward Oren, the man who rained down all this havoc on them in the first place. They settle for hovering near the back of the group.

Chase grits his teeth. "I. Said. Step. Aside."

Oren smiles. "I don't think so. Not until my faithful assistant gives me that detonator he has behind his back."

Echo spins around to see Tuff with one hand behind him, shuffling his feet nervously. Which is odd, because Echo was certain Tuff had given the detonator to Flora. But there'd been a lot going on. Oren couldn't possibly have seen everything, and Tuff knows that.

"I'm on your side," Tuff grunts, although surely he can't expect Oren to believe that.

"I watched you rig this place with explosives," says Oren calmly. "I've been watching you for a long time now. You thought you were so clever, playing both sides. You're really going to regret that."

Tuff freezes, realizing there's no point in arguing. Oren knows who he's really working for. And it isn't him.

Oren removes a venom gun from his belt and licks his lips.

Echo's eyes widen to see six yellow lines circling the canister. It's not just loaded with any venom. It's loaded with queen bee venom. And Oren has it pointed directly at Tuff.

"Give me the detonator, Tuff," says Oren calmly. "Or you'll be dead before you have the chance to use it."

"He doesn't have it," shouts River, patting his pocket. "He gave it to me."

"No, he didn't." Echo steps forward. "I have it."

"That's a lie," says Nola. "I've got it. And I'll never give it up."

"Unless I'm the one who has it." Vern grins at Oren, his enjoyment of the game reminding Echo of when he used to play Sting Roulette.

"Hilarious." Oren rolls his eyes. "But I know Tuff has it. And I'm giving him to the count of three to hand it over."

"And what if he doesn't have it?" Echo asks.

"Oh well." Oren shrugs, closing one eye to improve his aim. "One. Two—"

"Stop!" Flora steps out in front of Tuff. "Leave him alone. Don't you think you've made him suffer enough? Look what you've done to this poor man! If you want the detonator, you're going to have to get it from me." She holds up a small plastic device, showing Oren exactly who's got it.

River lets out a strangled gasp beside Echo but she's having enough trouble dealing with her own shock to give him any comfort. Flora is risking her life to save Tuff. A flush of shame washes over Echo to think about everything she'd accused Flora of. River had insisted she's a good person and it would appear he's right. What Flora's doing now takes incredible selflessness. Let alone courage.

Echo edges her way across to Flora before River can notice and stop her. Echo's the only one here who's Immune to queen bee venom. If anyone should be standing in front of Oren's gun, it's her.

"Flora," she whispers urgently. "Give me the detonator."

Oren laughs. "No, no no. Leave it with my daughter. It's much more fun that way. You people seem to enjoy a good game. Flora doesn't think I'll shoot her because of who she is to me. What do you think, Dead Born? Do you think I'll shoot her?"

Echo blinks, realizing he's asking her. "There's nobody you wouldn't kill if you thought it was going to advance your position."

"Smart." Oren nods. "Your time in the Green Zone served you well."

Flora waves the detonator. "I'll press the button if you shoot me. Even if it's the very last thing I do."

"And murder all these people?" Oren asks. "Let alone all the people you'll kill when you wipe out the Hive and make the production of Immunity impossible. My sweet daughter is far too kind to be capable of doing that."

"You don't know what I'm capable of," Flora sneers.

"In that case..." Oren clears his throat. "Proelium."

The giant Worker whirrs to life in the corner of the room and rises to her full height, the disc on her back glowing. People rear back and scream as the Worker charges at Flora.

"Pax!" Flora shouts. "Pax!"

But the Worker doesn't respond to her command. The word only seems to make the mechanical bee even more furious as she advances. Oren must have reprogrammed her. The only reason she'd responded to the word earlier, must have been because Oren had allowed it. He's been playing with them this whole time.

Flora presses the button on the detonator and squeezes her eyes closed.

"Get down!" Chase shouts, also seeing what Flora's done. "It's going to blow!"

People throw themselves into the far corner of the room and hide their faces while River and Echo try their best to shelter them.

Chase dives in front of Flora, sending her skittering away

from the Worker as a rumbling noise shakes the Sting, followed by an enormous bang.

But it's not the Hive that explodes.

The large window that connects to Oren's office shatters and glass rains down on them in tiny fragments.

A Worker careers through the window frame, knocking out more glass, and lands in front of Oren's Worker.

"Nectar!" Echo gasps, realizing the disc on the metallic beast's back is glowing silver. That wasn't the detonator Flora had been holding. It was Nectar's remote. And she obediently came to rescue her master when she was called.

Nectar rears up on her hind legs and makes a high-pitched buzzing sound. Echo covers her ears as the other Worker does the same, and they face each other, long legs thrashing and antennae flicking as they take swipes at each other.

Oren's Worker lands a direct blow across Nectar's head, sending her wobbling as she tries to steady herself. Just like her evil master, the Worker pounces on the opportunity and advances, forcing Nectar to take a few steps back.

Not willing to concede, Nectar throws out one of her forelegs and slams it down on the Worker's back. The glow from the bee's disc flickers and Echo lets out a gasp, hoping somehow Nectar's managed to damage the electronics inside this evil creature.

"Morsus, Nectar!" Flora shouts over the sound of the incessant buzzing. "Morsus!"

Echo turns to River. "What does that mean?"

His face is white, and he opens his mouth to answer without tearing his eyes from the clashing beasts before them. "It means bite. Or in this case, I think it means sting."

But Nectar seems to do the opposite to Flora's command. She crouches down and falls silent. Echo wonders if somehow Oren's managed to shut her down. He's still standing in the doorway to his office, and she's certain she didn't hear him breathe a word.

The other Worker scurries back away from Nectar and stares intently at her opponent.

"What's happening?" Nola asks. "Is it over?"

"I hope so," Vern mutters.

But as soon as the words are out of his mouth, the two bees launch themselves into the air with giant wings flapping. The buzzing noise rises to a pitch so high it can no longer be heard.

Oren's Worker flies forward, tilting her body so all six of her powerful legs are pointed ahead. They clack and thrash like a set of razor-sharp swords.

"Morsus!" Flora shouts again. "Morsus!"

Nectar seems to hear Flora this time. She zooms forward and lowers her head, pointing her giant stinger forward.

The two machines collide. The vibration from the crash of metal shakes the Hive as a chorus of gasps erupts from the people who are cowering closely together in a mountain of quivering human flesh.

Nectar bears the brunt of the other Worker's fury as she's pummeled by her legs, but she holds steady. Surging forward, she drives her stinger into the underbelly of the other Worker.

Both bees drop instantly to the floor as their buzzing morphs into a hum. Echo squints, trying to figure out which giant piece of tangled metal belongs to which beast. Oren's Worker is sprawled on her back, legs twitching, and lights flashing. Nectar's stinger is still inside her abdomen, and she withdraws it slowly, remaining sprawled on the floor as she turns to look at Flora, waiting for her praise.

Oren's Worker goes still and the light from her disc darkens.

Flora runs forward and crouches down, patting Nectar with tears trailing down her cheeks. Nectar just saved her life.

Although, given Flora rebuilt and reprogrammed her, perhaps Flora just saved her own life.

"Good girl," Flora coos, nuzzling her face against Nectar's. "You're my good, good girl."

"Impressive display," says Oren, lifting his venom gun and pointing it back at Tuff. "But you still haven't given me the detonator."

Echo doesn't hesitate this time. She races forward, diving in front of Tuff and Flora. Pushing down her fear, she realizes how much courage it must have taken when Flora did the same to protect Tuff. She may have questioned River's sister's motives in the past, but she now knows she was wrong. Nobody with an evil heart would risk their life to save someone else.

Flora stands and Echo quickly looks behind her to see Nectar trying to rise with her. But it seems she's sustained some damage in the battle and her back legs can't keep her steady. She wobbles and Flora works to keep her steady as Nectar rebalances to take her weight on her middle legs.

"The game's over," says Echo, glaring at Oren. "Your Worker's dead. And if you don't move out of the way, our Worker will kill you in exactly the same way."

"You do realize you're not the Sovereign, don't you?" Oren keeps the aim of his gun steady. "I tested you."

"Then you made a mistake," says River from behind Echo. "It's her."

Echo puts her hands on her hips, trying to make herself appear larger than she is. "I've been injected with queen bee venom twice and survived. How do you explain that?"

"Why don't you ask my daughter?" Oren sneers.

Echo goes to defend Flora, but words fail her. She grunts, hating that this man has her questioning River's twin again.

There's a rush of air behind them and Echo spins around to

see Nectar losing her balance and toppling, sending Flora sprawling.

"No!" Tuff shouts, pointing.

The detonator—the real one this time—has fallen out of Flora's hand and is skittering across the tiles.

Right toward Oren.

"No!" Tuff shouts again.

Echo flies forward, throwing herself at the detonator. She lands with a thud in front of it and her hand darts out. Her fingertips make contact with the hard plastic casing just as an intense pain shoots through her arm.

Oren's slammed his foot onto her wrist, pinning her to the floor. He bends down and scoops up the detonator, not removing his foot as Echo writhes in pain. Doing the only thing she can to protect herself, she grabs Oren's ankle with her other hand and pulls herself toward him, sinking her teeth into his ankle.

River gives Oren a shove and he lets out a howl, releasing her wrist as he's forced back. She clutches her arm to her chest and looks up to see Oren's pointing his gun at her face.

"You filthy Dead Born," he growls, holding the detonator with his other hand.

Echo rises to her knees and looks him directly in the eye. "Do it."

Oren smiles and she sees the tendons in his hand tense as he prepares to pull the trigger.

"Go on." She narrows her gaze. "I said do it."

There's talking behind her, and Echo hears River tell someone she'll be okay. His unwavering belief in her helps her hold her nerve right when she needs it. She's the Sovereign. The queen bee venom can't kill her. She's totally got this.

Oren presses down on the trigger just as a force slams into

Echo's side. She's knocked to the floor and looks up to see Flora wrestling with Oren for the detonator.

"No, Flora!" Echo cries as father and daughter declare war on each other. Both of them are prepared to fight to the death for this. And only one of them can win.

River scoops Echo up to her feet, and they race forward to help Flora, but it's already too late.

She's managed to get the detonator and lifts it above her head. Eyes wild with triumph, her hand clenches.

And her thumb presses down.

"Run!" River shouts, grabbing his father by the collar of his shirt and pulling him out of the doorway. Chase finishes the job, sending Oren flying into the room toward the Hive.

The hexagonal cell furthest from them bursts into flames with a loud bang, causing the one beside it to do the same as it sets off a chain reaction.

Tuff and Chase waste no time in ushering the frightened people through the door. Some climb through the broken glass that's clinging to the frame of the window in their desperation to get to safety as more cells of the Hive burst into flame. Echo scans the chaos for Flora but doesn't find her. She can't see Nectar either.

"No!" cries Oren as he tries to get to his feet but is knocked down by the force of the next explosion. The front casing of one of the hexagonal cells on the top row breaks away and tumbles down, engulfing him in flames and he rolls on the ground howling as he tries to put himself out.

"We have to go!" Echo grabs River by the arm and drags him to the door as he watches the father who betrayed him burn. "Leave him. He doesn't deserve to be saved!"

She's not sure if River agrees, but he allows himself to be led. The idea of leaving someone to die doesn't sit well with Echo, either. But there's no time to debate it. The room is quickly filling with smoke. They have to get out of here right now. If they don't burn in the next explosion, they'll suffocate. Hopefully Flora was one of the first to make it out.

With one last look to make sure nobody's left behind whose name isn't Oren, Echo takes River's hand and they follow the trail of people into the LaB.

Chase is hovering at the back of the crowd. "Where's Flora?"

"Isn't she with you?" River asks, scanning the frightened faces for his twin.

"She never left the Hive," says Chase.

"She must have." Echo pushes both of them forward. "Because she's not in there. I checked. And Nectar's missing too. They must be together."

"Maybe they left first," says River.

"Come on!" Echo shouts.

There's a thunderous explosion inside the Hive, followed by several loud pops. This seems to convince Chase. Together, they run into the corridors of the Sting, hardly daring to believe what just happened.

They blew up the Hive, taking Oren with it.

Artificial Immunity no longer exists.

Which means that aside from the handful of true Immunes left in the world, everyone else is Vulnerable.

CHAPTER
TWENTY-TWO
RIVER

"Flora!" River screams, even as he ushers the terrified people toward the stairs. "Flora!"

But he can't see his sister anywhere.

It's the smoke, he tells himself. And the panic.

And the absolute chaos.

They weren't meant to be inside the Sting when the Hive was detonated. But everything went wrong.

River doesn't let himself dwell on the image of his father's still body stretched out on the tiled floor of the Hive, his suit no longer white. Instead, it was ashen and charred as flames still danced on his back. The thought that his father's dead isn't one River can process right now.

Not when they have to get back to the Dead Zone.

Not when Flora's missing.

They reach the next floor down and someone stumbles as they go to take the set of stairs, his knees giving out beneath him. He clutches the railing just as River's mother steps in and slips under his arm.

She stumbles as they both straighten. "Our bodies aren't

used to moving," she says to him, smiling encouragingly. "They're adjusting to freedom."

River realizes the people trapped in the Hive are weak, their muscles having wasted away as they lay in their cells, treated as little more than a source of spinal fluid. Getting everyone back to the Dead Zone is going to be more of a challenge than they'd thought.

To his left, a young woman gasps, but Echo grabs her before she can fall. She wraps her arm around her shoulder, nodding toward the stairs. "We need to keep going."

The young woman, probably not much older than Echo, frowns in concentration as if what little strength she has she's going to channel into escaping. River can't help but respect her courage and grit. Especially when Echo's right, they have to get to the ground floor.

And then River has to find Flora.

Chase is at the lead and he reaches the next floor down, only to rear back when the door is shoved open. He instantly raises his fists as Green Borns pour into the stairwell.

Except their faces are just as panicked as the freed prisoners. They stream for the stairs, barely even glancing at the people already there.

"Fire!"

"I heard explosions!"

"We have to get out of here!"

Below, more Green Borns burst through the doors into the stairs designed as a fire escape. It's just that no one thought they'd have to use them in the safe bubble that is the Green Zone.

River glances at Echo, realizing this is actually to their advantage. No one is paying attention to them.

"Quick!" Echo says. "We need to become part of the crowd. Turn toward the atrium when you get to the ground floor."

River and Echo usher the people they freed forward as they blend into the rush of Green Borns clattering down the stairs. Each time, Echo tells them to meet at the atrium. Each time, River glances back up the way they came, hoping to see his twin rushing down.

When everyone has blended in, River and Echo join them. No one pays attention to the fact there are two bodies not dressed in the usual white sleeping attire everyone else is wearing. Their entire focus is on getting out of the Sting.

A rumble above has people instinctively ducking and crying out and the panic finally seeps into River's consciousness. Surely the Sting won't collapse...

A crash, then the sound of an explosion and glass shattering is his answer.

"Move!" River roars. "Get out of the Sting!"

The throng of people surge forward, now shoving and jostling. One of the freed prisoners crumples, unable to keep up with the terrified momentum. Vern quickly lifts her up, only to stumble to his knees himself. River pushes his way toward them, helping them both up. Vern looks at him gratefully, and with something else that feels strangely like pride.

"Only a couple more floors," River tells them, already turning back to the stairs as he focuses on not tripping.

The people fleeing the Sting are like a tide, drawing him and the others with them. River finds that as long as he stays upright as he and Vern support the woman they're helping, it's almost easier. He glances over his shoulder, trying to spot Echo, except he can no longer see her.

A fresh wave of panic surges through him. His father's probably dead. Flora's missing. Now Echo...

River pushes away the insidious thoughts. They don't know anything for sure, and Echo was beside him only a second ago.

They reach the ground floor and the people pour out, some sobbing in relief as they make their way to the door. As many people as possible are cramming into the airlock at once.

River glances at them as he and Vern lead the woman they're carrying toward the atrium and away from the crowd. The people are assuming they're safe outside...

They'll be fine while it's nighttime. The smoke billowing from the Hive will also keep the bees away.

But once daybreak is here. Once the fire is doused...

Every Green Born will have to start being careful. There are so few true Immunes left in the world. Everyone else's Immunity's been progressively waning since the moment they took their last sip of water.

Chase meets them inside the atrium, looking like he's counting heads. River allows the woman to sink onto a nearby chair, Vern bending over as he breathes hard beside her. River's mother limps over to him, and he reaches out to take her hand without looking up, as if he knew she was there. Their fingers intertwine with more strength than either seems to possess.

River scans the group frantically. "Where's Echo?" he asks, trying not to let his voice hike and failing.

"I'm here."

River spins to his right, finding her beside the young woman she helped. His breath comes out in a whoosh as relief rushes through him. Echo's lips soften in an almost-smile, and his chest loosens.

Although it's short lived. Another scan reveals someone else is missing.

"And Flora?" River demands, turning back to Chase. "Have you seen her?"

"She must've got out first," Chase replies, his face hard. "She's probably waiting by the net with Nectar."

"And if she's not?" River demands.

"She could still be up there!" comes another voice. River turns, surprised to find Vern standing beside him, vibrating with anger. "We can't leave her behind."

Chase scowls. "No one is going back to the Hive. It's too dangerous."

Anger roars through River as he crowds in on Chase. "I'm not leaving without her!"

"You saw that Oren had queen bee venom! And we don't know if he got her with it," Chase shouts, pain twisting his features. "She's safe or she's dead! Either way, we keep moving."

River recoils, just as much from the words as the agony in Chase's gaze. He doesn't want to consider the possibility Flora's gone. Or that Chase is hurting, even as he insists they keep moving forward.

A hand lands on River's arm and he finds his mother beside him. "Flora's fine. I would feel it if she weren't. We need to get these people back."

Echo appears beside her. "Or all of this would've been for nothing. Besides, she has Nectar with her."

River shakes his head, even though he knows they're right. "I can't leav..."

"Damn straight we can't," Vern snaps, just as he stumbles and River's mother has to catch him.

That's the moment River knows he can't go back. That he has to believe his mother. Has to cling to the same hope as Chase.

He looks to Vern. "If we don't find her, I'll come back," he vows.

River left the Green Zone to find his sister. He'll return to do the same if necessary.

Vern looks as if he's going to object, but someone lets out a sob behind them. "Please, I can't go back there."

"Come on," Chase bites out. "We have to keep moving."

Echo slips her hand into River's and squeezes. He draws in a shuddering sigh, trying to draw the comfort she's offering from the simple gesture. Of course Flora's alive. He'd feel if anything happened to her, just like his mother would. He and his twin have been connected since their time in the womb.

"Okay, everyone," Chase says, keeping his voice low but clear. "We're getting out of here. Move quickly and stay quiet. The Dead Zone is the safest place for you right now."

The people glance at each other but no one objects. Various shades of fear and determination grace their faces. They're escaping a life of repeated torture yet leaving everything they know and love behind.

Chase strides to the rear door and opens it, ushering people through. River's mother takes Vern's hand and leads him out, both leaning against each other. Without needing to be asked, Echo slips under the arm of the young woman she helped and walks with her out of the atrium. The others quickly follow and River comes up the rear, telling himself he's there to keep an eye on any stragglers, when the truth is he's still hoping Flora will burst through the door at any second.

Leif turns to him. "I saw her, River. Flora's alive, I know it."

River pauses. Leif not only went through his Confirmation with them, but also chose to go into the Hive in River's stead. When there's time, he's going to have to thank him for that. "Are you sure?"

Leif nods. "I'm sure." He indicates with his head toward the door. "Now let's hurry up and get out of here."

The rush of relief almost makes River's head spin. "Yes, let's go."

Catching up to the others, they slip out of the atrium and into the night, only to discover they're not alone. A growing mass of people is spilling from the Sting, the edge of the crowd several feet to their left.

Except everyone's looking up at the gaping hole pouring smoke from the top of the sting. Flames flicker in the thick, black smog that seems to be growing by the second. A wail sounds somewhere and River knows the people who trained for these emergencies, even as they assumed they'd never happen, will start the work of putting out the fire.

The few who aren't gazing up look lost as they cling to each other, faces blank. There's no Daphne to give them directions. No Oren to provide leadership.

And their assumption that the Sting is infallible is as much a myth as Immunity.

"Quick," Chase hisses, directing people in the opposite direction. "Straight to the Dead Zone."

Everyone moves silently, not wanting to bring attention to themselves, blending into the night as soon as they can. The tension in River's chest is just about to loosen when someone from the crowd calls out.

"Leif!"

River spins around as Leif does the same. An older woman and a man who looks like Leif, only a few years older, have broken away and are running toward them.

"Mom," Leif whispers. "Glen."

Before River can do anything, Leif breaks into a sprint and the three have grasped each other in a fierce hug, the sounds of soft tears coming from the trembling trio.

Leif's mother is the first to pull back. She frames his face with her hands. "What are you doing here?"

Leif's lips twist. "I haven't been where you think I've been."

His brother grips his arm. "It doesn't matter. You're staying. We'll hide you. Wait here and I'll get Dad."

Alarm shoots through River. As much as he wants to see

200

this family reunited, they can't leave any of the prisoners behind. Anyone loyal to Oren will try to capture them again to keep them quiet.

Then the brother looks beyond Leif and his eyes widen. "That's River," he gasps. "Oren's son!"

"That's right," says Leif. "I've been helping him."

River freezes, unsure of what to do. He doesn't want to hurt these people, but Leif can't stay, nor can he even remotely explain why.

But Leif is already shaking his head as he extricates himself. "I have to go," he says urgently. He grips her arms, gazing intently into her face. "Stay inside. Stay safe. No one is Immune."

"What are you talking about—"

But he's already turned away and broken into a jog. As one of those who's spent the least amount of time in the Hive, he's one of the strongest. River quickly joins him, glad that Leif's mother and brother simply watch them disappear, mute and in shock.

Their world has crumbled around them, and in ways they can't even comprehend yet.

The way through the Green Zone is slow and difficult. Anyone who is more able-bodied ends up supporting those who spent longer wasting away inside the Hive. By the time they reach the net, some people are rasping and wheezing even more than River is.

He finds Echo and Chase standing beside the net and he instantly realizes what the issue is. With the black door locked and no Alphadome, the only way to get through is by tearing their way through the net.

Yet they need it now, more than ever. The Dead Zone is the only place safe from bees. The net needs to remain intact.

A cry has them all spinning around simultaneously to find

an old man pointing at the sky. "She's coming for us! There was no way she was going to let us go!"

The outline of a Worker is visible in the dark, the faint glow of her disc illuminating it. A silver disc.

"Run! Hide!"

"No!" River cries before anyone can scatter. "This Worker is a friend! She's the one who fought for us in the Hive."

"He's telling the truth," Echo says, appearing beside him. "She's called Nectar and she's been reprogrammed. She's the one who will get us through the net."

No one runs, but everyone gives Nectar a wide berth when she lands a few moments later, some cowering behind shrubs and trees. River watches as the Worker walks toward the net and undoes it, then steps through. He knows this is a good thing, but one question is caught in a loop in his head.

If Nectar's here, where's Flora?

It's only Leif's assurances that he saw River's twin that stops him from turning and running straight back to the Sting. It's possible that Flora herself sent Nectar to help them.

"Quick," Chase says, indicating for people to file through the hole. "We can't let any bees in."

Everyone slips through as quickly as possible and Nectar sews up the hole, closing them in. River finds himself almost letting out a sigh of relief. His lungs will now loosen, and these people are safe.

"We're almost there," Echo tells everyone. "Then you can rest."

Her words are the impetus the exhausted prisoners need to cover the last distance to the bunker. River's glad it's dark and they don't have to see the reality of the Dead Zone. They have enough to come to terms with already.

Most of the people collapse the moment they're in the bunker. One or two need to be carried the last few feet, rather than remaining in a heap in the entrance. They all sink to the floor the moment they can, faces drawn and skin pale. River's exhausted himself.

"We need to get them water," Echo says, compassion softening her features.

River nods in agreement and they make their way toward the crypt. To his surprise, his mother joins them, even though she's limping.

He frowns, reaching out to stop her. "We've got it. You just rest."

His mother brushes his hands away. "I'll rest when I'm ready," she says sharply.

Echo chuckles. "Ah, there's Nola."

River's lips twitch. His memories had held onto all the sweet times with his mother, but he's fast remembering she was also quick with her words. He's looking forward to remembering all of her.

Chase and Vern also come, along with Leif. At least they'll be able to look after everyone quicker and then they can all get some rest.

The moment River's mother enters, she stops. "My chair!" She gasps, her hand shooting to her mouth.

"Flora knew Echo would want it here," Chase says, screwing his face up.

Echo shrugs, glancing at River's mother. "It seemed so important to you."

River's mother engulfs her in a hug. "You always did right by me." Before Echo can even return the gesture, River's mother releases her and rushes to the chair.

She bends over, spearing her arm deep behind the threadbare cushion. River's about to ask her what she's doing, but Echo draws in a sharp breath.

"That's why you were so possessive of it."

River's mother nods, straightening. With a wide smile, she lifts a piece of carefully folded paper. "I told you it held important memories. Including the most important memory in any of the zones."

She doesn't have to say what it is. The slight tremble in her hand as she unfolds it says it all.

So does the thick silence that fills the room.

And the stillness in River's every cell.

His mother is holding the very thing they've all been searching for. And it was right under their noses this whole time.

The piece of paper contains the Sovereign Code.

Now, finally, Immunity can be given to all.

CHAPTER

TWENTY-THREE

ECHO

Echo wakes in the bunker, unsure where she is for a moment. It feels different in this cavernous room that used to belong only to her and River. There are at least a dozen bodies sleeping on the floor around them. Along with Nola, who's fast asleep in her beloved chair with Vernon snoring at her feet.

Looking at the chair in the dim light, Echo still can't believe it had been holding the Sovereign Code all this time. She really should have guessed after that note Nola left for her. Perhaps if she hadn't had so many demands on her attention she would have. Then again, Nola had always been attached to that filthy chair. It was completely in character for her to ask Echo to keep it safe.

Vern lets out a particularly loud snore and Nola nudges him with her foot. The relationship between those two had been a surprise to Echo, even though River had told her how fondly Vern had spoken of his mother over the years. It's nice they've found each other, especially when they've lost so much. Including Vern's beloved kasi. Not that she's heard him complain even once. Perhaps the kasi had been his crutch to help cope with the loss of Nola? It doesn't seem like he needs it now.

River stirs beside Echo, having tossed and turned all night.

"Let's go to the LaB," he whispers.

She nods, knowing he's keen to head out and look for Flora now that it's daylight.

They creep out of the crypt and make their way past more sleeping bodies in the corridor as they head into Flora's work-shop. It's the one place they'd asked the people not to access. There are too many dangerous things kept there. Deadly things. Things they're going to need to produce Immunity once they find Flora. If they ever do... There's been no word of her since leaving the Hive. Chase insists she died, either in the explosion or from the queen bee venom. This theory doesn't match Leif's story of seeing her leave, which makes Echo completely unsure what to think.

They enter the LaB to find Chase asleep sitting up, leaning against the wall. His bloodshot eyes fly open, and he runs a hand through his tangle of blond curls.

"Any news?" he asks, which tells Echo he's still holding onto just a sliver of hope Flora might be alive.

River shakes his head. "The sun should be up now though, so we can head out."

"I'm going to hold a Razers' meeting," says Chase. "We need to move things forward as quickly as possible. It's time to take the next step."

River nods. "Where should we start? I was thinking we should check for her in the grounds around the Sting first."

Chase's brows shoot up. "I didn't mean to look for Flora. I told you that's a waste of time. There's no way she survived."

"You don't know that." River is a lot more reluctant to give up on his twin than Chase seems to be.

"She'd have come back if she were alive," Chase says firmly. "It's been hours."

River shakes his head. "Maybe she's injured."

Echo heard this debate a number of times before they agreed to get some rest and wait for daylight, and it's going in the same direction now as it had then. A never-ending circle. And it's starting to make her dizzy.

"What next step were you talking about?" she asks Chase, trying to steer the conversation in a more productive direction.

"Well, we have the Sovereign and the Code," says Chase. "The two things we need."

Echo nods. "Except we're missing the person who knows how to put those two things together. Maybe we need to get Reed back. He taught Flora everything she knows."

Chase nods. "Do we trust him?"

River seems surprised by this. "Of course."

"I'm not entirely sure," says Echo gently. "I think we can trust him. He's helped us along the way, but there's a part of him that's still loyal to Oren."

"Oren's dead." Chase hauls himself to his feet and paces. "Maybe that's enough to bring Reed to our side."

"Maybe," Echo agrees. "Let's hope so anyway."

"You can look for Flora if you like," says Chase, heading for the door. "I'm going to gather the Razers. That's the next step. We'll meet in the scoring grounds. It would be good to have you both there."

"Sure." Echo crosses her arms and gives him a smile.

River immediately turns to Echo when he leaves. "It's like he doesn't care about Flora at all."

Echo shakes her head. "He cares a lot. He's just dealing with it differently to you."

"But Leif saw her leave." River throws out his hands.

"There was a lot going on," Echo says cautiously. "He might have been mistaken."

"I'd feel it if she were dead," says River. "She's out there somewhere. What if she's hurt? I'm going to look for her."

Echo slips her arms around River's waist and rests her head on his chest. She can feel the frantic beating of his aching heart. "Flora's tough."

"I still have to find her," River says.

"Maybe she doesn't want to be found." Echo bites down on her lip as she waits for River's reaction.

He sighs, pressing his cheek to the top of her head. "She didn't want to be found last time either and that didn't stop me."

Echo pulls back so she can look at River. "I know you love your sister, but there's nothing you can do right now. Chase is right. It's unlikely she made it out alive. And if she did, then there could be a good reason she hasn't come back. Our focus has to stay on finishing what we started here. The Green Borns' Immunity will already be waning. Many will die if we don't act fast. Why don't we see what happens at the Razers' meeting before we make any decisions?"

A storm of emotions passes through River's eyes as he turns this over. Eventually, he nods. "Okay."

"Okay?" she checks.

"I'm never going to give up on her," he says. "But I'll go to the meeting first."

Echo presses up on her toes and kisses his lips, knowing this is the best answer she's going to get out of him for now.

"You're a good brother," she tells him. "Flora's lucky to have you."

He shakes his head. "I'm the lucky one. Not only to have her, but to have you."

There's a sound in the doorway and they look across to see Blossom, the woman Echo helped walk from the Hive.

"Can I talk to you?" she says, glancing around.

Echo smiles. "Come in. What's the matter?"

"I'll wait outside." River lets go of Echo.

"No." Blossom holds up a hand. "I want to talk to you, too. Please."

"Oh." River leans against the bench Nectar had carved from dirt. "Is everything okay?"

Blossom enters the LaB. She's small in stature, making her initially appear younger than she is. Echo quickly worked out she could tell how long someone had spent in the Hive by the length of their hair. Blossom's blonde locks are hanging right down to her waist.

"I need to tell you something about your sister," she says. "I would have told you sooner, but I didn't want to say anything while that guy was around."

Echo tilts her head. "You mean Chase?"

Blossom nods. "He's pretty intimidating."

This makes Echo laugh. "Not when you get to know him. Everything he does is to help the people."

"The Dead Borns," Blossom points out. "You don't see the way he looks at the rest of us."

"What about my sister?" River interrupts. "You said you had something to tell me about her. Did you see her leave?"

Blossom shakes her head, wringing her hands in front of her. "I saw Oren inject her with the venom when they were fighting over the detonator. Well, at least I think I did. She jumped like she'd been stabbed, then she went all wobbly."

"Leif said he saw her get out," says River firmly. "So, she couldn't have been injected."

Blossom draws in another breath. "How well do you know Leif?"

"Not very well," says River. "But he volunteered to take my place in the Hive, so I know his heart is good."

"He volunteered because he was afraid of the Dead Zone," Blossom blurts out. "He had no idea what he was choosing. He thought he'd be able to break out of the Hive and get back to his family. He didn't do it for you. He did it for himself."

"What does that have to do with Flora?" River asks, seeming impatient.

Echo puts a hand on his arm. "Let's hear her out."

Blossom shrugs. "It's just that...I think maybe he made up his story about seeing her leave."

"Why would he do that?" River runs a hand through his hair.

"If you thought she was still in there, you'd never have left." Blossom bites down on her lip. "He told you that so we could all get out before things got worse."

River draws in a breath. "That's a pretty serious accusation."

Blossom steps closer and lowers her voice. "Leif's not as nice as you think he is. Don't be fooled. I've known him and his family all my life."

"Thanks for the information, Blossom." Echo ushers her out of the LaB, not wanting River to get even more frustrated. He needs time to process what she just said. "Could you do me a favor and wake everyone up? There's a meeting about to start that we want you all to come to."

"A meeting with who?" Blossom arches a brow.

"The Razers." Echo gives her a smile, not wanting to explain Chase is the one who leads them. "They're working to help make things fair between the zones."

Blossom doesn't seem convinced, but she nods. No matter her suspicions about Leif, Echo knows she has her loyalty after rescuing her from the Hive.

When Echo turns back to River, he hasn't moved. It's like the information Blossom gave him has frozen him to the spot.

"She meant well," Echo tells him.

"But what are we supposed to do with that?" River shakes his head.

"Nothing," she says. "Just keep it in the back of our minds. And keep our eyes open. It's a good reminder not to trust anyone around here."

"Except each other." He pulls her back to his chest.

"Except each other," she repeats. It's true. He really is the only person in the world she truly trusts.

She embraces him, holding him for long moments before they break apart. Then Echo heads up the stairs into the heat of the day while River goes to round everyone up and see if his mom and Vern need any help.

Makk and Jupiter are waiting outside the hatch and greet her with a smile. She gives Jupiter a quick hug, not having seen them for a while.

"It's so good to see you," Jupiter gushes. "When I smelled all that smoke coming from the Hive, I was so worried."

"Echo's tough." Makk flexes his barely existent biceps and grins. "If she didn't waste so much time talking, she'd rule the world by now."

Echo looks in the direction of the Sting. She can see the tip of it from here, and while the top section has sustained some serious damage, miraculously, the structure is still standing.

"Who do you think's going to lead the Green Borns now?" Makk asks.

"Maybe nobody," says Jupiter with a shrug. "Or then again, knowing them, maybe everybody."

Makk waves at someone and Echo turns to see Tuff approaching, clasping Goldie's hand in his own. He'd been wise to leave the Green Zone. There's nothing left for him there. Finally, he gets to be with his family.

"It must be good to have your dad with you," Echo says, watching as Cascade sidles up to Tuff to tell him something.

"He takes up a lot of room." Makk rolls his eyes but his affection for his father is clear. "Our house feels like it's shrunk."

"At least he doesn't talk too much," Echo points out.

Makk laughs. "He barely talks at all."

"Unlike his son." Echo pokes Makk in his stomach and he leaps back and squeals.

Chase claps his hands to get everyone's attention, and the Razers contract closer to hear what he has to say. River emerges from the bunker with the rest of the people, and the Razers stare at them like they're walking ghosts. Which in some ways they are. They've most certainly been to hell and back.

Sledge and Fray are in the crowd, along with Cascade. They look even more frail than the last time Echo had seen them. They need to get these people some food as soon as they can.

"The war has begun!" Chase calls out.

The Razers throw their fists in the air and cheer.

"As you know, we destroyed the Hive, and rescued the people Oren was torturing in there. And we left him there to burn!" Chase sneers and Echo sees a glimpse of why Blossom's afraid of him.

"We need to steal their food!" Sledge calls out. "Tear down the net!"

Chase shakes his head. "Not yet."

"I'd rather take my chances with the bees than starve to death," Fray says. "We can't wait."

"You won't starve," Chase promises. "The days of Immunity in the Green Zone are over. Everyone is Vulnerable now."

Echo frowns. This isn't strictly true. While most people who passed their Confirmation were selected by Oren to be Immune, there are a few true Immunes among them. Like Echo. And Tuff. And it's impossible to tell which category the Green Borns belong to. Unless they get stung by a bee, of course.

"The Dead Zone is about to become the safest place anyone can be," Chase announces. "Pretty soon the Green Borns will be lining up to get in here."

"Don't let them in," sneers a man near the front.

"That's tempting," says Chase. "But we'll let them in. As long as each of them brings enough food to feed ten people for a week."

"And what do we do after a week?" Jupiter asks.

"We'll all be Immune by then." Chase grins. "Because we have the Sovereign and now we have the Code. We'll make Immunity for everyone, then we'll tear down the net and eat so much food we'll all feel sick!"

Excitement ripples through the crowd and Echo looks across at River, who gives her a worried smile.

He knows as well as she does that a week is far too ambitious. They need to find Reed, gather all the ingredients for Immunity, and follow the Code to make enough for every single person in both the zones. Then they need to administer it and wait for it to take effect. Even a year would seem close to impossible.

But they don't have a year. They may not even have a week.

Because anarchy has already arrived.

And it's their job to find their way out.

CHAPTER
TWENTY-FOUR
RIVER

River hangs back as everyone makes their way into the bunker, glancing at the faint outline of the Sting in the distance. Flora's there. He knows she is.

Or her body is...

He shoves the thought away ruthlessly. Blossom's story can't be true. Everything was chaos as the explosions erupted. She can't have seen what she thought she did. And it's the opposite of what Leif told River.

Unless he's confused, too...

Echo comes up beside him, concern tightening the edges of her mouth, and he tries to smile at her reassuringly. "Getting Reed here is the logical next step," he says.

And that means returning to the Sting.

"Except we can't go until it's dark," she says, chewing her lip as she watches him. "I know it's hard for you to wait."

He's about to tell her it's impossible when Blossom stumbles ahead and they both rush to help. With River on one side and Echo on the other, they support her as they descend

214

underground into the bunker. She smiles at them gratefully as they reach the main room, sinking to the ground with a soft sigh. River looks around, seeing most of the others have done the same, including his mother.

In fact, she smiles at him with such love it makes his chest ache, then closes her eyes and promptly falls asleep, even though it's barely morning. Vern is beside her, stroking her hair back from her face in ways that River has seen more than once, yet isn't sure how he feels about it.

"They're all so tired," Echo murmurs.

River notes that just the walk out to the scoring grounds has taken its toll. After spending so much time in the Hive, followed by the desperate escape into the Dead Zone, these people have little strength left. The road to recovery will be a long one.

"Rest is the best thing for them right now," he says, agreeing with her.

"Let's go to the LaB then," Echo suggests. "We want it as ready as it can be for when Reed gets here."

Chase appears behind them. "If he does," he mutters under his breath.

"He will," River assures him. "Reed is an ally."

Chase doesn't say anything, although his expression communicates nothing but doubt. He turns for the LaB and Echo joins him.

River quickly grabs her hand. "I'm just going to check on Nectar."

Her brows twitch a little closer, no doubt knowing that Nectar's powered down and there's nothing to check, but she nods. "Sure. I'll see you in a sec."

River almost hugs her, grateful that she understands he needs a moment. That Nectar is his last link to Flora. That he still doesn't know how he feels that the Worker his sister programmed is here, but she's not.

He carefully picks his way through the dozing or sleeping people and enters the crypt. A few people are tucked up along the walls, yawning, some even already asleep like his mother. Yet, everyone is as far away from the Worker as they can.

River walks quietly to the slumbering machine, noting the way her silver disc pulses softly like a heartbeat. For some reason, it feels like proof Flora's also alive, that her heart is beating just as steadily as Nectar's.

He rests his hand on the smooth metal of her head, letting out a slow breath. "Where are you, Flora? Why haven't you come back?"

"Are you going to find out the answers to those questions?"

River spins around at the softly spoken words, finding Vern only a few feet away, gazing at him steadily. In a way that has River shifting his weight, thinking of everything he's seen between Vern and his mother.

Vern was always there when River was growing up. Even with the kasi drinking, he was a friend. A mentor. Someone to help him smile after the death of his mother when he wasn't sure he'd be able to smile again.

Someone who always seemed more honest and real than anyone else in the Green Zone. Yet, it turns out he's been lying to him as much as anyone else.

River suppresses the need to clench his hands. "You have feelings for my mother," he says, keeping his voice low. Maybe Vern hung around just so he could get close to her.

Vern nods. "Magnolia is the love of my life," he says honestly. Simply.

River blinks, trying to reconcile that information with his childhood. Along with the way he's seen his mother look at

Vern, the way she touches him whenever she can. "But she was with my father."

"I found your mother in the orchard one day, only two years after she married your father," Vern says, letting out a sigh. "She was crying."

Frowning, River considers shaking his head. The mother of his childhood was happy, loving, keen to smile. But his childhood was a lie. And now he knows exactly the kind of man Oren is...

Vern takes a step closer. "Oren was angry with her because she hadn't borne him children yet. He was blaming her. She was so sad, so beautiful. It was inevitable that I comfort her." His gaze holds River's. "That we'd keep meeting."

River takes a step back and bumps into Nectar. A part of him wants to hop on her and fly out of here. The part that knows more lies are about to be peeled away.

Yet an even bigger part wants to hear this. The part that craves the truth.

"Within a few weeks, Magnolia was pregnant with you and Flora," Vern finishes, his voice soft so it can't be heard by the sleeping bodies around them.

Yet the words are like a boulder slamming through River. "You're saying..."

He can't finish the sentence. That means...

"Oren was never your father," Vern says, his eyes swimming with emotion. "From what we could tell, he was infertile."

Every molecule of air rushes out of River's lungs. His unblinking eyes take in the tears trickling down Vern's cheeks, reaching the soft smile gracing his face.

Oren wasn't his father.

Vern is.

A broken, strangled sound erupts from River, and Vern covers the distance between them in one stride, engulfing him in a hug. River wraps his arms around him, holding on tight as he tries to figure out whether he should laugh or cry. Whether he should be angry at this revelation, or just relieved.

Turns out, he doesn't do any of that. He just holds the man who loved his mother the way she deserved.

"I wanted to tell you so many times, but we both knew that Oren couldn't find out the truth," Vern says, holding River tightly. "There was no telling what he'd do."

He would've sent River and Flora to the Dead Zone. If he was feeling merciful, he would've sent them to the Moon Zone, like Daphne did with her daughter.

River pulls back, understanding starting to sink in. "You were always there, in the periphery, waiting to see if we needed you."

"I should've done better by you and Flora. When I thought Magnolia died..." Vern's face twists. "Kasi was the only thing that numbed the crater my soul became."

Someone groans, then whimpers in their sleep, reminding them they're far from alone. And that there's still work to be done. The pained sound was reminiscent of the screams River remembers pouring out of him when he was in the Hive.

Which brings River back to the reason he was here, with Nectar. Because the thought of focusing on Immunity when Flora's still missing isn't one he can reconcile...

Vern arches a brow in a way that reminds River of the times he challenged him to play Sting roulette. "So, are we going to go get Flora or what?"

River draws in a sharp breath. "That's a dangerous suggestion, Vern."

"That's my daughter out there, River," he growls. "I'm not sitting by and waiting to see if she turns up."

River finds himself grinning. Ever since he escaped to the Dead Zone, he's been worried a part of him is like his father. When that father was Oren, the thought was terrifying. But now that he knows the truth, he also realizes something else. Just like Vern, he had no intention of sitting around and waiting. He came here to go after Flora.

Now, he's okay with sharing some traits with his father. With Vern.

He turns and leaps onto Nectar's back, then looks down, knowing this is going to take some time to process. "I can go on my own."

Vern snorts as he extends his hand. "Help an old man up, will you?"

River reaches down and they grasp each other, the hold feeling far more than just a lift onto Nectar. He hauls Vern up, trying not to think too much about it. Not considering what they're about to do.

Vern settles himself behind River. "Ready."

River instinctively glances toward the door, thinking of Echo and hoping she's not about to come looking for him. Only two can ride Nectar at once. By going with Vern, Echo stays here, safe. She doesn't need to put her life on the line for someone she's not even sure she trusts.

Still, it feels odd to leave her like this. They've barely been apart since the fight for Immunity started. Maybe he should at least tell her... River shakes his head. Echo's safety is more important, and if any of the people in the crypt watch them leave, they'll tell her what's happened. Even if they don't, the absence of Nectar will be pretty self-explanatory.

River leans down and whispers, "To the Sovereign graveyard."

To his delight, Nectar whirrs to life, her wings silently snapping out. He then realizes Echo is about to find out exactly what he's doing. There's only one way out of the bunker, and that's past the LaB.

Surprisingly, Nectar turns toward the rear of the crypt rather than the exit that will take them to the main room. She walks to the back wall, then rears up on her hind legs, leaving River and Vern to clutch her smooth body. With short, sharp movements, her front legs rip away some black material, making River gasp.

A tunnel! Just like the one Chase created in the Alphadome.

"Flora's one clever girl," Vern says, pride evident in his voice.

River agrees, but at the same time, he can't help but wonder why Flora kept it a secret, even as he wishes the question didn't just rise in his mind.

A few people wake, moaning in horror to see Nectar looming before them. They hurry to the back of the room just as Nectar scrabbles up the hole, this one much wider than the one Chase dug with little more than planks of wood.

And it turns out, much longer.

River and Vern tuck in low over Nectar as she crawls through the tunnel that feels like it goes on forever as it slowly angles up. When they come out, River squints against the light, even though it's still early morning. He looks around, seeing the scoring grounds in the distance, the Green Zone even further away. They've exited somewhere they're not likely to be seen. Beyond the net of the Dead Zone, in the Extinction Zone.

"Yep, she's a genius," Vern says.

River doesn't say anything. This is an ideal escape route. It's just that Flora never mentioned it. He straightens, setting his sight on the blur of green ahead. Once he finds Flora, he'll get answers.

Nectar lifts into the air and Vern's arms clamp around

River. He's silent for the next several minutes of the trip, either in wonder or fear, mostly likely both. But when they circle the Green Zone without approaching it, Vern seems to realize they're not going to the Sting.

"Is this thing lost?"

"The Sovereign graveyard is underground, beneath the Sting," River tells him, glad they have the sun behind them, making it harder for them to be spotted up in the air. "With a tunnel that leads to it just like the bunker. It means we can enter with less chance of being seen."

"The Sovereign graveyard?"

"Yeah." River's insides twist. "Most people who die in the search for the Sovereign end up there."

And that won't be Flora.

"With Oren dead and everyone trying to figure out what to do next," River continues. "It's our best bet for getting in."

Vern grunts. "Until I see a body, Oren ain't dead."

River doesn't reply. He hasn't considered how he feels if either scenario eventuates. Even though he now knows Oren isn't his biological father, the man still raised him. And is the one responsible for all the suffering River's trying to undo.

The red sand of the Extinction Zone stretches out beneath them as Nectar angles down, and River scans for the hatch that will lead to the Sovereign graveyard. He sees it a second before Nectar rapidly descends, Vern once more clinging to him.

"You know riding a robot bee isn't normal, don't you?" Vern grouches.

River almost smiles. "Nothing's been normal in the search for Immunity."

The metal lid covering the tunnel lifts automatically as Nectar approaches and she dives in as it closes behind them. They're plunged into darkness, her silver disc the only light illuminating their way. River's body tightens as they fly through the labyrinthine tunnels, conscious of what he'll be seeing soon.

The first shelves are empty.

But after the next turn, they start filling up.

Bodies are stacked one on top of each other, lining the walls.

"Is that..." Vern gasps.

"This is where Oren keeps people from both Zones." Bile scorches River's throat. "So he can test everyone."

"I almost hope Oren's not dead," Vern spits. "So I can kill him myself."

River doesn't say anything, conscious that Oren's death was a blessing to the fight for Immunity, although he understands the sentiment. Oren had a lot to answer for.

"We need to check each body as we pass," River says, his voice turning hoarse. "In case it's Flora."

"It won't be," Vern growls, even as his head spins from side to side, scanning the corpses.

River's stomach feels like it holds nothing but acid as he does the same. He looks at body after body, face after face, each time relieved it's not Flora. Each time grieving for the loss of another life in Oren's relentless pursuit of Immunity for the very same people he claimed he was trying to save.

A light ahead tells River they're almost at the central room, so he orders Nectar to land. He and Vern climb off, looking around cautiously. "We need to be careful," River says quietly.

Vern glances back the way they came. "She's not here," he mutters, as if just saying the words aloud will make them true.

Except it's another voice who answers him. "He's right. Flora's not here."

River spins to find Reed standing in the opening of the tunnel. The hands that were on his hips explode outward. "Are you crazy, River? What are you doing here?"

"You know why I'm here." River walks toward him, but Reed quickly enters the tunnel. "I'm looking for Flora."

"She's not here," Reed says again. "I'd know if she was."

Vern steps closer to River. "I don't trust him."

Reed barely glances at him. "You can't be here, River. You need to leave."

"If Flora's not in here, then I want to see the Hive for myself." It's a long shot, but maybe there will be a clue as to what happened to his sister.

"That's a terrible idea," Reed snaps. "The Hive is little more than a shell. I know because I helped cleaned up your mess."

River shakes his head. "You know it was time people knew the truth."

Reed sighs. "Leif's brother has been talking. He's not only telling people that Immunity is a myth, he also said he saw you. That you're the one who destroyed the Sting."

River shrugs. "Technically, it's the truth."

"Most people aren't listening," Reed continues. "But once someone gets stung..."

Then there will be proof.

And panic.

"Which is why you can't be here, River. It's too dangerous," Reed says, his voice hardening. "There are a lot of people loyal to Oren who want revenge."

River slashes his hand through the air. "They can't stop what's coming. We have the Sovereign, and now we have the Code. It's time to make Immunity."

Reed's eyes widen. "Wow, you really did it."

"And Flora was as much a part of this as any of us," River says. "I'm not leaving her behind."

Reed frowns, hesitates, then seems to reach a decision. "Flora's not who you think she is, River."

Vern growls as he steps forward. "I told you we can't trust him. He doesn't know what he's talking about."

"This isn't about trust," River says, taking a step forward, intending to walk around Reed so he can get to the lift. "This is about finding my sister."

"This is about far more than that," Reed says, right before he leaps back and darts out of the tunnel. He spins around, looking at River almost in apology before slamming his hand against the wall beside it.

In a blink, a black wall shoots down, cutting him off. And trapping River and Vern inside the tunnel.

Vern curses. "I knew he couldn't be trusted!"

River spins and runs back to Nectar, not even bothering to try and get through the wall. It's clear Reed doesn't want them entering the Sting. He leaps on Nectar, holding out a hand for Vern to do the same. "We need to get back to the hatch!"

Adrenaline and dread pump furiously through River, making his head spin and his mouth dry as Vern clambers on behind him.

"The bunker," he tells Nectar. "Celer."

The Latin word for fast has the effect he was hoping for. Nectar shoots forward and their surroundings become a blur.

River just has to hope it's fast enough.

They race back through the tunnels, River's heart thrumming as if he's the one flying. Vern clings to him like his life depends on it. "What if Reed's locked it down," he gasps.

River doesn't answer. That's not a possibility he wants to consider.

They reach the hatch and Nectar flies toward it with more speed than River's comfortable with. Yet all he does is brace himself, hoping it's a good sign. Nectar must know the hatch is about to open.

Yet all that comes closer and larger is a black metal plate. It remains motionless, hard and unyielding. Shut.

Nectar slows to a stop at the last moment, preventing them from crashing into the hatch and River falls forward as he works to hold on. He closes his eyes as he realizes what this means.

It didn't open.

They're trapped.

TWENTY-FIVE

ECHO

E cho runs into the crypt to see what the commotion is all about.

Nola immediately grabs her arm. "River's gone! And Vern. They left on that awful flying thing."

"Why didn't you stop them?" Echo asks. "And how did they get out? I was right outside the door!"

"I was asleep." Nola drags her over to the far corner of the room, almost tripping over a black cloth on the floor. "Leif said they went through there."

Echo spins around to find Leif behind her, nodding. "I heard a whirring sound. I thought I was dreaming but I opened my eyes just in time to see the mechanical bee climbing up through that hole in the ceiling. And River and Vern were on its back."

There are a few people gathered around, straining their necks as they try to peer into the darkness of the hole above their heads. With no shelves underneath like in the original crypt, there's no way to get up there. Unless you can fly, like Nectar, of course.

"I have to go after them." Echo looks around for something she can stand on. But there's nothing. All the furniture in the bunker has been carved from solid earth. Even standing on Leif's shoulders wouldn't make her tall enough.

"You'll never get up there," says Nola. "Or I'd already have gone myself."

"Then I'll get rocks from the scoring grounds." Echo walks toward the corridor. "If I pile them high enough, I should be able to reach."

"You'd need hundreds of them," Leif calls after her. "River and Vern will be long gone by the time you finish. Or they might even be back."

"Urgh." Echo comes to a halt, realizing he's right. "Then I'll find a way through the net. I'll break down the black door if I have to."

"Echo." Nola goes to her, placing a hand on each of her shoulders as she tries to catch her gaze. "What was your advice to River last night when he wanted to go after Flora?"

Echo rolls her eyes, seeing where this is headed. "That it was too dangerous."

"That's right," Nola nods. "River also told me you said that maybe Flora didn't want to be found."

"And?" Echo is losing her patience. She needs to go after River, not stand here talking about it!

"Maybe River doesn't want to be found." Nola lets go of her to cross her arms. "Or he doesn't want you to go after him. He'd have told you where he was going if he wanted you there."

Anguish churns in Echo's gut.

This is exactly how River must have felt when Flora went missing.

He knew with his head he shouldn't go after his twin, yet his heart refused to listen.

"What's going on?" Chase asks, marching into the crypt.

"River and Vern left on Nectar." Echo points to the hole in the ceiling. "Did you know that was there?"

Chase doesn't need words to answer. The shock on his face does it for him. So Flora hadn't told him either.

"When did this happen?" he asks.

"Nectar must have dug it out a while ago," says Echo. "But they only just went missing now."

"Where does it lead?" Nola asks, squinting.

Chase goes forward to have a closer look. "The Green Zone."

"What?" Nola screeches, reminding Echo of her old friend. "I thought it just went straight outside here."

Echo shakes her head. "This place is a replica of another bunker we used to visit. That one had a tunnel too, and it went directly to the Green Zone."

"Then we need to go after them!" Nola is the one heading for the corridor, having completely changed her tune. "Hurry, we need some rocks to stand on."

"What happened to River not wanting to be found?" Echo asks, running after her. Nola doesn't have the strength to climb through the tunnel, let alone make her way through the Green Zone. Then when River returns it will be to a missing mother, along with his sister. Echo needs to go alone.

"That was before I knew where he went." Nola continues to shuffle down the corridor.

Echo takes her arm and brings her to a stop. "Let me go and look for them. I can move faster by myself."

"Terrible idea," Nola scoffs. "You're the Sovereign. Someone has to keep you safe."

"And you think that should be you?" Echo asks. "You might look ten years younger since you got out of the Hive, but you move like you're one hundred."

Nola blinks at her. She's never been one to coat her words in sugar. All Echo is doing is being equally direct in return.

"If you're going, then so am I." It seems Nola is as stubborn as her son.

"Nola." Echo puts a hand on her friend's arm. She has no idea what River was thinking, but she knows he'll be counting on her for one thing—to look after his mother while he's gone. Which means convincing her to stay behind. "Trust me. I'll find him. It's better if you wait here."

Nola nods, tears filling her eyes. "I'll stay at the tunnel and wait for them."

Echo breathes a sigh. "I still don't understand why he left without letting me know."

"I think Vern must have told him," Nola says quietly. "He wasn't thinking straight."

Echo tilts her head. "Told him what?"

"That..." Nola looks to the floor, then straight back at Echo. "Have you really not worked it out yet?"

Echo sighs. "Nola, please just tell me what you're talking about. We've had enough riddles to solve already."

"Vern's his father," she says. "Flora's too. Obviously."

Echo's jaw drops. "Vern? Not Oren?"

Nola shrugs as she nods. "I tried for years to give Oren a child. I desperately wanted one for myself too. I needed someone to love who would love me in return. But it wasn't until I met Vern that...well, you can put it together for yourself."

"Oren wasn't River's father." Echo knows she's stating the obvious, but hopes that saying it out loud will help her take it in.

"Vern gave me the children I yearned for," says Nola. "Then he couldn't have them for himself. Until now."

"Did Oren know about this?" Echo asks.

"I don't think so." Nola shakes her head. "He died thinking he was their father. If I had my time again, I'd have told him the truth just before he choked on his last breath."

Echo's heart breaks for the damaged woman standing in front of her. She doesn't have to ask how Oren treated her to know it would have been awful. She only has to look at what he did to the two people he believed to be his own children to understand. It's no wonder she's so bitter. Which makes Echo even more determined to bring her son back to her.

Chase appears in the corridor. "I'm going to the black door."

"It's locked," Echo reminds him.

"Not from the other side." He moves past them. "I'm meeting the Razers there. We're going to wait for the Green Borns to start asking to come through, then we'll prop the door open and cover the gap with a net."

"I'll come," Echo says. "If the door opens, I can get some food from the Betadome." *And sneak away to find River when Chase isn't looking.* That has to be easier than trying to find a way to climb up to the tunnel.

Chase shakes his head. "No, you won't."

"Excuse me?" Echo draws in a breath.

He rolls his eyes. "You're the Sovereign, Echo. If anything were to happen to you... We have to keep you safe."

"But the people need food." Echo realizes it's going to be harder to sneak away than she thought.

"Tuff will go in," says Chase. "He passed his Confirmation, remember? He's a true Immune. One of the lucky few."

"Fine." Echo huffs. "But I'm still coming with you. I might be able to spot Nectar if I keep an eye on the sky."

Echo nods goodbye to Nola who gives her a conspiring wink. She knows full well that Echo will take the first chance she gets to go into the Green Zone.

She follows Chase out of the corridor and up the stairs, already imagining what she'll say to River when she finds him. She won't know whether to hug him or tell him off for disappearing on her. She'll probably do both.

"It's like old times," Chase says when they emerge into the bright sunlight. "Just the two of us."

"No offense, but it's been a while since that idea excited me." Echo gives him a playful shove.

"It's like we were different people back then," says Chase. "You especially."

She opens her mouth to protest but he cuts her off before she can speak.

"I meant that in a good way!" He holds up his hands. "I always knew you had a kind heart, but I had no idea you were so gutsy."

She shoots up her brows. "Gutsy?"

"Yeah." He gives her a gentle shove right back. "You're brave. And smart."

"And hungry," she adds. "You need to let me help Tuff get some food from the Betadome. If we don't bring enough out, people will start going in there themselves, no matter the risk."

"I take back the smart bit," says Chase. "Immunity is more important than food. And for that, we need you alive."

"Immunity is useless if we all die from starvation," Echo points out.

"We have water," he reminds her. "And our bellies are used to being empty. We can survive a bit longer."

She remains unconvinced. It's been too long already since anyone here had anything to eat. Maybe that's where River went? To fill the storage compartment in Nectar's belly with food? But why wouldn't he wait until night when the bees are asleep? And why wouldn't he tell her he was leaving?

Because he's gone to look for Flora.

And Vern went with him because he's her father. As much as Echo doesn't like it, it's the only explanation that makes sense. Which is why she has no choice but to go after him.

Echo and Chase pick their way through the scoring grounds and head to the black door where there's a group of Razers ready and waiting with a metal bar to prop the door open and a net. They can't rely on the smoke alone to protect the entrance. If bees get inside the Dead Zone, it will spell disaster. Then they not only won't have any food, they won't have their safety. And that's the only bargaining chip they have right now.

"Any visitors?" Chase asks.

"Not yet." Sledge shakes his head while Tuff grunts.

"They'll come," Chase says with certainty.

Fray peers into the Betadome. "Why wouldn't they just hide inside the Sting?"

"Because the top's been blown right off it," says Chase. "Which means bees can get in. And we don't know how those blasts might have weakened the structure."

There's a flash of movement and Fray lets out a gasp. "Look! Someone's coming."

"Remember," says Chase. "Enough food for ten people, or they don't come in."

"Got it." Sledge pats his stomach. "I'm looking forward to a feed."

A group of three people make their way across the Beta-dome, tiptoeing and pale faced. They're wearing bee suits, but the sleeves are torn and they're missing their masks, rendering them useless. The hum of bees can be heard even at a distance and the people glance around nervously as they move closer.

Echo recognizes them as Leif's family. It makes sense they'd be the first to come looking for refuge given Leif had told them they were no longer safe in the Green Zone.

232

Leif's brother, Glen, pulls open the door and waits for the smoke that never arrives.

"Not so fast," growls Sledge, barring the entrance as one of the Razers jams the metal bar in the door and drapes the net over the gap.

"Please, let us in," Leif's mother sobs, glancing around nervously in case a bee has decided to target her. "People are dying. The bees. They're everywhere. There aren't enough suits. People are fighting over them."

Echo shakes her head. That explains the torn state of their suits. She's not really sure why they bothered wearing them at all.

"We need safety," Leif's father says firmly.

"And we need food." Sledge blocks the door and Tuff backs him up with his large frame. "Enough for ten people for a week. Each."

Leif's family glance around at the trees inside the Beta-dome. They're heavy with fruit. But also heavy with bees.

"We're not Immune," Glen says. "If the bees sting us, we'll die!"

"And if we don't eat, so will we." Sledge is unmoved by their desperation, but it's tugging on Echo's heart. She can't stand to see anyone in pain. Except perhaps Oren...

"Listen," Leif's father hisses, trying to keep his voice down so he doesn't stir up the bees. "Our son is in there. He told us he's been helping River. You owe it to us to help us in return."

"Ten people. One week." Sledge talks slowly and loudly as if Leif's father has a hearing problem. "Now."

Another family appears cautiously at the door behind Leif's family. They have scarves tied around their heads, reminding Echo of how Nola used to look when she greeted her in her tiny hut. Sledge explains the condition of entry. The people glance at each other nervously through their scarves.

"We can't carry that much food," the mother says. "Please. At least let my daughter go through. She's too young to die."

"All my daughters died before they were born." Fray shoves a sack at them. "And don't take anything from the Betadome. We have that covered. Food from there doesn't count."

Tuff pushes his way through the door with a sack of his own and heads for the nearest tree. He picks the fruit carefully, not wanting to stir up the bees more than they already are. Dead Borns are starting to gather at the net, the news of the possibility of food spreading faster than fire.

"Wait here," the father of the new family whispers to his wife and daughter.

He takes a sack and quickly makes his way out of the Beta-dome, keeping his head tucked under his scarf while his family press themselves against the net, trying to get as far away from the bees as they can.

Echo edges forward. "This isn't right. They could get stung. Let them in."

"We need food." Chase holds her back, tilting his head toward the gathering crowd of Dead Borns. "And lots of it. Weren't you just telling me that Immunity is useless if we're all dead?"

Echo feels ill. He's right. Because she was right when she'd said it the first time. The people of the Dead Zone need food. Desperately. And thanks to Oren, this is the only way they can get it.

Tuff returns and passes a full sack of fruit to Chase, who gives him another so he can go back in for more. Chase hauls the bounty to a crate they have set up and Jupiter starts distributing the fruit one piece at a time. More Razers stand guard to make sure nobody takes more than their allocation. Echo's mouth waters but she knows there are people who need the food more than she does. When she manages to get inside the Betadome to look for River, she can eat as much as she likes.

The father returns several minutes later with a sack bulging with walnuts. He tries to squeeze past Glen, who blocks his path, not having made any attempt to get food of his own.

"We were here first." Glen shoulders him out of the way. "Wait your turn."

"But we have what they asked for!" the father exclaims. "You haven't picked anything."

"Then give us your food." Glen forcibly rips the sack of nuts from the father's hands and shoves it at Sledge. "There. That should cover the three of us."

"Hey!" The father grabs Glen by the arm but gets pushed hard in the chest and lands heavily on the ground.

The humming of the bees intensifies in response to the shouting and movement and Echo winces, hoping none of them come to investigate.

"Get your own food," Glen snarls.

"That's what he did," the mother of the new family huffs back, keeping her scarf pulled across the lower part of her face.

Echo waits for Sledge to make things right, and allow the new family through, but he's so dazed at the sight of all the walnuts that he's almost delirious. He takes one and cracks it open, shoveling it in his mouth before passing the sack to Chase, who takes it over to the crate. Sledge closes his eyes as he chews on the nut, then steps back, allowing Leif's family to come through.

Echo remembers what Blossom had told them about not trusting Leif, saying she'd known his family all her life. She thinks she might now understand what she'd meant by that. Which throws into question what Leif had said about seeing Flora get out of the Hive alive. Maybe he really was just trying to get them all to move on without waiting to search for her?

Leif's family stalks off into the Dead Zone. Echo doesn't bother to point them in the direction of the bunker so they can find their son. They can figure that out for themselves.

Sledge rearranges the net around the gap in the door, conscious the frenzied movements of the people must be stirring up the bees. The father who was knocked to the ground gets back on his feet and glances around nervously until he's satisfied the bees are paying him no attention.

Echo feels ill. Surely, it's just a matter of time before this man's luck runs out? Hopefully he's retained some of the Immunity from the water he's been drinking.

"Stay very still," the man whispers to his family, before heading off to fill another sack with food.

"You let the wrong people in." Echo steps up to Sledge and points at the disappearing backs of Leif's family. "They didn't collect that food."

"Food's food. Doesn't matter how they get it." Sledge pulls the net aside to let Tuff through with another load of fruit for the crate. Echo considers darting inside but the bees are already disturbed. The last thing they need is her to make it worse. Especially while that man and his family are still in there. She's going to have to wait until everyone else is out until she goes in.

"I need one more piece," a woman at the crate begs Jupiter. "For my daughter at home."

"One each," Jupiter says sternly.

"He got two!" someone else complains.

Echo sees the problem Sledge had identified first. If they don't start quickly distributing food, there's going to be a riot. There's no time to sort out arguments between the Green

Borns. They have enough to deal with, keeping their own people calm.

Another desperate family arrives at the door, their faces turning pale when Sledge explains the condition of entry. Echo wonders what kind of welcome they'd expected after the way the Green Zone has treated the Dead Borns all their lives. Surely, they hadn't thought they'd be greeted with open arms?

There's a terrible scream and Echo's head snaps up to see the father who had his food stolen by Glen. He's staggering toward his family, dragging a heavy sack. He rips off his scarf to reveal his face is purple and swelling fast.

"I was stung!" he cries out, passing the sack to his daughter. "Quickly, take this. Go through to safety."

"We need adrenacure!" his wife shouts to Sledge. "Hurry!"

Echo swallows. There are a few canisters back in the bunker, but she'd never be able to get them in time. And they need those for when they make Immunity.

"We don't have none of that stuff here," Sledge tells her. "You can blame yourselves for that."

The woman's shock turns to panic as her husband collapses to the ground, his face swelling as he struggles to drag air into his lungs. A bee circles him and the woman and her daughter are forced to step back. Two more join the frenzy.

"This is your fault!" the woman hisses at Sledge, trying and failing to keep her voice down. "If you'd let us in instead of those thieves this wouldn't be happening."

Sledge blinks at her, unmoved, his hatred for the Green Borns clear.

"Go!" the father chokes out from the ground. "Hurry!"

The daughter grips the top of the sack, her face streaming with tears as she drags it toward the door. Her mother follows her to the one place she must never have imagined would offer her the security they so desperately need.

They disappear from sight for a moment as they pass behind the black door, and when they emerge on the other side there are three people.

"Reed!" Echo gasps, seeing who's with them.

"Where's your food?" Sledge asks, having no idea who Reed is.

"Let him through," says Echo, taking Reed by the arm. "He's here to help. Besides, there was enough in that sack for three."

Sledge grunts, allowing Reed to pass.

"Have you seen River?" Echo asks, pulling him away from Sledge. "Is that why you're here?"

Reed shakes his head. "Why would I have seen River?"

"Because he went to the Green Zone." Echo rakes her fingers through her hair.

"I haven't seen him," says Reed. "I came here to check if you needed my help. I brought the last of the serpentwood."

Echo lets out a sigh.

They have the Code.

They have the Sovereign.

And now they have serpentwood, along with the one person other than Flora who knows how to put all of them together.

Everything is finally falling into place. Except River isn't here to see it. Which means as much as she hates the idea, she needs to put off going to look for him. Because if Reed says he's not in the Green Zone, there's not a lot of point going after him.

But that only raises another question...

If River's not in the Green Zone, then where is he?

CHAPTER

TWENTY-SIX

RIVER

River rounds the bend in the tunnel, having to make a conscious effort to pick up his feet as hopelessness drags at him. He should never have come here without telling anyone.

He should never have come here without telling Echo.

And now he and Vern are trapped in the Sovereign grave-yard, without a soul knowing they're here.

All because Reed betrayed them.

River's hands form hot, ineffectual fists. He wanted to believe Reed was their ally. He could see the battle within his old friend as he tried to fight for what's right. It turns out, River wanting Reed to choose Immunity for all wasn't enough.

He shakes his head. He can blame Reed for betraying them, but ultimately it's himself who's at fault. He chose to come here with Vern. He chose to come after his sister.

He chose this as if he's not answerable to anyone, not part of a team.

As if he's not going to let down the girl he loves if he fails to come back.

Nectar's legs tap quietly behind him, the soft light of her disc illuminating his way as he returns to the end of the tunnel where Vern's waiting. Where the hatch has remained tightly closed no matter what they tried. Pushing. Hitting. Ramming it with Nectar's solid metal body. Shouting every Latin word for 'open the heck up' River could think of.

The shelves around him are now empty, which is a small blessing. River left Vern to rest while he surveyed the entire length of the tunnel, hoping to find some way out. A door. A vent. A crack in the cement. Except there was nothing but rows and rows of dead bodies.

River even recognized a few of them, his stomach recoiling each time a familiar set of features registered. Three were from the Green Zone, one was from the Dead Zone. All desiccated, their skin stretched over their bones so tightly it revealed every skeletal bump and depression. He wondered how long before they'd start decomposing now that there aren't Workers caring for them, feeding as they embalm them. But he'd quickly shut that thought down. That implies he and Vern will be here for long enough for decay to start.

And River can't afford for that to happen.

His fists now rhythmically clenching and unclenching, he lengthens his stride. Somehow, he has to make this right.

"River?" Vern's voice carries from the end of the tunnel, full of caution, possibly a thread of fear.

"It's me," River assures him as he comes closer, seeing that Vern's on his feet, tense and coiled.

Vern lets out a breath. "I can never tell with that Worker. Could be one of Oren's, for all I knew."

"Her disc is silver," River tells him, ordering Nectar to power down. "It's what differentiates her from the others."

Vern studies him as he gets closer. "Did you find

anything?" he asks, his tone suggesting he already knows the answer.

River shakes his head, resting his back against the wall and sliding down. "The place is a tomb."

Vern snorts, coming over to sit beside him. "It was designed to be."

Designed to hold the growing death toll as Oren ruthlessly sought out the Sovereign.

River's fists are now resting on his knees as he stares straight ahead. He lets his head fall back and thud against the concrete behind him as he stares up at the closed hatch. "I should've told Echo what I was doing," he says, voicing the thought that won't stop battering his mind.

"Anyone who loves you knows how big your heart is." Vern reached out to squeeze River's arm. "And that it's forged from loyalty. Echo will understand."

If he gets back to her...

River forcefully shoves the thought away. He *has* to get back to Echo. He just hopes she doesn't come looking for him while he figures out how to do that.

"Echo's a good one," Vern adds. "I should've known your match wouldn't be in the Green Zone. You needed someone with more backbone. Someone who would give life to the questions you didn't know were alive inside you."

"She's the best," River says quietly, meaning every word. Vern's words come back to him. "She's the love of my life."

"Then you'll get back to her. Just like I did with Magnolia."

River nods, comforted and uneasy at the same time. Vern and his mother's love brought them back together. He just hopes it doesn't take five years and the assumption he's dead for it to happen.

Vern shifts his weight, settling against the hard wall a little more. "Whatever happened to the girl who was sniffing around you from the moment she set eyes on you?"

"Clover?" River asks, remembering how Vern interrupted them on Harvest Day as she failed to take the hint he wasn't interested. Even Vern could see what was happening when River couldn't and was trying to protect him. "It's a long story but she died," River says heavily.

"That's too bad," Vern grunts, not sounding too sad about it. "That's what aligning yourself with Oren will do."

"She meant well," River says, conscious of how lame that sounds. Clover may have been manipulative and self-centered, but she also just wanted to be loved. His own sister craves the same thing after a lifetime with a father who never accepted her.

Who turned out not to be her father.

Finding Flora would mean River could tell her the truth. Maybe it would give her some peace.

Vern snorts again. "Of course you'd think that." Before River can answer, he continues. "At least we know Flora's not here."

"Yeah, it wasn't a total waste," River agrees dryly.

They may have confirmed his twin isn't in the Sovereign graveyard. But they still have no idea where she is.

"Maybe we rest and then do another scout around," Vern suggests.

"Good idea," River says, even as his stomach revolts at the idea of scanning the shelves again. But they don't have a choice. It's their only chance of escaping. If he has to, he'll dig his way out. One little crack is all he needs.

In fact, maybe Nectar can do exactly that! She dug out the bunker, surely she can dig their way out of this tunnel, even if it is lined with concrete!

River's about to turn to Vern to relay the idea when something catches his eye. He angles his head up, shocked to find the pinprick of light that caught his attention is growing. It lengthens, running its way around the outer edge of the hatch.

River shoots to his feet. "The hatch, it's opening!"

Vern leaps up, too. "The question is why."

River's first thought is that Reed's letting them out. Maybe he kept them here for a reason. Not that it matters. Freedom is slowly being revealed as the line of light grows into a crescent, then thickens.

Behind them, Nectar comes alive, whirring as if she's excited. She lifts, walking toward them. River drags his gaze away from the opening hatch, shocked.

Vern grins, then must see something on River's face. "Did you just use one of them fancy words?"

River shakes his head. "No."

Nectar's preparing for something he doesn't know about.

"We have to get on her," Vern says urgently. "The hatch is almost open!"

River snaps his gaze back to the hatch, seeing that Vern's right. Blazing sunlight pours through the large hole, making him squint. They've been in the tunnel longer than he thought.

There's no time to wonder why this is happening or how. He grips Vern's arm, prepared to haul him up if needed. "Get ready."

Vern hangs onto River's forearm as they both turn to Nectar. Her disc shines brighter and brighter as she approaches, the lights behind her eyes flashing frantically. It's not something River's seen before, which is just as unsettling as the surprise opening of the hatch. But if it means getting out of here, if there's a chance of getting back to Echo, then he's going to take it.

In a blink, Nectar's wings snap out and she lifts into the air, shooting forward. At first, River prepares to leap, but she ascends as quickly as she surges forward. All he and Vern have time to do is duck as she flies over them.

And straight out the hatch.

"What the hell?" Vern demands.

River stares in shock, trying to figure out what just happened. "Revenite!" he shouts, trying the Latin term for 'come back.' When nothing happens, he tries again. "Reditus!" But 'return' doesn't work either.

Nectar abandoned them.

Which means someone just called her.

"She's coming back!" Vern gasps.

River registers six dangling legs lowering into the hatch and he lets out a sigh of relief. He takes a step forward, only to freeze.

The Worker that drops down hovers in the bright light pouring through the hatch. Her antennae twitch. Her jaws clack as if she's getting ready to eat.

The whirring sound sends ice skittering down River's spine.

Vern grabs River as he takes a step back. "Her disc ain't silver," he says, his voice low.

And neither are the two other Workers who descend after her.

Nectar hasn't returned. Three Workers with red discs are now hovering in a line, bobbing gently.

"Run!" River shouts.

He and Vern turn and break into a frantic sprint into the bowels of the tunnel. Behind them, the whirring reaches fever pitch and one panicked look over River's shoulder reveals what he wishes wasn't true.

They're coming after them, now in a deadly trident formation.

"Faster!" he shouts to Vern.

River's breath is already sawing in and out of his lungs as they round the first bend. With each pounding footstep, the whirring becomes louder. Beside him, Vern stumbles, and he quickly catches him, trying not to lose what little head start they have.

Vern rights and River holds onto him even more tightly.

Even as he knows running is futile. They're heading for a dead end.

There is no escape.

They round another bend just as one of the Workers spears down, her black legs snatching at Vern's shoulders.

"Get away!" River screams, using his momentum to leap at the mechanical beast.

He grabs hold of one of her legs and pulls with all his strength, making the Worker pitch sideways. Landing back on the ground, he scoops up Vern as he stumbles again. Above them, the Worker tries to right herself, but one of her wings clips the shelves lining the walls. Wood splinters and bones go flying, making River and Vern duck.

But they don't stop. Barely slow.

Behind them, there's a clash as two of the Workers collide, meaning they fall back a few feet. River doesn't have time to try and guess how much of a reprieve it's granted them. Not when the door to the central room is ahead.

He and Vern throw themselves against the door, digging their fingers into the tight gap at the base and trying to lift it up. River's fingers strain, the tendons on his arms stand out in stark relief. He clenches his teeth so hard they grind.

But the door doesn't open.

"River," Vern gasps, spinning around and plastering himself against the cool metal.

The three Workers land on the ground, their combined legs clattering on the cement floor as they stalk forward. River

TAMAR SLOAN & HEIDI CATHERINE

steps in front of Vern, prepared to fight with everything he has.

Except it won't count for much. He doesn't stand a chance against the might of three machines programmed to kill.

Behind him, Vern gasps and leaps forward, shoving River. He spins around, assuming Vern's trying to take his place to fight too, only to register the door is moving. Lifting. Opening.

A glance back reveals the Workers have stopped several feet away, watching this unfold in the same way River is. He grabs Vern by the shirt, yanking him closer, conscious they have a deadly threat behind them and now have no idea what's about to be before them.

Has Reed come to save them?

The door lifts, revealing a man on the other side, flanked by two more Workers.

At first, River doesn't recognize the scarred, melted face, but then he takes an involuntary step back.

The white hair, although only a patchwork dispersed among shiny areas of skin, is familiar. So is the height, the tilt of the chin. And the eyes, glaring at him from beneath stretched eyelids without lashes.

Despite the scars, the scalded skin, the liquified features. He knows them all.

Oren survived the fire.

The man who River believed was his father smiles, his lipless mouth twisting. "I told you it was only a matter of time before you came running back to me."

CHAPTER
TWENTY-SEVEN
ECHO

"So, you're sure you didn't see River?" Echo asks Reed for what must be the tenth time since they arrived at the bunker.

"I told you, no." He's starting to look a little annoyed, so she decides to drop it for now. "I'd have seen him if he went into the Green Zone. Especially if he was flying on a giant bee."

Echo nods, still struggling to understand why River hadn't told her where he was going. She can't help but feel hurt, even though she knows he'll have a perfectly good explanation. He always does.

Setting the serpentwood down on the workbench, Reed studies the crumpled piece of paper Echo had handed him with the Sovereign Code written down in Nola's messy scrawl.

"Any surprises on there?" Echo cranes her neck to look over his shoulder.

"The whole thing's a surprise," he says. "Not so much the ingredients. We had pretty much all of them figured out. Although, the quantity of aluminum salt is a surprise. I thought we'd need a lot more."

"Where do we even get that?" Echo asks.

Reed retrieves a small package from his pocket. "I brought some with me. I was worried it wouldn't be enough, but this will be plenty. It's the serpentwood I'm concerned about. Does River still have those seeds Clover gave him?"

"He carries them with him," says Echo through gritted teeth. "Although, there aren't many left. And he's not here..."

"Never mind." Reed tucks the piece of paper in his pocket. Echo doesn't blame him for not wanting to put it down. It had taken them so long to find it. They can't afford for it to go missing again. "Where did Flora keep the other ingredients?"

Echo points to a cupboard that's really a hole dug out of the wall. "Everything should be in there. Apart from whatever it is you need to take from me." A shudder runs down her spine.

"About that..." An emotion Echo can't identify crosses Reed's face. For a moment, she thinks it's excitement, but it couldn't possibly be that. He's going to need to extract her spinal fluid while she's experiencing great fear. Only a psychopath would get excited about the prospect of that.

"What about it?" she prompts when he fails to finish his sentence. "I've done it before. I know what's involved."

Reed shakes his head. "It's not that."

"Then what?"

"Oren already had me test your blood," he says. "And you're not the Sovereign. You had no immunity to queen bee venom at all."

"Then why have I survived being stung by a queen?" She jams her hands on her hips. "And I injected myself with venom a second time."

Reed shakes his head. "I can't explain that. I also can't explain why the Immunity Flora made from your spinal fluid didn't work. If you really are Immune to queen bee venom, then it should have been successful."

"She didn't have the Code." Echo remembers Flora's explanation.

"She should still have been able to make Immunity," says Reed. "The Code is more important for producing large batches."

"Then we must be doing something wrong." Echo shrugs. "Or the blood sample you took from me got mixed up somehow."

"Were you frightened when Flora took your spinal fluid?" he asks, taking the Code out of his pocket and frowning at it.

"I was terrified!" She remembers how she'd truly believed Chase was about to kill River and the fear that gripped her. The thought of losing him is the worst possible thing she could imagine. Which is why she's so determined to get him back.

Reed taps the paper. "Would you be open to being injected again? Before I take your sample, I mean."

"Sure." She'll do anything if Reeds thinks it will work. They're running out of time. If they don't get Immunity to the people soon, they may as well give up.

"The vaccine is designed to mimic your immune response," Reed explains. "Which will be stronger if your body is actually fighting venom at the time. See this line here on the Code?"

He points at a line of scribble and Echo nods, even though she doesn't have a hope of understanding what it says with her limited literacy skills.

"The Code calls for the protein that primes your immune system to cancel out the bee venom," he says, although it really doesn't make anything clearer. "I think that's where Flora got it wrong. Your body wasn't fighting any venom at the time of your extraction, which limited the effect."

"And you think that will make the difference?" she asks.

"It will make *all* the difference." He points again at the paper before folding it and putting it back in his pocket. "It's all written here in black and white."

"Then let's do it now." Echo straightens her back, trying to look braver than she feels. "While everyone's out getting their food. The bunker may never be this quiet again."

In truth, she doesn't want to frighten the people. They've been through enough already, including their own extractions. Some of them dozens of times. They don't need to witness her screams. It's best to do it before anyone returns. Besides, time isn't exactly on their side. The sooner they make Immunity, the more lives they can save.

Reed nods. "That could work. Assuming I can scare you, of course. How do you feel about spiders?"

She shrugs. "They're okay. Except when their legs get caught in my throat."

Reed reels back, unsure if she's joking—which she most certainly isn't. Spiders are a great source of protein in the Dead Zone.

"It's okay," he says. "I have a better idea."

Echo crinkles her brow, curious. But she doesn't ask what he means. Things are usually far scarier when they're unknown.

Reed retrieves Flora's box of supplies and sets it down on the bench. He takes out a canister of queen bee venom and stares at it in awe.

"Sit down," he tells her, pointing to a chair that's little more than a carved out lump of dirt.

Her heart rate picks up as she sits, despite not having any idea how Reed intends to frighten her. The last time she was extracted, River was there. As he was the two times she'd encountered queen bee venom. It doesn't feel right to be doing this without him. She's not even sure she can.

"You look upset," says Reed, fiddling with a syringe.

"Wouldn't you be?" she asks.

"Fair call." He sets down the syringe and takes a long length of thin cord from his pocket.

"What's that for?" she asks.

"I need to tie you up, so you stay still," he explains, looping the rope around her waist and then tying her ankles together.

"Flora didn't have to do this to me." Her heart is beating hard now. Perhaps that's what Reed had meant when he said he intended to scare her. If so, it's working. "I can sit still."

"Put your hands behind your back," he instructs.

She hesitates, unsure about handing over full control to a guy she's never really fully trusted. But River trusts Reed. And she trusts River. It will be okay.

"Hands," he says. "I said to put them behind your back."

There's something about his tone that sets her on edge. Has the scaring part started already? If so, she's not sure she's comfortable with this. She far preferred it when he talked about spiders.

"Maybe we should wait for River to get back," she suggests, trying to buy herself just a little time. River could walk back in that door at any moment. Then she knows she could go through with this. He always makes her stronger.

"People are dying," Reed reminds her as he forcibly takes her hands and binds her wrists behind her. While she's not tied to the chair, she's most certainly immobile. There's no way she could run from this room if she wanted to. Which admittedly, she does. More than anything.

"There." Reed stares at her as that inscrutable expression on his face returns. It's all she can do to hope that he's not actually a psychopath. "And now for this."

He takes a cloth from his pocket and before she can react, he's stuffed it in her mouth, using another cord to gag her.

She chokes on the revolting taste of the cloth that pushes on the back of her throat, hoping he hasn't doused it in chemicals first. Feeling faint, she tries to draw in air through her nose, needing more oxygen to keep up with her racing heart.

"Reed!" she tries to shout, but it comes out more like "Reeegh".

Tears sting at her eyes as she wriggles, trying to tell him she's changed her mind. She doesn't mind being extracted. It's necessary. She's the Sovereign. Everyone is depending on her.

But not like this.

And not without River.

This is too much. She can't do it. She just can't.

But she has to. Because there's nothing she can do to stop Reed now that he has her in this vulnerable position.

"You want River, do you?" he asks, picking up the canister of venom.

She nods, mumbling out her reply. She wants River more than she's wanted anything in her life.

"Well, it's time I told you a little secret." Reed grins. "I *did* see him in the Green Zone. He was with Vernon, riding on the Worker that Flora stole from Oren."

Echo's eyes widen as she struggles against the cords that are now cutting into her wrists and ankles. She hadn't told him that River had been with Vern. If he knows this, then he must be telling the truth!

"How else do you think I knew you had the Code?" Reeds ask. "River told me. But you were so busy trying to get me to make Immunity to save the filthy Dead Borns that you never stopped to think about that, did you?"

Salty tears slide down Echo's cheeks as she realizes she was fooled. He's right. She didn't think about any of that. There's no way Reed could have known they had the Code unless someone told him. And that someone was undoubtedly River.

"Do you want to know where he is?" Reed taps the canister of venom, making sure it's functioning as he prepares to jam it into her leg.

Echo nods, begging him to tell her. If she can get out of this alive, she's going straight to River. No waiting for permission from Chase. Or Sledge. Or anyone. Nothing and nobody will stop her. And when she finds him, they'll never be separated again.

"River's in the Sovereign graveyard." Reed slams the canister into Echo's leg, far harder than required and she cries out in response, both at the pain and his words.

The graveyard! He can't be in there! Because if he's there, then he must be...

"That's right." Reed tosses the canister aside and picks up the syringe. "Your boyfriend is dead. Oren killed him. And he's coming for you next."

The words slide down her spine like ice, just as Reed stabs her with the syringe in the back of the neck, extracting something that goes beyond fear. It's pure grief as her every cell explodes in agony.

Black spots cloud her vision, and she feels herself tipping as she slides from the chair and lands on the floor with a thud. She doesn't feel the pain of the fall. It's impossible to feel anything other than the torment that's swirling through her mind.

Oren is alive. He killed River. And Reed is working for him.

Which means that Oren now has everything.

And Echo has nothing.

CHAPTER
TWENTY-EIGHT
RIVER

River's first thought is he's glad the monster in front of him isn't his father. His second thought is Oren's charred, twisted features now match his soul.

Oren grins, victory puffing out his chest. "Captis," he growls.

The two Workers walk forward, their discs flashing bright red. River keeps his gaze on Oren as he speaks. "He's ordered them to capture us," he tells Vern, keeping his voice low. "Don't fight it."

They don't stand a chance against these two machines. They need to save their energy.

A Worker snatches River, making him grimace as her metallic legs clamp around him. Beside him, Vern groans at the rough handling. River grits his teeth, vowing Oren will pay for every hurt he's ever inflicted.

Oren turns to look at the Worker holding Vern. "Processus."

Process?

The Worker dutifully carries Vern to the next tunnel, already whirring with excitement.

"No!" River shouts. Vern can't have finally been free of the Hive, only to die. River can't have found his father, only to lose him. "Stop! Prohibere! Pax!"

But the Worker keeps going, now entering the tunnel.

Oren chuckles. "These ones are programmed to only listen to my voice."

River struggles against the metal vise holding him, ignoring the pain as the immovable legs dig into his sides. "Please, no!"

Oren waves a dismissive hand, the tips of two fingers melted down to the first knuckle. "I'm not going to kill him." His forehead twitches as if he just raised a non-existent eyebrow. "Right now, he's useful to me."

River goes still. He just showed Oren that Vern means something to him. And he's going to use it against him.

The Worker carrying Vern disappears into the tunnel, and River almost groans out loud. There's the sound of a struggle, then Vern grunting, and she returns a moment later, empty handed. The door slams closed behind her.

Oren turns his back on the tunnel. "He can lie on the shelves just like every other disappointment in here." He draws in a steadying breath. "Now, we're going to have a chat. Don't give me any trouble and he'll remain unharmed."

Without glancing at River, he limps to the elevator, and the Worker still holding him dutifully follows. Oren steps back and the Worker enters, turning around so she's facing the open door. He joins them, turning his back as if to prove how little a threat River is.

River's jaw tightens, hating he's right. He's not going to risk Vern.

Oren presses the button for the uppermost level. They're going to the Hive.

River studies the man in front of him as they silently rise through the Sting. The back of Oren's head is patchy like the rest of it, spurts of white hair erupting from the melted, contorted skin. The strands are shorter than they used to be, no doubt singed in the explosion. And he's holding himself more stiffly than before, no doubt because his body still has a lot of healing to do. River wonders why Oren's bringing him back to the site that almost killed him. As punishment? To exact his revenge?

River draws in a steadying breath, trying to dissipate some of the impotent fury storming through him. What happens next, what's said next, is going to count. His only advantage is that Oren believes he's his son. Otherwise, he'd be dead. It's an advantage he's going to have to use.

The elevator comes to a stop and the doors open. Oren exits into the LaB. The area is almost untouched, although it's eerily empty. The benches and shelves are bare, even the glass columns that once housed plants are vacant. Oren limps past it all with barely a glance, heading straight to the door that leads to the Restricted Area. River has no choice but to follow as the Worker carries him.

Inside, his eyes widen as he takes in the carnage they wrought.

The entire back wall that once housed the Hive is gone, revealing an expansive view that goes as far as the Dead Zone. The cerulean sky is breathtaking, the gossamer clouds feeling like they're almost at eye level this high up. A gentle breeze ruffles River's hair, stirring up the scent of charcoal and ash.

Oren stops where the glass wall to his office once was, although the desk and shelves behind him are spotless. "Dimittis."

The Worker releases River the instant the order is given, and he lands in a heap. His feet have barely touched the floor when he's pushing up, ready to defend himself. Hoping to run.

But the Worker steps back, blocking the door. River's gaze darts around. The only way out is the monstrous wound on the side of the Sting, and that would be nothing but a sheer drop for hundreds of feet.

For now, he's trapped.

Oren's cold gaze settles on River. "You think you've won, don't you?"

River doesn't answer. Even if he dies here, they have the Sovereign and the Code.

"Fools," Oren spits. "Echo isn't the Sovereign."

"Liar," River hisses, unable to stay quiet. "She's been stung by a queen bee more than once. And survived."

Oren waves a dismissive hand, taking a limping step toward River. He instantly takes one to the right, maintaining the distance between them. "I thought it was her, too. Everything seemed to suggest she was. But then I tested her. She's most definitely not the Sovereign."

River shakes his head, moving once more when Oren shifts to the left. "We tested her too. With actual venom. And she survived."

"Which has always been an anomaly. One that sent you down the wrong path because you wanted to believe it so much."

River glares at him. "Or she's the Sovereign."

"She most likely had some remaining Immunity from her time in the Green Zone. Added to her natural Immunity, which she most certainly possesses, and she was able to withstand the venom." Oren's lipless mouth twitches. "But that will wear off. I predict the next time she's injected, she'll die. In fact, I believe Reed is injecting her right now."

River wants to roar a denial, but there's something about Oren's smugness that has him hesitating. The need to get back to Echo, when he's the furthest away he's ever been, is overwhelming.

Oren shuffles to the left as he watches River with interest.

River takes the corresponding steps around the room to maintain the distance between them. A breeze runs up his back, telling him the gaping hole in the Hive is behind him, but somehow, being closer to that jagged ledge feels safer than being within arm's reach of the evil man watching his every move.

"I don't believe you," he snarls. "Everything you say is a lie."

A grotesque parody of a smile twists across Oren's mouth. "Here's a truth for you." His gaze slips past River, coasting over the horizon, the Dead Zone, before returning to him. "There is no Sovereign. Which means it's time to make tough choices."

"Your specialty," River spits.

Oren snaps a glare at him before turning toward his office. River watches, tense and coiled, as he limps to the rear wall and presses a button. The white expanse opens like sliding doors, revealing something that has River reflexively stepping back. He quickly stops himself, conscious of the sheer fall behind him.

But the need to get away, to undo what he's seeing, doesn't fade.

Behind thick glass, the wall is covered in honeycomb, each cell holding a wriggling, twitching bee.

Another Hive. Smaller, yet it feels far more deadly.

"Queen bees," Oren says proudly. "Hundreds of them. Each with a tiny transmitter attached so I can control them as completely as I control my Workers."

River's frozen in horror. He's looking at a tiny army that could wipe out thousands of people in less than an hour.

"Tonight, I'll be sending my Workers out to create holes in the net surrounding the Dead Zone." Oren runs his deformed hand over the glass front gently, almost affectionately. The skin on the back cracks, creating jagged lines of blood. "Tomorrow, my queens are going to do what I should've done all along. Without the Vulnerables, this never would've happened."

River's snapped out of his stupor. Oren's talking about exterminating every soul in the Dead Zone! "Without the inequity this never would've happened!" he shouts.

Oren inclines his head. "Which is why there will no longer be any inequality. I'll ensure the true Immunes are spared. Vulnerables will meet the fate they would have if we hadn't built any of this. They were never meant to survive."

"This is mass murder," River spits, bile scorching his throat.

Oren stalks forward, fury rippling over his melted features. "This is necessary. We'll start all over again. Once only Immunes are breeding, thriving thanks to the riches of the Green Zone, then maybe a Sovereign will appear. Or maybe this is how humanity will continue." Oren shrugs. "Either way, humankind survives."

River breaks into a run, his fury rupturing from his throat as a roar. Oren grins, as if he was expecting this, maybe even relishing it, but River doesn't care. In fact, he welcomes the fight, too. It's time to end this. To stop Oren's evil.

Except Oren takes a handful of steps and then slaps his palm against the wall with a grimace of pain. Followed by a grin of victory. The glass wall dividing the Restricted Area shoots up right in front of River, halting his trajectory as he crashes into it. He's thrown backward, landing on the smooth tiles and skidding much too fast.

Frantically, River crashes his hands down, trying to slow his momentum. The ledge is only a few feet away! He digs his fingers into the floor, his nails catching on the grout lines, but unable to gain purchase.

He can already feel the weightlessness of falling. The inevitability as gravity multiplies his speed.

But the little jolts turn out to be enough.

He slows to a stop, his head hanging over the edge. Heart pounding so hard it hurts, River scrabbles back. One glance at the dizzying drop and he almost throws up. The ground is so far below it's a blur of pale cement and indistinguishable green.

River leaps to his feet and away from the deadly drop, fury and adrenaline creating a potent cocktail in his bloodstream. "You can't do this!" he screams, realizing Oren can't hear him.

Oren walks over to the control panel and presses a button. "And your punishment for betraying me is to watch everyone you thought you could protect die," he says, his voice coming through a speaker to River's left.

River throws himself at the glass wall, pounding it. "No! This is wrong! It's murder!"

Oren smirks, a sick look of anticipation suffusing his face. He presses the button again. "So will be what I'm going to do to your father."

Without waiting for a response, without acknowledging River's furious, frantic beating of the glass wall, he leaves the Restricted Area, taking his Worker with him.

Closing River off on a man-made cliff. He beats the glass over and over. Trying to smash it. Trying to keep the helplessness at bay.

Trying to escape the truths that are his only companions.

Oren knows Vern is River's father. That's a betrayal that won't go unpunished. Vern will pay with his life.

And tomorrow, Oren will exterminate the Dead Zone so he can start with a clean slate of Immunes. Thousands of people will die painful, suffocating deaths. And River will have a bird's eye view of it all.

Exhausted, defeated, and powerless, River finally stops. He turns and slides down the glass wall, hot tears scaling his cold cheeks.

If everything Oren said was true, what is there to fight for?

There is no Sovereign.

And if there's no soul carrying the genetic code that would save them all, then that means Echo's dead.

THE END

Ready for the final book in The Sovereign Code?

Check out Sting Wars now!

http://mybook.to/StingWars

THE THAW CHRONICLES

Tamar Sloan and Heidi Catherine are the authors of the bestselling series, The Thaw Chronicles.

Get your free prequel now!
http://mybook.to/BurningThaw

WANT TO STAY IN TOUCH?

If you'd like to be the first for to hear all the news from Tamar and Heidi, be sure to sign up to our newsletter. Subscribers receive bonus content, early cover reveals and sneaky snippets of upcoming books. We'd love you to join us!

SIGN UP HERE:

https://sendfox.com/tamarandheidi

ABOUT THE AUTHORS

Tamar Sloan hasn't decided whether she's a psychologist who loves writing, or a writer with a lifelong fascination with psychology. She must have been someone pretty awesome in a previous life (past life regression indicated a Care Bear), because she gets to do both. When not reading, writing or working with teens, Tamar can be found with her husband and two children enjoying country life in their small slice of the Australian bush.

Heidi Catherine loves the way her books give her the opportunity to escape into worlds vastly different to her own life in the burbs. While she quite enjoys killing her characters (especially the awful ones), she promises she's far better behaved in real life. Other than writing and reading, Heidi's current obsessions include watching far too much reality TV with the excuse that it's research for her books.

MORE SERIES TO FALL IN LOVE WITH...

ALSO BY TAMAR SLOAN AND HEIDI CATHERINE

The Thaw Chronicles

Elemental Games

ALSO BY TAMAR SLOAN

Keepers of the Grail

Keepers of the Light

Keepers of the Chalice

Keepers of Excalibur

Zodiac Guardians

Descendants of the Gods

Prime Prophecy

ALSO BY HEIDI CATHERINE

The Kingdoms of Evernow

The Soulweaver